Morgan Robertson

Where Angels Fear to Tread

Morgan Robertson

Where Angels Fear to Tread

ISBN/EAN: 9783337075828

Printed in Europe, USA, Canada, Australia, Japan

Cover: Foto ©Andreas Hilbeck / pixelio.de

More available books at **www.hansebooks.com**

"WHERE ANGELS FEAR TO TREAD"

And Other Tales of the Sea

BY

MORGAN ROBERTSON

McKINLAY, STONE & MACKENZIE
NEW YORK

" ' Where Angels Fear to Tread ' " was first published in the " Atlantic Monthly "; " Salvage " in the " Century Magazine "; " The Brain of the Battle-Ship," " The Wigwag Message," " Between the Millstones," and " The Battle of the Monsters," in the " Saturday Evening Post "; " The Trade-Wind " in " Collier's Weekly "; " From the Royal-Yard Down " in " Ainslee's Magazine "; " Needs Must When the Devil Drives " and " When Greek Meets Greek " in McClure's Syndicate; and " Primordial " in " Harper's Monthly Magazine."

To the publishers of these periodicals I am indebted for the privilege of republishing the stories in book form.

MORGAN ROBERTSON.

CONTENTS

"WHERE ANGELS FEAR TO TREAD"

"I have seen wicked men and fools, a great many of each; and I believe they both get paid in the end, but the fools first."

ROBERT LOUIS STEVENSON.

PART I

THE first man to climb the *Almena's* side-ladder from the tug was the shipping-master, and after him came the crew he had shipped. They clustered at the rail, looking around and aloft with muttered profane comments, one to the other, while the shipping-master approached a gray-eyed giant who stood with a shorter but broader man at the poop-deck steps.

"Mr. Jackson—the mate here, I s'pose?" inquired the shipping-master. A nod answered him. "I've brought you a good crew," he continued; "we'll just tally 'em off, and then you can sign my receipt. The captain'll be down with the pilot this afternoon."

"I'm the mate—yes," said the giant; "but what dry-goods store did you raid for that crowd? Did the captain pick 'em out?"

"A delegation o' parsons," muttered the short, broad man, contemptuously.

"No, they're not parsons," said the shipping-master, as he turned to the man, the slightest trace of a smile on his seamy face. "You're Mr. Becker, the second mate, I take it; you'll find 'em all right, sir. They're sailors, and good ones, too. No, Mr.

Jackson, the skipper didn't pick 'em—just asked me for sixteen good men, and there you are. Muster up to the capstan here, boys," he called, "and be counted."

As they grouped themselves amidships with their clothes-bags, the shipping-master beckoned the chief mate over to the rail.

"You see, Mr. Jackson," he said, with a backward glance at the men, "I've only played the regular dodge on 'em. They've all got the sailor's bug in their heads and want to go coasting; so I told 'em this was a coaster."

"So she is," answered the officer; "round the Horn to Callao is coasting. What more do they want?"

"Yes, but I said nothin' of Callao, and they were all three sheets i' the wind when they signed, so they didn't notice the articles. They expected a schooner, too, big enough for sixteen men; but I've just talked 'em out of that notion. They think, too, that they'll have a week in port to see if they like the craft; and to make 'em think it was easy to quit, I told 'em to sign nicknames—made 'em believe that a wrong name on the articles voided the contract."

"But it don't. They're here, and they'll stay—that is, if they know enough to man the windlass."

"Of course—of course. I'm just givin' you a pointer. You may have to run them a little at the start, but that's easy. Now we'll tally 'em off. Don't mind the names; they'll answer to 'em. You see, they're all townies, and bring their names from home."

The shipping-master drew a large paper from his pocket, and they approached the men at the capstan, where the short, broad second mate had been taking their individual measures with scowling eye.

It was a strange crew for the forecastle of an out-ward-bound, deep-water American ship. Mr. Jackson looked in vain for the heavy, foreign faces, the greasy canvas jackets and blanket trousers he was accustomed to see. Not that these men seemed to be landsmen—each carried in his face and bearing the indefinable something by which sailors of all races may distinguish each other at a glance from fisher-men, tugmen, and deck-hands. They were all young men, and their intelligent faces—blemished more or less with marks of overnight dissipation—were as sunburnt as were those of the two mates; and where a hand could be seen, it showed as brown and tarry as that of the ablest able seaman. There were no chests among them, but the canvas clothes-bags were the genuine article, and they shouldered and handled them as only sailors can. Yet, aside from these externals, they gave no sign of being anything but well-paid, well-fed, self-respecting citizens, who would read the papers, discuss politics, raise families, and drink more than is good on pay-nights, to repent at church in the morning. The hands among them that were hidden were covered with well-fitting gloves—kid or dogskin; all wore white shirts and fashionable neck-wear; their shoes were polished; their hats were in style; and here and there, where an unbuttoned, silk-faced overcoat exposed the garments beneath, could be seen a gold watch-chain with tasteful charm.

"Now, boys," said the shipping-master, cheerily, as he unfolded the articles on the capstan-head, "an-swer, and step over to starboard as I read your names. Ready? Tosser Galvin."

"Here." A man carried his bag across the deck a short distance.

"Bigpig Monahan." Another—as large a man as the mate—answered and followed.

"Moccasey Gill."

"Good God!" muttered the mate, as this man responded.

"Sinful Peck." An undersized man, with a cultivated blond mustache, lifted his hat politely to Mr. Jackson, disclosing a smooth, bald head, and passed over, smiling sweetly. Whatever his character, his name belied his appearance; for his face was cherubic in its innocence.

"Say," interrupted the mate, angrily, "what kind of a game is this, anyhow? Are these men sailors?"

"Yes, yes," answered the shipping-master, hurriedly; "you'll find 'em all right. And, Sinful," he added, as he frowned reprovingly at the last man named, "don't you get gay till my receipt's signed and I'm clear of you."

Mr. Jackson wondered, but subsided; and, each name bringing forth a response, the reader called off: "Seldom Helward, Shiner O'Toole, Senator Sands, Jump Black, Yampaw Gallagher, Sorry Welch, Yorker Jimson, General Lannigan, Turkey Twain, Gunner Meagher, Ghost O'Brien, and Poop-deck Cahill."

Then the astounded Mr. Jackson broke forth profanely. "I've been shipmates," he declared between oaths, "with freak names of all nations; but this gang beats me. Say, you," he called,—"you with the cro'-jack eye there,—what's that name you go by? Who are you?" He spoke to the large man who had answered to "Bigpig Monahan," and who suffered from a slight distortion of one eye; but the man, instead of civilly repeating his name, answered curtly and coolly:

"I'm the man that struck Billy Patterson."

Fully realizing that the mate who hesitates is lost, and earnestly resolved to rebuke this man as his insolence required, Mr. Jackson had secured a belaying-pin and almost reached him, when he found himself looking into the bore of a pistol held by the shipping-master.

"Now, stop this," said the latter, firmly; "stop it right here, Mr. Jackson. These men are under my care till you've signed my receipt. After that you can do as you like; but if you touch one of them before you sign, I'll have you up 'fore the commissioner. And you fellers," he said over his shoulder, "you keep still and be civil till I'm rid of you. I've used you well, got your berths, and charged you nothin'. All I wanted was to get Cappen Benson the right kind of a crew."

"Let's see that receipt," snarled the mate. "Put that gun up, too, or I'll show you one of my own. I'll tend to your good men when you get ashore." He glared at the quiescent Bigpig, and followed the shipping-master—who still held his pistol ready, however—over to the rail, where the receipt was produced and signed.

"Away you go, now," said the mate; "you and your gun. Get over the side."

The shipping-master did not answer until he had scrambled down to the waiting tug and around to the far side of her deck-house. There, ready to dodge, he looked up at the mate with a triumphant grin on his shrewd face, and called:

"Say, Mr. Jackson, 'member the old bark *Fair*

Wind ten years ago, and the ordinary seaman you triced up and skinned alive with a deck-scraper? D' you 'member, curse you? 'Member breakin' the same boy's arm with a heaver? You do, don't you? I'm him. 'Member me sayin' I'd get square? "

He stepped back to avoid the whirling belaying-pin sent by the mate, which, rebounding, only smashed a window in the pilot-house. Then, amid an exchange of blasphemous disapproval between Mr. Jackson and the tug captain, and derisive jeers from the shipping-master,—who also averred that Mr. Jackson ought to be shot, but was not worth hanging for,—the tug gathered in her lines and steamed away.

Wrathful of soul, Mr. Jackson turned to the men on the deck. They had changed their position; they were now close to the fife-rail at the mainmast, surrounding Bigpig Monahan (for by their names we must know them), who, with an injured expression of face, was shedding outer garments and voicing his opinion of Mr. Jackson, which the others answered by nods and encouraging words. He had dropped a pair of starched cuffs over a belaying-pin, and was rolling up his shirt-sleeve, showing an arm as large as a small man's leg, and the mate was just about to interrupt the discourse, when the second mate called his name. Turning, he beheld him beckoning violently from the cabin companionway, and joined him.

"Got your gun, Mr. Jackson? " asked the second officer, anxiously, as he drew him within the door. " I started for mine when the shippin'-master pulled. I can't make that crowd out; but they're lookin' for fight, that's plain. When you were at the rail they were sayin': ' Soak him, Bigpig.' ' Paste him, Bigpig.' 'Put a head on him.' They might be a lot o' prize-fighters."

Mr. Becker was not afraid; his position and duties forbade it. He was simply human, and confronted with a new problem.

"Don't care a rap what they are," answered the mate, who was sufficiently warmed up to welcome any problem. They'll get fight enough. We'll overhaul their dunnage first for whisky and knives, then turn them to. Come on—I'm heeled."

They stepped out and advanced to the capstan amidships, each with a hand in his trousers pocket.

"Pile those bags against the capstan here, and go forrard," ordered the mate, in his most officer-like tone.

"Go to the devil," they answered. "What for?— they're our bags, not yours. Who in Sam Hill are you, anyhow? What are you? You talk like a p'liceman."

Before this irreverence could be replied to Bigpig Monahan advanced.

"Look here, old horse," he said; "I don't know whether you're captain or mate, or owner or cook; and I don't care, either. You had somethin' to say 'bout my eyes just now. Nature made my eyes, and I can't help how they look; but I don't allow any big bullheads to make remarks 'bout 'em. You're spoilin' for somethin.' Put up your hands." He threw himself into an aggressive attitude, one mighty fist within six inches of Mr. Jackson's face.

"Go forrard," roared the officer, his gray eyes sparkling; "forrard, all o' you!"

"We'll settle this; then we'll go forrard. There'll

be fair play; these men'll see to that. You'll only have me to handle. Put up."

Mr. Jackson did not "put up." He repeated again his order to go forward, and was struck on the nose—not a hard blow; just a preliminary tap, which started blood. He immediately drew his pistol and shot the man, who fell with a groan.

An expression of shock and horror overspread every face among the crew, and they surged back, away from that murderous pistol. A momentary hesitance followed, then horror gave way to furious rage, and carnage began. Coats and vests were flung off, belaying-pins and capstan-bars seized; inarticulate, half-uttered imprecations punctuated by pistol reports drowned the storm of abuse with which the mates justified the shot, and two distinct bands of men swayed and zigzagged about the deck, the center of each an officer fighting according to his lights—shooting as he could between blows of fists and clubs. Then the smoke of battle thinned and two men with sore heads and bleeding faces retreated painfully and hurriedly to the cabin, followed by snarling maledictions and threats.

It was hardly a victory for either side. The pistols were empty and the fight taken out of the mates for a time; and on the deck lay three moaning men, while two others clung to the fife-rail, draining blood from limp, hanging arms. But eleven sound and angry men were left—and the officers had more ammunition. They entered their rooms, mopped their faces with wet towels, reloaded the firearms, pocketed the remaining cartridges, and returned to the deck, the mate carrying a small ensign.

"We'll run it up to the main, Becker," he said

thickly,—for he suffered,—ignoring in his excitement
the etiquette of the quarter-deck.

"Aye, aye," said the other, equally unmindful
of his breeding. "Will we go for 'em again?" The
problem had defined itself to Mr. Becker. These men
would fight, but not shoot.

"No, no," answered the mate; "not unless they
go for us and it's self-defense. They're not sailors
—they don't know where they are. We don't want
to get into trouble. Sailors don't act that way.
We'll wait for the captain or the police." Which,
interpreted, and plus the slight shade of anxiety
showing in his disfigured face, meant that Mr. Jackson was confronted with a new phase of the problem:
as to how much more unsafe it might be to shoot
down, on the deck of a ship, men who did not know
where they were, than to shoot down sailors who did.
So, while the uninjured men were assisting the
wounded five into the forecastle, the police flag was
run up to the main-truck, and the two mates retired
to the poop to wait and watch.

In a few moments the eleven men came aft in a
body, empty-handed, however, and evidently with
no present hostile intention: they had merely come
for their clothes. But that dunnage had not been
searched; and in it might be all sorts of dangerous
weapons and equally dangerous whisky, the possession of which could bring an unpleasant solution to
the problem. So Mr. Jackson and Mr. Becker
leveled their pistols over the poop-rail, and, the chief
mate roared: "Let those things alone—let 'em alone,
or we'll drop some more o' you."

The men halted, hesitated, and sullenly returned
to the forecastle.

"Guess they've had enough," said Mr. Becker, jubilantly.

"Don't fool yourself. They're not used to blood-letting, that's all. If it wasn't for my wife and the kids I'd lower the dinghy and jump her; and it isn't them I'd run from, either. As it is, I've half a mind to haul down the flag, and let the old man settle it. Steward," he called to a mild-faced man who had been flitting from galley to cabin, unmindful of the disturbance, "go forrard and find out how bad those fellows are hurt. Don't say I sent you, though."

The steward obeyed, and returned with the information that two men had broken arms, two flesh-wounds in the legs, and one—the big man—suffered from a ragged hole through the shoulder. All were stretched out in bedless bunks, unwilling to move. He had been asked numerous questions by the others —as to where the ship was bound, who the men were who had shot them, why there was no bedding in the forecastle, the captain's whereabouts, and the possibility of getting ashore to swear out warrants. He had also been asked for bandages and hot water, which he requested permission to supply, as the wounded men were suffering greatly. This permission was refused, and the slight—very slight— nautical flavor to the queries, and the hopeful condition of the stricken ones, decided Mr. Jackson to leave the police flag at the masthead.

When dinner was served in the cabin, and Mr. Jackson sat down before a savory roast, leaving Mr. Becker on deck to watch, the steward imparted the additional information that the men forward expected to eat in the cabin.

"Hang it!" he mused; "they can't be sailor-men."

Then Mr. Becker reached his head down the sky-light, and said: "Raisin' the devil with the cook, sir —dragged him out o' the galley into the forecastle."

"Are they coming aft?"

"No, sir."

"All right. Watch out."

The mate went on eating, and the steward hurried forward to learn the fate of his assistant. He did not return until Mr. Jackson was about to leave the cabin. Then he came, with a wry face and disgust in his soul, complaining that he had been seized, hustled into the forecastle, and compelled, with the Chinese cook, to eat of the salt beef and pea-soup prepared for the men, which lay untouched by them. In spite of his aches and trouble of mind, Mr. Jackson was moved to a feeble grin.

"Takes a sailor or a hog to eat it, hey, Steward?" he said.

He relieved Mr. Becker, who ate his dinner hurriedly, as became a good second mate, and the two resumed their watch on the poop, noticing that the cook was jabbering Chinese protest in the galley, and that the men had climbed to the topgallant-forecastle—also watching, and occasionally waving futile signals to passing tugs or small sailing-craft. They, too, might have welcomed the police boat.

But, either because the *Almena* lay too far over on the Jersey flats for the flag to be noticed, or because harbor police share the fallibility of their shore brethren in being elsewhere when wanted, no shiny black steamer with blue-coated guard appeared to investigate the trouble, and it was well on toward three o'clock before a tug left the beaten track to the eastward and steamed over to the ship. The officers took her lines as she came alongside, and two men climbed the side-ladder—one, a Sandy Hook pilot, who need not be described; the other, the captain of the ship.

Captain Benson, in manner and appearance, was as superior to the smooth-shaven and manly-looking Mr. Jackson as the latter was to the misformed, hairy, and brutal second mate. With his fashionably cut clothing, steady blue eye, and refined features, he could have been taken for an easy-going club-man or educated army officer rather than the master of a working-craft. Yet there was no lack of seamanly, decision in the leap he made from the rail to the deck, or in the tone of his voice as he demanded:

"What's the police flag up for, Mr. Jackson?"

"Mutiny, sir. They started in to lick me 'fore turning to, and we've shot five, but none of them fatally."

"Lower that flag—at once."

Mr. Becker obeyed this order, and as the flag fluttered down the captain received an account of the crew's misdoing from the mate. He stepped into his cabin, and returning with a double-barreled shot-gun, leaned it against the booby-hatch, and said quietly: "Call all hands aft who can come."

Mr. Jackson delivered the order in a roar, and the eleven men forward, who had been watching the newcomers from the forecastle, straggled aft and clustered near the capstan, all of them hatless and coatless, shivering palpably in the keen December air. With no flinching of their eyes, they stared at Captain Benson and the pilot.

"Now, men," said the captain, "what's this trouble about? What's the matter?"

"Are you the captain here?" asked a red-haired, Roman-nosed man, as he stepped out of the group. "There's matter enough. We ship for a run down to Rio Janeiro and back in a big schooner; and here we're put aboard a square-rigged craft, that we don't know anything about, bound for Callao, and 'fore we're here ten minutes we're howled at and shot. Bigpig Monahan thinks he's goin' to die; he's bleedin'—they're all bleedin', like stuck pigs. Sorry Welch and Turkey Twain ha' got broken arms, and Jump Black and Ghost O'Brien got it in the legs and can't stand up. What kind o' work is this, anyhow?"

"That's perfectly right. You were shot for assaulting my officers. Do you call yourselves able seamen, and say you know nothing about square-rigged craft?"

"We're able seamen on the Lakes. We can get along in schooners. That's what we came down for."

Captain Benson's lips puckered, and he whistled softly. "The Lakes," he said—"lake sailors. What part of the Lakes?"

"Oswego. We're all union men."

The captain took a turn or two along the deck, then faced them, and said: "Men, I've been fooled as well as you. I would not have an Oswego sailor aboard my ship—much less a whole crew of them. You may know your work up there, but are almost useless here until you learn. Although I paid five dollars a man for you, I'd put you ashore and ship a new crew were it not for the fact that five wounded men going out of this ship requires explanations, which would delay my sailing and incur expense to my owners. However, I give you the choice—to go to sea, and learn your work under the mates, or go to jail as mutineers; for to protect my officers I must prosecute you all."

"S'pose we do neither?"

"You will probably be shot—to the last resisting man—either by us or the harbor police. You are up against the law."

They looked at each other with varying expressions on their faces; then one asked: "What about the bunks in the forecastle? There's no bedding."

"If you failed to bring your own, you will sleep on the bunk-boards without it."

"And that swill the Chinaman cooked at dinner-time—what about that?"

"You will get the allowance of provisions provided by law—no more. And you will eat it in the forecastle. Also, if you have neglected to bring pots, pans, and spoons, you will very likely eat it with your fingers. This is not a lake vessel, where sailors eat at the cabin table, with knives and forks. Decide this matter quickly."

The captain began pacing the deck, and the listening pilot stepped forward, and said kindly: "Take my advice, boys, and go along. You're in for it if you don't."

They thanked him with their eyes for the sympathy, conferred together for a few moments, then their spokesman called out: "We'll leave it to the fellers forrard, captain"; and forward they trooped. In five minutes they were back, with resolution in their faces.

"We'll go, captain," their leader said. "Bigpig can't be moved 'thout killin' him, and says if he lives he'll follow your mate to hell but he'll pay him back; and the others talk the same; and we'll stand by 'em—we'll square up this day's work."

Captain Benson brought his walk to a stop close to the shot-gun. "Very well, that is your declaration," he said, his voice dropping the conversational tone he had assumed, and taking on one more in accordance with his position; "now I will deliver mine. We sail at once for Callao and back to an American port of discharge. You know your wages—fourteen dollars a month. I am master of this ship, responsible to my owners and the law for the lives of all on board. And this responsibility includes the right to take the life of a mutineer. You have been such, but I waive the charge considering your ignorance of salt-water custom and your agreement to start anew. The law defines your allowance of food, but not your duties or your working- and sleeping-time. That is left to the discretion of your captain and officers. Precedent—the decision of the courts—has decided the privilege of a captain or officer to punish insolence or lack of respect from a sailor with a blow—of a fist or missile; but, understand me now, a return of the blow makes that man a mutineer, and his prompt killing is justified by the law of the land. Is this plain to you? You are here to answer and obey orders respectfully, adding the word 'sir' to each response; you are never to go to windward of an officer, or address him by name without the prefix 'Mr.'; and you are to work civilly and faithfully, resenting nothing said to you until you are discharged in an American port at the end of the voyage. A failure in this will bring you prompt punishment; and resentment of this punishment on your part will bring—death. Mr. Jackson," he concluded, turning to his first officer, "overhaul their dunnage, turn them to, and man the windlass."

A man—the bald-headed Sinful Peck—sprang forward; but his face was not cherubic now. His blue eyes blazed with emotion much in keeping with his sobriquet; and, raising his hand, the nervously crooking fingers of which made it almost a fist, he said, in a voice explosively strident:

"That's all right. That's *your* say. You've described the condition o' nigger slaves, not American voters. And I'll tell you one thing, right here—I'm a free-born citizen. I know my work, and can do it, without bein' cursed and abused; and if you or your mates rub my fur the wrong way I'm goin' to claw back; and if I'm shot, you want to shoot sure; for if you don't, I'll kill that man, if I have to lash my knife to a broom-handle, and prod him through his window when he's asleep."

But alas for Sinful Peck! He had barely finished his defiance when he fell like a log under the impact of the big mate's fist; then, while the pilot, turning his back on the painful scene, walked aft, nodding and shaking his head, and the captain's strong language and leveled shot-gun induced the men to an agitated acquiescence, the two officers kicked and stamped upon the little man until consciousness left him. Before he recovered he had been ironed to a stanchion in the 'tween-deck, and entered in the captain's official log for threatening life. And by this time the dunnage had been searched, a few sheath-knives tossed overboard, and the remaining ten men were moodily heaving in the chain.

And so, with a crippled crew of schooner sailors, the square-rigger *Almena* was towed to sea, smoldering rebellion in one end of her, the power of the law in the other—murder in the heart of every man on board.

PART II

FIVE months later the *Almena* lay at an outer mooring-buoy in Callao Roads, again ready for sea, but waiting. With her at the anchorage were representatives of most of the maritime nations. English ships and barks with painted ports, and spider-web braces, high-sided, square-sterned American half-clippers, clumsy, square-bowed "Dutchmen," coasting-brigs of any nation, lumber-schooners from "'Frisco," hide-carriers from Valparaiso, pearl-boats and fishermen, and even a couple of homesick Malay proas from the west crowded the roadstead; for the guano trade was booming, and Callao prosperous. Nearly every type of craft known to sailors was there; but the postman and the policeman of the seas—the coastwise mail-steamer and the heavily sparred man-of-war—were conspicuously absent. The Pacific Mail boat would not arrive for a week, and the last cruiser had departed two days before.

Beyond the faint land- and sea-breeze, there was no wind nor promise of it for several days; and Captain Benson, though properly cleared at the custom-house for New York, was in no hurry, and had taken advantage of the delay to give a dinner to some captains with whom he had fraternized on shore. " I've a first-rate steward," he had told them, " and I'll treat you well; and I've the best-trained crew that ever went to sea. Come, all of you, and bring your first officers. I want to give you an object-lesson on the influence of matter over mind that you can't learn in the books."

So they came, at half-past eleven, in their own ships' dinghies, which were sent back with orders to return at nightfall—six big-fisted, more or less fat captains, and six big-fisted, beetle-browed, and embarrassed chief mates. As they climbed the gangway they were met and welcomed by Captain Benson, who led them to the poop, the only dry and clean part of the ship; for the *Almena's* crew were holystoning the main-deck, and as this operation consists in grinding off the oiled surface of the planks with sandstone, the resulting slime of sand, oily woodpulp, and salt water made walking unpleasant, as well as being very hard on polished shoe-leather. But in this filthy slime the men were on their knees, working the six-inch blocks of stone, technically called " bibles," back and forth with about the speed and motion of an energetic woman over a washboard.

The mates also were working. With legs clad in long rubber boots, they filled buckets at the deck-pump and scattered water around where needed, occasionally throwing the whole bucketful at a doubtful spot on the deck to expose it to criticism. As the visitors lined up against the monkey-rail and looked down on the scene, Mr. Becker launched such a bucketful as only a second mate can—and a man who happened to be in the way was rolled over by the unexpected impact. He gasped a little louder than might have been necessary, and the wasting of the bucketful of water having forced Mr. Becker to make an extra trip to the pump, the officer was duly incensed.

"Get out o' the way, there," he bawled, eying the man sternly. "What are you gruntin' at? A little water won't hurt you—soap neither."

He went to the pump for more water, and the man crawled back to his holystone. It was Bigpig Monahan, hollow-eyed and thin, slow in his voluntary movements; minus his look of injury, too, as though he might have welcomed the bowling over as a momentary respite for his aching muscles.

Now and then, when the officers' faces were partly turned, a man would stop, rise erect on his knees, and bend backward. A man may work a holystone much longer and press it much harder on the deck for these occasional stretchings of contracted tissue; but the two mates chose to ignore this physiological fact, and a moment later, a little man, caught in the act by Mr. Jackson, was also rolled over on his back, not by a bucket of water, but by the boot of the mate, who uttered words suitable to the occasion, and held his hand in his pocket until the little man, grinning with rage, had resumed his work.

"There," said Captain Benson to his guests on the poop; "see that little devil! See him show his teeth! That is Mr. Sinful Peck. I've had him in irons with a broken head five times, and the log is full of him. I towed him over the stern running down the trades to take the cussedness out of him, and if he had not been born for higher things, he'd have drowned. He was absolutely unconquerable until I found him telling his beads one time in irons and took them away from him. Now to get an occasional chance at them he is fairly quiet."

"So this is your trained crew, is it, captain?" said a grizzled old skipper of the party. "What ails that fellow down in the scuppers with a prayer-book?" He pointed to a man who with one hand was rubbing a small holystone in a corner where a large one would not go.

"Ran foul of the big end of a handspike," answered Captain Benson, quietly; "he'll carry his arm in splints all the way home, I think. His name is Gunner Meagher. I don't know how they got their names, but they signed them and will answer to them. They are unique. Look at that outlaw down there by the bitts. That is Poop-deck Cahill. Looks like a prize-fighter, doesn't he? But the steward tells me that he was educated for the priesthood, and fell by the wayside. That one close to the hatch—the one with the red head and hang-dog jib—is Seldom Helward. He was shot off the cro'-jack yard; he fell into the lee clew of the cro'-jack, so we pulled him in."

"What did he do, captain?" asked the grizzled skipper.

"Threw a marlinespike at the mate."

"What made him throw it?"

"Never asked. I suppose he objected to something said to him."

"Ought to ha' killed him on the yard. Are they all of a kind?"

"Every man. Not one knew the ropes or his place when he shipped. They're schooner sailors from the Lakes, where the captain, if he is civil and respectful to his men, is as good as any of them. They started to clean us up the first day, but failed, and I went to sea with them. Since then, until lately, it has been war to the knife. I've set more bones, mended more heads, and plugged more shot-holes on this passage than ever before, and my officers have grown perceptibly thinner; but little by little, man by man, we've broken them in. Still, I admit, it was a job. Why, that same Seldom Helward I ironed and ran up on the fall of a main-buntline. We were rolling before a stiff breeze and sea, and he would swing six feet over each rail and bat against the mast in transit; but the dog stood it eight hours before he stopped cursing us. Then he was unconscious. When he came to in the forecastle, he was ready to begin again; but they stopped him. They're keeping a log, I learn, and are going to law. Every time a man gets thumped they enter the tragedy, and all sign their names."

Captain Benson smiled dignifiedly in answer to the outburst of laughter evoked by this, and the men below lifted their haggard, hopeless faces an instant and looked at the party with eyes that were furtive —cat-like. The grinding of the stones prevented their hearing the talk, but they knew that they were being laughed at.

"Never knew a sailor yet," wheezed a portly and asthmatic captain, "who wasn't ready to sue the devil and try the court in hell when he's at sea. Trouble is, they never get past the first saloon."

"They got a little law here," resumed Captain Benson, quietly. "I put them all in the guardo. The consul advised it, and committed them for fear they might desert when we lay at the dock. When I took them out to run to the islands, they complained of being starved; and to tell the truth, they didn't throw their next meal overboard as usual. Nevertheless, a good four weeks' board-bill comes out of their wages. I don't think they'll have a big pay-day in New York: the natives cleaned out the forecastle in their absence, and they'll have to draw heavily on my slop-chest."

" That's where captains have the best of it," said one of the mates, jocularly—and presumptuously, to judge by his captain's frown; " we hammer 'em round and wear out their clothes, and it's the captain that sells 'em new ones."

" Captain," said the grizzled one, who had been scanning the crew intently, " I'd pay that crew off if I were you; you ought to ha' let 'em run, or worked 'em out and saved their pay. Look at 'em— look at the devils in their eyes. I notice your mates seldom turn their backs on 'em. I'd get rid of 'em."

" What! Just when we have them under control and useful? Oh, no! They know their work now, and I'd only have to ship a crowd of beach-combers and half-breeds at nearly double pay. Besides, gentlemen, we're just a little proud of this crew. They are lake sailors from Oswego, a little port on Lake Ontario. When I was young I sailed on the Lakes a season or two and became thoroughly acquainted with the aggressive self-respect of that breed. They would rather fight than eat. Their reputation in this regard prevents them getting berths in any but Oswego vessels, and even affects the policy of the nation. There's a fort at Oswego, and whenever a company of soldiers anywhere in the country become unmanageable—when their officers can't control them outside the guard-house—the War Department at

Washington transfers them to Oswego for the tutelage they will get from the sailors. And they get it; they are well-behaved, well-licked soldiers when they leave. An Oswego sailor loves a row. He is possessed by the fighting spirit of a bulldog; he inherits it with his Irish sense of injury; he sucks it in with his mother's milk, and drinks it in with his whisky; and when no enemies are near, he will fight his friends. Pay them off? Not much. I've taken sixteen of those devils round the Horn, and I'll take them back. I'm proud of them. Just look at them," he concluded vivaciously, as he waved his hand at his men; " docile and obedient, down on their knees with bibles and prayer-books."

" And the name o' the Lord on their lips," grunted the adviser; " but not in prayer, I'll bet you."

" Hardly," laughed Captain Benson. " Come below, gentlemen; the steward is ready."

From lack of facilities the mild-faced and smiling steward could not serve that dinner with the style which it deserved. He would have liked, he explained, as they seated themselves, to bring it on in separate courses; but one and all disclaimed such frivolity. The dinner was there, and that was enough. And it was a splendid dinner. In front of Captain Benson, at the head of the table, stood a large tureen of smoking terrapin-stew; next to that a stuffed and baked freshly caught fish; and waiting their turn in the center of the spread, a couple of brace of wild geese from the inland lakes, brown and glistening, oyster-dressed and savory. Farther along was a steaming plum-pudding, overhead on a swinging tray a dozen bottles of wine, by the captain's elbow a decanter of yellow fluid, and before each man's plate a couple of glasses of different size.

"We'll start off with an appetizer, gentlemen," said the host, as he passed the decanter to his neighbor. "Here is some of the best Dutch courage ever distilled; try it."

The decanter went around, each filling his glass and holding it poised; then, when all were supplied, they drank to the grizzled old captain's toast: "A speedy and pleasant passage home for the *Almena*, and further confusion to her misguided crew." The captain responded gracefully, and began serving the stew, which the steward took from him plate by plate, and passed around.

But, either because thirteen men had sat down to that table, or because the Fates were unusually freakish that day, it was destined that, beyond the initial glass of whisky, not a man present should partake of Captain Benson's dinner. On deck things had been happening, and just as the host had filled the last plate for himself, a wet, bedraggled, dirty little man, his tarry clothing splashed with the slime of the deck, his eyes flaming green, his face expanded to a smile of ferocity, appeared in the forward doorway, holding a cocked revolver which covered them all. Behind him in the passage were other men, equally unkempt, their eyes wide open with excitement and anticipation.

"Don't ye move," yelped the little man, "not a man. Keep yer hands out o' yer pockets. Put 'em over yer heads. That's it. You too, cappen."

They obeyed him (there was death in the green eyes and smile), all but one. Captain Benson sprang to his feet, with a hand in his breast pocket.

"You scoundrels!" he cried, as he drew forth a

pistol. "Leave this—" The speech was stopped by a report, deafening in the closed-up space; and Captain Benson fell heavily, his pistol rattling on the floor.

"Hang me up, will ye?" growled another voice through the smoke.

In the after-door were more men, the red-haired Seldom Helward in the van, holding a smoking pistol. "Get the gun, one o' you fellows over there," he called.

A man stepped in and picked up the pistol, which he cocked.

"One by one," said Seldom, his voice rising to the pitch and timbre of a trumpet-blast, "you men walk out the forward companionway with your hands over your heads. Plug them, Sinful, if two move together, and shoot to kill."

Taken by surprise, the guests, resolute men though they were, obeyed the command. As each rose to his feet, he was first relieved of a bright revolver, which served to increase the moral front of the enemy, then led out to the booby-hatch, on which lay a newly broached coil of hambro-line and pile of thole-pins from the boatswain's locker. Here he was searched again for jack-knife or brass knuckles, bound with the hambro-line, gagged with a thole-pin, and marched forward, past the prostrate first mate, who lay quiet in the scuppers, and the erect but agonized second mate, gagged and bound to the fife-rail, to the port forecastle, where he was locked in with the Chinese cook, who, similarly treated, had preceded. The mild-faced steward, weeping now, as much from professional disappointment as from stronger emotion, was questioned sternly, and allowed his freedom

on his promise not to "sing out" or make trouble.
Captain Benson was examined, his injury diagnosed
as brain-concussion, from the glancing bullet, more
or less serious, and dragged out to the scuppers,
where he was bound beside his unconscious first officer.
Then, leaving them to live or die as their subconsciousness determined, the sixteen mutineers sacrile-
giously reëntered the cabin and devoured the dinner.
And the appetites they displayed—their healthy,
hilarious enjoyment of the good things on the table
—so affected the professional sense of the steward
that he ceased his weeping, and even smiled as he
waited on them.

When you have cursed, beaten, and kicked a slave
for five months it is always advisable to watch him
for a few seconds after you administer correction,
to give him time to realize his condition. And when
you have carried a revolver in the right-hand trousers
pocket for five months it is advisable occasionally to
inspect the cloth of the pocket to make sure that it
is not wearing thin from the chafe of the muzzle.
Mr. Jackson had ignored the first rule of conduct,
Mr. Becker the second. Mr. Jackson had kicked
Sinful Peck once too often; but not knowing that it
was once too often, had immediately turned his back,
and received thereat the sharp corner of a bible on
his bump of inhabitiveness, which bump responded in
its function; for Mr. Jackson showed no immediate
desire to move from the place where he fell. Beyond binding, he received no further attention from
the men. Mr. Becker, on his way to the lazarette in
the stern for a bucket of sand to assist in the holystoning, had reached the head of the poop steps
when this occurred; and turning at the sound of his

superior's fall, had bounded to the main-deck without touching the steps, reaching for his pistol as he landed, only to pinion his fingers in a large hole in the pocket. Wildly he struggled to reclaim his weapon, down his trouser leg, held firmly to his knee by the tight rubber boot; but he could not reach it. His anxious face betrayed his predicament to the wakening men, and when he looked into Mr. Jackson's revolver, held by Sinful Peck, he submitted to being bound to the fife-rail and gagged with the end of the topgallant-sheet—a large rope, which just filled his mouth, and hurt. Then the firearm was recovered, and the descent upon the dinner-party quickly planned and carried out.

Have you ever seen a kennel of hunting-dogs released on a fine day after long confinement—how they bark and yelp, chasing one another, biting playfully, rolling and tumbling over and over in sheer joy and healthy appreciation of freedom? Without the vocal expression of emotion, the conduct of these men after that wine dinner was very similar to that of such emancipated dogs. They waltzed, boxed, wrestled, threw each other about the deck, turned handsprings and cart-wheels,—those not too weak,—buffeted, kicked, and clubbed the suffering Mr. Becker, reviled and cursed the unconscious captain and chief officer, and when tired of this, as children and dogs of play, they turned to their captives for amusement. The second mate was taken from the fife-rail, with hands still bound, and led to the forecastle; the gags of all and the bonds of the cook were removed, and the forecastle dinner was brought from the galley. This they were invited to eat. There was a piece of salt-beef, boiled a little longer than usual on account of

the delay; it was black, brown, green, and iridescent
in spots; it was slippery with ptomaïnes, filthy to the
sight, stinking, and nauseating. There were potatoes, two years old, shriveled before boiling—hard
and soggy, black, blue, and bitter after the process.
And there was the usual "weevily hardtack" in the
bread-barge.

Protest was useless. The unhappy captives surrounded that dinner on the forecastle floor (for there
was neither table to sit at, nor chests, stools, or boxes
to sit on, in the apartment), and, with hands behind
their backs and disgust in their faces, masticated and
swallowed the morsels which the Chinese cook put to
their mouths, while their feelings were further out-
raged by the hilarity of the men at their backs, and
their appetites occasionally jogged into activity by
the impact on their heads of a tarry fist or pistol-
butt. At last a portly captain began vomiting, and
this being contagious, the meal ended; for even the
stomachs of the sailors, overcharged as they were
with the rich food and wine of the cabin table, were
affected by the spectacle.

There were cool heads in that crowd of mutineers
—men who thought of consequences: Poop-deck Cahill, square-faced and resolute, but thoughtful of eye
and refined of speech; Seldom Helward, who had shot
the captain—a man whose fiery hair, arching eye-
brows, Roman nose, and explosive language indicated
the daredevil, but whose intelligent though humorous
eye and corrugated forehead gave certain signs of
repressive study and thought; and Bigpig Monahan,
already described. These three men went into session
under the break of the poop, and came to the conclusion that the consul who had jailed them for

nothing would hang them for this; then, calling the rest to the conference as a committee of the whole, they outlined and put to vote a proposition to make sail and go to sea, leaving the fate of their captives for later consideration—which was adopted unanimously and with much profanity, the central thought of the latter being an intention to " make 'em finish the holystonin' for the fun they had laughin' at us." Then Bigpig Monahan sneaked below and induced the steward to toss through the storeroom dead-light every bottle of wine and liquor which the ship contained. " For Seldom and Poop-deck," he said to him, " are the only men in the gang fit to pick up navigation and git this ship into port again; but if they git their fill of it, it's all day with you, steward."

Six second mates on six American ships watched curiously, doubtingly, and at last anxiously, as sails were dropped and yards mastheaded on board the *Almena*, and as she paid off from the mooring-buoy before the land breeze and showed them her stern, sent six dinghies, which gave up the pursuit in a few minutes and mustered around the buoy, where a wastefully slipped shot of anchor-chain gave additional evidence that all was not right. But by the time the matter was reported to the authorities ashore, the *Almena*, having caught the newly arrived southerly wind off the Peruvian coast, was hull down on the western horizon.

Four days later, one of the *Almena's* boats, containing twelve men with sore heads, disfigured faces, and clothing ruined by oily wood-pulp,—ruined particularly about the knees of their trousers,—came wearily into the roadstead from the open sea, past the shipping and up to the landing at the custom-house docks. From here the twelve proceeded to the American consul and entered bitter complaint of inhuman treatment received at the hands of sixteen mutinous sailors on board the *Almena*—treatment so cruel that they had welcomed being turned adrift in an open boat; whereat, the consul, deploring the absence of man-of-war or steamer to send in pursuit, took their individual affidavits; and these he sent to San Francisco, from which point the account of the crime, described as piracy, spread to every newspaper in Christendom.

PART III

A NORTHEAST gale off Hatteras: immense gray combers, five to the mile, charging, shoreward, occasionally breaking, again lifting their heads too high in the effort, truncated as by a knife, and the liquid apex shattered to spray; an expanse of leaden sky showing between the rain-squalls, across which heavy background rushed the darker scud and storm-clouds; a passenger-steamer rolling helplessly in the trough, and a square-rigged vessel, hove to on the port tack, two miles to windward of the steamer, and drifting south toward the storm-center. This is the picture that the sea-birds saw at daybreak on a September morning, and could the sea-birds have spoken they might have told that the square-rigged craft carried a navigator who had learned that a whirling fury of storm-center was less to be feared than the deadly Diamond Shoals—the outlying guard of Cape Hatteras toward which that steamer was drifting, broadside on.

Clad in yellow oilskins and sou'wester, he stood by the after-companionway, intently examining through a pair of glasses the wallowing steamer to leeward, barely distinguishable in the half-light and driving spindrift. On the main-deck a half-dozen men paced up and down, sheltered by the weather rail; forward, two others walked the deck by the side of the forward house, but never allowed their march to extend past the after-corner; and at the wheel stood a little man who sheltered a cheerful face under the lee of a big coat-collar, and occasionally peeped out at the navigator.

"Poop-deck," he shouted above the noise of the wind, "take the wheel till I fire up."

"Thought I was exempt from steering," growled the other, good-humoredly, as he placed the glasses inside the companionway.

"You're getting too fat and sassy; steer a little."

Poop-deck relieved the little man, who descended the cabin stairs, and returned in a few moments, smoking a short pipe. He took the wheel, and Poop-deck again examined the steamer with the glasses.

"There goes his ensign, union down," he exclaimed; "he's in trouble. We'll show ours."

From a flag-locker inside the companionway he drew out the Stars and Stripes, which he ran up to the monkey-gaff. Then he looked again.

"Down goes his ensign; up goes the code pennant. He wants to signal. Come up here, boys," called Poop-deck; "give me a hand."

As the six men climbed the steps, he pulled out the corresponding code signal from the locker, and ran it up on the other part of the halyards as the ensign fluttered down. "Go down, one of you," he said, "and get the signal-book and shipping-list. He'll show his number next. Get ours ready—R. L. F. T."

While a man sprang below for the books named, the others hooked together the signal-flags forming the ship's number, and Poop-deck resumed the glasses.

"Q. T. F. N.," he exclaimed. "Look it up."

The books had arrived, and while one lowered and hoisted again the code signal, which was also the answering pennant, the others pored over the shipping-list.

"Steamer *Aldebaran* of New York," they said.

The pennant came down, and the ship's number went up to the gaff.

"H. V.," called Poop-deck, as he scanned two flags now flying from the steamer's truck. "What does that say?"

"Damaged rudder—cannot steer," they answered.

"Pull down the number and show the answering pennant again," said Poop-deck; "and let me see that signal-book." He turned the leaves, studied a page for a moment, then said: "Run up H. V. R. That says, 'What do you want?' and that's the nearest thing to it."

These flags took the place of the answering pennant at the gaff-end, and again Poop-deck watched through the glasses, noting first the showing of the steamer's answering pennant, then the letters K. R. N.

"What does K. R. N. say?" he asked.

They turned the leaves, and answered: "I can tow you."

"Tow us? We're all right; we don't want a tow.

He's crazy. How can he tow us when he can't steer?" exclaimed three or four together.

"He wants to tow us so that he *can* steer, you blasted fools," said Poop-deck. "He can keep head to sea and go where he likes with a big drag on his stern."

"That's so. Where's he bound—'you that has knowledge and eddication'?"

"Didn't say; but he's bound for the Diamond Shoals, and he'll fetch up in three hours, if we can't help him. He's close in."

"Tow-line's down the forepeak," said a man. "Couldn't get it up in an hour," said another. "Yes, we can," said a third. Then, all speaking at once, and each raising his voice to its limit, they argued excitedly: "Can't be done." "Coil it on the forecastle." "Yes, we can." "Too much sea." "Run down to wind'ard." "Line'ud part, anyhow." "Float a barrel." "Shut up." "I tell you, we can." "Call the watch." "Seldom, yer daft." "Needn't get a boat over." "Hell ye can." "Call the boys." "All hands with heavin'-lines." "Can't back a topsail in this." "Go lay down." "Soak yer head, Seldom." "Hush." "Shut up." "Nothin' *you* can't do." "Go to the devil." "I tell you, we can; do as I say, and we'll get a line to him, or get his."

The affirmative speaker, who had also uttered the last declaration, was Seldom Helward. "Put me in command," he yelled excitedly, "and do what I tell you, and we'll make fast to him."

"No captains here," growled one, while the rest eyed Seldom reprovingly.

"Well, there ought to be; you're all rattled, and

don't know any more than to let thousands o' dollars slip past you. There's salvage down to looward."

" Salvage? "

" Yes, salvage. Big boat—full o' passengers and valuable cargo—shoals to looward of him—can't steer. You poor fools, what ails you? "

" Foller Seldom," vociferated the little man at the wheel; " foller Seldom, and ye'll wear stripes."

" Dry up, Sinful. Call the watch. It's near seven bells, anyhow. Let's hear what the rest say. Strike the bell."

The uproarious howl with which sailors call the watch below was delivered down the cabin stairs, and soon eight other men came up, rubbing their eyes and grumbling at the premature wakening, while another man came out of the forecastle and joined the two pacing the forward deck. Seldom Helward's proposition was discussed noisily in joint session on the poop, and finally accepted.

" We put you in charge, Seldom, against the rule," said Bigpig Monahan, sternly, " 'cause we think you've some good scheme in your head; but if you haven't,—if you make a mess of things just to have a little fun bossin' us,—you'll hear from us. Go ahead, now. You're captain."

Seldom climbed to the top of the afterhouse, looked to windward, then to leeward at the rolling steamer, and called out:

" I want more beef at the wheel. Bigpig, take it; and you, Turkey, stand by with him. Get away from there, Sinful. Give her the upper maintopsail, the rest of you. Poop-deck, you stand by the signal-halyards. Ask him if he's got a tow-line ready."

Protesting angrily at the slight put upon him,

Sinful Peck relinquished the wheel, and joined the rest on the main-deck, where they had hurried. Two men went aloft to loose the topsail, and the rest cleared away gear, while Poop-deck examined the signal-book.

"K. S. G. says, 'Have a tow-line ready.' That ought to do, Seldom," he called.

"Run it up," ordered the newly installed captain, "and watch his answer." Up went the signal, and as the men on the main-deck were manning the top-sail-halyards, Poop-deck made out the answer: "V. K. C."

"That means, 'All right,' Seldom," he said, after inspecting the book.

"Good enough; but we'll get our line ready, too. Get down and help 'em masthead the yard first, then take 'em forrard and coil the tow-line abaft the wind-lass. Get all the heavin'-lines ready, too."

Poop-deck obeyed; and while the maintopsail-yard slowly arose to place under the efforts of the rest, Seldom himself ran up the answering pennant, and then the repetition of the steamer's last message: "All right." This was the final signal displayed between the two craft. Both signal-flags were lowered, and for a half-hour Seldom waited, until the others had lifted a nine-inch hawser from the fore-peak and coiled it down. Then came his next orders in a continuous roar:

"Three hands aft to the spanker-sheet! Stand by to slack off and haul in! Man the braces for wearing ship, the rest o' you! Hard up the wheel! Check in port main and starboard cro'-jack braces! Shiver the topsail! Slack off that spanker!"

Before he had finished the men had reached their

posts. The orders were obeyed. The ship paid off, staggered a little in the trough under the right-angle pressure of the gale, swung still farther, and steadied down to a long, rolling motion, dead before the wind, heading for the steamer. Yards were squared in, the spanker hauled aft, staysail trimmed to port, and all hands waited while the ship charged down the two miles of intervening sea.

"Handles like a yacht," muttered Seldom, as, with brow wrinkled and keen eye flashing above his hooked nose, he conned the steering from his place near the mizzenmast.

Three men separated themselves from the rest and came aft. They were those who had walked the forward deck. One was tall, broad-shouldered, and smooth-shaven, with a palpable limp; another, short, broad, and hairy, showed a lamentable absence of front teeth; and the third, a blue-eyed man, slight and graceful of movement, carried his arm in splints and sling. This last was in the van as they climbed the poop steps.

"I wish to protest," he said. "I am captain of this ship under the law. I protest against this insanity. No boat can live in this sea. No help can be given that steamer."

"And I bear witness to the protest," said the tall man. The short, hairy man might have spoken also, but had no time.

"Get off the poop," yelled Seldom. "Go forrard, where you belong." He stood close to the bucket-rack around the skylight. Seizing bucket after bucket, he launched them at his visitors, with the result that the big man was tumbled down the poop steps head first, while the other two followed, right side up, but hurriedly, and bearing some sore spots. Then the rest of the men set upon them, much as a pack of dogs would worry strange cats, and kicked and buffeted them forward.

There was no time for much amusement of this sort. Yards were braced to port, for the ship was careering down toward the steamer at a ten-knot rate; and soon black dots on her rail resolved into passengers waving hats and handkerchiefs, and black dots on the boat deck resolved into sailors standing by the end of a hawser which led up from the bitts below on the fantail. And the ship came down, until it might have seemed that Seldom's intention was to ram her. But not so; when a scant two lengths separated the two craft, he called out: " Hard down! Light up the staysail-sheet and stand by the forebraces ! "

Around the ship came on the crest of a sea; she sank into the hollow behind, shipped a few dozen tons of water from the next comber, and then lay fairly steady, with her bow meeting the seas, and the huge steamer not a half-length away on the lee quarter. The foretopmast-staysail was flattened, and Seldom closely scrutinized the drift and heave of the ship.

" How's your wheel, Bigpig? " he asked.

" Hard down."

" Put it up a little; keep her in the trough."

He noted the effect on the ship of this change; then, as though satisfied, roared out: " Let your forebraces hang, forrard there! Stand by heavin'-lines fore and aft! Stand by to go ahead with that steamer when we have your line! " The last injunction, delivered through his hands, went down the wind like a thunder-clap, and the officers on the steamer's bridge, vainly trying to make themselves heard against the gale in the same manner, started perceptibly at the impact of sound, and one went to the engine-room speaking tube.

Breast to breast the two vessels lifted and fell. At times it seemed that the ship was to be dropped bodily on the deck of the steamer; at others, her crew looked up a streaked slope of a hundred feet to where the other craft was poised at the crest. Then the steamer would drop, and the next sea would heave the ship toward her. But it was noticeable that every bound brought her nearer to the steamer, and also farther ahead, for her sails were doing their work.

"Kick ahead on board the steamer!" thundered Seldom from his eminence. "Go ahead! Start the wagon, or say your prayers, you blasted idiots!"

The engines were already turning; but it takes time to overcome three thousand tons of inertia, and before the steamer had forged ahead six feet the ship had lifted above her, and descended her black side with a grinding crash of wood against iron. Fore and main channels on the ship were carried away, leaving all lee rigging slack and useless; lower braces caught in the steamer's davit-cleats and snapped, but the sails, held by the weather braces, remained full, and the yards did not swing. The two craft separated with a roll and came together again with more scraping and snapping of rigging. Passengers left the rail, dived indoors, and took refuge on the opposite side, where falling blocks and small spars might not reach them. Another leap toward the steamer resulted in the ship's maintopgallant-mast falling in a zigzag whirl, as the snapping gear aloft impeded it; and dropping athwart the steamer's funnel, it neatly sent the royalyard with sail attached down the iron cylinder, where it soon blazed and helped the artificial draft in the stoke-hold. Next came the foretopgallantmast, which smashed a couple of boats. Then, as the round black stern of the steamer scraped the lee bow of the ship, jib-guys parted, and the jib-boom itself went, snapping at the bowsprit-cap, with the last bite the ship made at the steamer she was helping. But all through this riot of destruction—while passengers screamed and prayed, while officers on the steamer shouted and swore, and Seldom Helward, bellowing insanely, danced up and down on the ship's house, and the hail of wood and iron from aloft threatened their heads —men were passing the tow-line.

It was a three-inch steel hawser with a Manila tail, which they had taken to the foretopsail-sheet bitts before the jib-boom had gone. Panting from their exertions, they watched it lift from the water as the steamer ahead paid out with a taut strain; then, though the crippled spars were in danger of falling and really needed their first attention, they ignored the fact and hurried aft, as one man, to attend to Seldom.

Encouraged by the objurgations of Bigpig and his assistant, who were steering now after the steamer, they called their late commander down from the house and deposed him in a concert of profane ridicule and abuse, to which he replied in kind. He was struck in the face by the small fist of Sinful Peck, and immediately knocked the little man down. Then he was knocked down himself by a larger fist, and, fighting bravely and viciously, became the object of fist-blows and kicks, until, in one of his whirling staggers along the deck, he passed close to the short, broad, hairy man, who yielded to the excitement of the moment and added a blow to Seldom's punishment. It was an unfortunate mistake; for he took Seldom's place, and the rain of fists and boots descended on him until he fell unconscious. Mr. Helward himself delivered the last quieting blow, and then stood over him with a lurid grin on his bleeding face.

"Got to put down mutiny though the heavens fall," he said painfully.

"Right you are, Seldom," answered one. "Here, Jackson, Benson—drag him forrard; and, Seldom," he added, reprovingly, "don't you ever try it again. Want to be captain, hey? You can't; you don't know enough. You couldn't command my wheelbarrow. Here's three days' work to clear up the muss you've made."

But in this they spoke more, and less, than the truth. The steamer, going slowly, and steering with a bridle from the tow-line to each quarter, kept the ship's canvas full until her crew had steadied the yards and furled it. They would then have rigged preventer-stays and shrouds on their shaky spars, had there been time; but there was not. An uncanny appearance of the sea to leward indicated too close proximity to the shoals, while a blackening of the sky to windward told of probable increase of wind and sea. And the steamer waited no longer. With a preliminary blast of her whistle, she hung the weight of the ship on the starboard bridle, gave power to her engines, and rounded to, very slowly, head to sea, while the men on the ship, who had been carrying the end of the coiled hawser up the foretopmast rigging, dropped it and came down hurriedly.

Released from the wind-pressure on her strong side, which had somewhat steadied her, the ship now rolled more than she had done in the trough, and with every starboard roll were ominous creakings and grindings aloft. At last came a heavier lurch, and both crippled topmasts fell, taking with them the mizzentopgallantmast. Luckily, no one was hurt, and they disgustedly cut the wreck adrift, stayed the fore- and mainmasts with the hawser, and resigning themselves to a large subtraction from their salvage, went to a late breakfast—a savory meal of smoking fried ham and potatoes, hot cakes and coffee, served to sixteen in the cabin, and an unsavory meal of "hardtack-hash," with an infusion of burnt bread-crust, pease, beans, and leather, handed, but not served, to three in the forecastle.

Three days later, with Sandy Hook lighthouse showing through the haze ahead, and nothing left of the gale but a rolling ground-swell, the steamer slowed down so that a pilot-boat's dinghy could put a man aboard each craft. And the one who climbed the ship's side was the pilot that had taken her to sea, outward bound, and sympathized with her crew. They surrounded him on the poop and asked for news, while the three men forward looked aft hungrily, as though they would have joined the meeting, but dared not. Instead of giving news, the pilot asked questions, which they answered.

"I knew you'd taken charge, boys," he said at length. "The whole world knows it, and every man-of-war on the Pacific stations has been looking for you. But they're only looking out there. What

brings you round here, dismasted, towing into New
York?"

"That's where the ship's bound—New York. We
took her out; we bring her home. We don't want
her—don't belong to us. We're law-abidin' men."

"Law-abiding men?" asked the amazed pilot.

"You bet. We're goin' to prosecute those dogs of
ours forrard there to the last limit o' the law. We'll
show 'em they can't starve and hammer and shoot
free-born Americans just 'cause they've got guns in
their pockets."

The pilot looked forward, nodded to one of the
three, who beckoned to him, and asked:

"Who'd you elect captain?"

"Nobody," they roared. "We had enough o'
captains. This ship's an unlimited democracy—
everybody just as good as the next man; that is, all
but the dogs. They sleep on the bunk-boards, do as
they're told, and eat salt mule and dunderfunk—
same as we did goin' out."

"Did they navigate for you? Did no one have
charge of things?"

"Poop-deck picked up navigation, and we let him
off steerin' and standin' lookout. Then Seldom, here,
he wanted to be captain just once, and we let him—
well, look at our spars."

"Poop-deck? Which is Poop-deck? Do you
mean to say," asked the pilot when the navigator had
been indicated to him, "that you brought this ship
home on picked-up navigation?"

"Didn't know anything about it when we left
Callao," answered the sailor, modestly. "The
steward knew enough to wind the chronometer until I
learned how. We made an offing and steered due

south, while I studied the books and charts. It didn't take me long to learn how to take the sun. Then we blundered round the Horn somehow, and before long I could take chronometer sights for the longitude. Of course I know we went out in four months and used up five to get back; but a man can't learn the whole thing in one passage. We lost some time, too, chasing other ships and buying stores; the cabin grub gave out."

"You bought, I suppose, with Captain Benson's money."

"S'pose it was his. We found it in his desk. But we've kept account of every cent expended, and bought no grub too good for a white man to eat."

"What dismasted you?"

They explained the meeting with the steamer and Seldom's misdoing; then requested information about the salvage laws.

"Boys," said the pilot, "I'm sorry for you. I saw the start of this voyage, and you appear to be decent men. You'll get no salvage; you'll get no wages. You are mutineers and pirates, with no standing in court. Any salvage which the *Almena* has earned will be paid to her owners and to the three men whom you deprived of command. What you can get—the maximum, though I can't say how hard the judge will lay it on—is ten years in state's prison, and a fine of two thousand dollars each. We'll have to stop at quarantine. Take my advice: if you get a chance, lower the boats and skip."

They laughed at the advice. They were American citizens who respected the law. They had killed no one, robbed no one; their wages and salvage, independently of insurance liabilities, would pay for the stores bought, and the loss of the spars. They had no fear of any court of justice in the land; for they had only asserted their manhood and repressed inhuman brutality.

The pilot went forward, talked awhile with the three, and left them with joyous faces. An hour later he pointed out the *Almena's* number flying from the masthead of the steamer.

"He's telling on you, boys," he said. "He knew you when you helped him, and used you, of course. Your reputation's pretty bad on the high seas. See that signal-station ashore there? Well, they're telegraphing now that the pirate *Almena* is coming in. You'll see a police boat at quarantine."

He was but partly right. Not only a police boat, but an outward-bound man-of-war and an incoming revenue cutter escorted the ship to quarantine, where the tow-line was cast off, and an anchor dropped. Then, in the persons of a scandalized health-officer, a naval captain, a revenue-marine lieutenant, and a purple-faced sergeant of the steamboat squad, the power of the law was rehabilitated on the *Almena's* quarter-deck, and the strong hand of the law closed down on her unruly crew. With blank faces, they discarded—to shirts, trousers, and boots—the slop-chest clothing which belonged to the triumphant Captain Benson, and descended the side to the police boat, which immediately steamed away. Then a chuckling trio entered the ship's cabin, and ordered the steward to bring them something to eat.

Now, there is no record either in the reports for that year of the police department, or from any official babbling, or from later yarns spun by the sixteen prisoners, of what really occurred on the deck of that steamer while she was going up the bay. Newspapers of the time gave generous space to speculations written up on the facts discovered by reporters; but nothing was ever proved. The facts were few. A tug met the steamer in the Narrows about a quarter to twelve that morning, and her captain, on being questioned, declared that all seemed well with her. The prisoners were grouped forward, guarded by eight officers and a sergeant. A little after twelve o'clock a Battery boatman observed her coming, and hied him around to the police dock to have a look at the murderous pirates he had heard about, only to see her heading up the North River, past the Battery. A watchman on the elevator docks at Sixty-third Street observed her charging up the river a little later in the afternoon, wondered why, and spoke of it. The captain of the *Mary Powell*, bound up, reported catching her abreast of Yonkers. He had whistled as he passed, and though no one was in sight, the salute was politely answered. At some time during the night, residents of Sing Sing were wakened by a sound of steam blowing off somewhere on the river; and in the morning a couple of fishermen, going out to their pond-nets in the early dawn, found the police boat grounded on the shoals. On boarding her they had released a pinioned, gagged, and hungry captain in the pilot-house, and an engineer, fireman, and two deck-hands, similarly limited, in the lamp-room. Hearing noises from below, they pried open the nailed doors of the dining-room staircase, and liberated a purple-faced sergeant and eight furious officers, who chased their deliverers into their skiff, and spoke sternly to the working-force.

Among the theories advanced was one, by the editor of a paper in a small Lake Ontario town, to the effect that it made little difference to an Oswego sailor whether he shipped as captain, mate, engineer, sailor, or fireman, and that the officers of the New York Harbor Patrol had only under-estimated the caliber of the men in their charge, leaving them unguarded while they went to dinner. But his paper and town were small and far away, he could not possibly know anything of the subject, and his opinion obtained little credence.

Years later, however, he attended, as guest, a meeting and dinner of the Shipmasters' and Pilots' Association of Cleveland, Ohio, when a resolution was adopted to petition the city for a harbor police service. Captain Monahan, Captain Helward, Captain Peck, and Captain Cahill, having spoken and voted in the negative, left their seats on the adoption of the proposition, reached a clear spot on the floor, shook hands silently, and then, forming a ring, danced around in a circle (the tails of their coats standing out in horizontal rigidity) until reproved by the chair.

And the editor knew why.

THE BRAIN OF THE BATTLE-SHIP

BUILD an inverted Harvey-steel box about eight feet high, one hundred and fifty feet long, half as wide, with walls of eighteen-inch thickness, and a roof of three, and you have strong protection against shot and shell. Build up from the ends of the box two steel barbettes with revolving turrets as heavy as your side-walls; place in each a pair of thirteen-inch rifles; flank these turrets with four others of eight-inch wall, each holding two eight-inch guns; these again with four smaller, containing four six-inch guns, and you have power of offense nearly equal to your protection. Loosely speaking, a modern gun-projectile will, at short range, pierce steel equal to itself in cross-section, and from an elevated muzzle will travel as many miles as this cross-section measures in inches. Placed upon an outlying shoal, this box with its guns would make an efficient fortress, but would lack the advantage of being able to move and choose position.

Build underneath and each way from the ends of the box a cellular hull to float it; place within it, and below the box, magazines, boilers, and engines; construct above, between the turrets, a lighter super-structure to hold additional quick-fire guns and torpedo-tubes; cap the whole with a military mast supporting fighting-tops, and containing an armored conning-tower in its base; man and equip, provision and coal the fabric, and you can go to sea, confident of your ability to destroy everything that floats, except icebergs and other battle-ships.

Of these essentials was the first-class coast-defense battle-ship *Argyll.* She was of ten thousand tons' displacement, and was propelled by twin screws which received ten thousand horse-power from twin engines placed below the water-line. Three long tubes—one fixed in the stem, two movable in the superstructure —could launch Whitehead torpedoes,—mechanical fish carrying two hundred and twenty pounds of gun-cotton in their heads,—which sought in the water a twenty-foot depth, and hurried where pointed at a thirty-knot rate of speed. Their impact below the water-line was deadly, and only equaled in effect by the work of the ram-bow, the blow of the ship as a whole—the last glorious, suicidal charge on an enemy that had dismounted the guns, if such could happen.

Besides her thirteen-, eight-, and six-inch guns, she carried a secondary quick-fire battery of twenty six-pounders, four one-pounders, and four Gatling guns distributed about the superstructure and in the fighting-tops. The peculiar efficacy of this battery lay in its menace to threatening torpedo-boats, and its hostility to range-finders, big-gun sights, and op-posing gunners. A torpedo-boat, receiving the full attention of her quick-fire battery, could be disin-tegrated and sunk in a yeasty froth raised by the rain of projectiles long before she could come within range of torpedo action; while a simultaneous dis-charge of all guns would distribute over seven thou-sand pounds of metal with foot-tons of energy suffi-cient to lift the ship herself high out of water. Bristling, glistening, and massive, a reservoir of death potential, a center of radiant destruction, a spitting, chattering, thundering epitome of racial hatred, she bore within her steel walls the ever-growing burden of progressive human thought. She was a maker of history, a changer of boundaries, a friend of young governments; and it chanced that on a fine tropical morning, in company with three armored cruisers, four protected cruisers, and a fleet of tor-pedo-boats and destroyers, she went into action.

She was stripped to bare steel and signal-halyards. Davits, anchors, and cables were stowed and secured. Ladders, gratings, stanchions, and all movable deck-fittings were below the water-line. Wooden bulk-heads, productive of splinters, were knocked down and discarded, while all boats, with the plugs out, were overboard, riding to a sea-anchor made up of oars and small spars.

The crew was at quarters. Below, in the maga-zine, handling-rooms, stoke-holds, and bunkers, bare-waisted men worked and waited in stifling heat; for she was under forced draft, and compartments were closed, even though the enemy was still five miles away. The chief and his first assistant engineer watched the main engines in their twin compartments, while the subordinate aids and machinists attended to the dynamos, motors, and auxiliary cylinders that worked the turrets, pumps, and ammunition-hoists. All boilers were hot and hissing steam; all fire-pumps were working; all fire-hose connected and spouting streams of water. Perspiring men with strained faces deluged one another while they waited.

In the turrets were the gun-crews, six men to a gun, with an officer above in the sighting-hood; be-hind the superstructure-ports were the quick-fire men, sailors and marines; and above all, in the fight-ing-tops, were the sharp-shooters and men who handled the one-pounders and Gatling guns—the easiest-minded of the ship's company, for they could see and breathe. Each division of fighters and workers was overseen by an officer; in some cases by two and three.

Preparatory work was done, and, excepting the "black gang," men were quiescent, but feverish. Few spoke, and then on frivolous things, in tones that were not recognized. Occasionally a man would bring out a piece of paper and write, using for a desk a gun-breech or -carriage, a turret-wall, or the deck. An officer in a fighting-top used a telegraph-dial, and a stoker in the depths his shovel, in a chink of light from the furnace. These letters, written in instalments, were pocketed in confidence that some-time they would be mailed.

From the captain down each man knew that a large proportion of their number was foredoomed; but not a consciousness among them could admit the possibility of itself being chosen. The great first law forbade it. Senior officers pictured in their minds dead juniors, and thought of extra work after the fight. Junior officers thought of vacancies above them and promotion. Men in the turrets bade mental good-by to their mates in the superstructure; and these, secure in their five-inch protection, pitied those in the fighting-tops, where, cold logic says, no man may live through a sea-fight. Yet all would have volunteered to fill vacancies aloft. The healthy human mind can postulate suffering, but not its own extinction.

In a circular apartment in the military mast, pro-tected by twelve inches of steel, perforated by vertical and horizontal slits for observation, stood the captain and navigating officer, both in shirt-sleeves; for this, the conning-tower, was hot. Around the inner walls were the nerve-terminals of the structure—the indicators, telegraph-dials, telephones, push-buttons, and speaking-tubes, which communicated with gun-stations, turrets, steering-room, engine-rooms, and all parts of the ship where men were stationed. In the forward part was a binnacle with small steering-wheel, disconnected now, for the steering was done by men below the water-line in the stern. A spiral staircase led to the main-deck below, and another to the first fighting-top above, in which staircase were small platforms where a signal-officer and two quartermasters watched through slits the signals from the flag-ship, and answered as directed by the captain below with small flags, which they mastheaded through the hollow within the staircase.

The chief master-at-arms, bareheaded, climbed into the conning-tower.

"Captain Blake, what'll we do with Finnegan?" he said. "I've released him from the brig as you ordered; but Mr. Clarkson won't have him in the turret where he belongs, and no one else wants him around. They even chased him out of the bunkers. He wants to work and fight, but Mr. Clarkson won't place him; says he washes his hands of Finnegan, and sent me to you. I took him to the bay, but he won't take medicine."

Captain Blake, stern of face and kindly of eye, drew back from a peep-hole, and asked: "What's his condition?"

"Shaky, sir. Sees little spiders and big spiders crawling round his cap-rim. Him and the recording angel knows where he gets it and where he keeps it, sir; but I don't. I've watched him for six months."

" Send him to me."

" Very good, sir."

The master-at-arms descended, and in a few moments the unwanted Finnegan appeared—a graybearded, emaciated, bleary-eyed seaman, who brushed imaginary things from his neck and arms, and stammered, as he removed his cap: " Report for duty, sir."

" For duty? " answered the captain, eying him sternly. " For death. You will be allowed the honorable death of an English seaman. You will die in the fighting-top sometime in the next three hours."

The man shivered, elevated one shoulder, and rubbed his ear against it, but said nothing, while Mr. Dalrymple, the navigating officer, with his eyes at a peep-hole and his ears open to the dialogue, wondered (as he and the whole ship's company had wondered before) what the real relation was between the captain and this wretched, drunken butt of the crew. For the captain's present attitude was a complete departure. Always he had shielded Finnegan from punishment to the extent that naval etiquette would permit.

" I have tried for six years," continued the captain, " to reform you and hold you to the manhood I once knew in you; but I give you up. You are not fit to live, and will never be fitter to die than this morning, when the chance comes to you to die fighting for your country. But I want you to die fighting. Do you wish to see the surgeon or the chaplain? "

" No, no, no, cappen; one's bad as t'other. The chaplain'll pray and the doctor'll fill me up wi' bromide, and it just makes me crazy, sir. I'm all right, cappen, if I only had a drink. Just give me a drink, cappen—the doctor won't,—and send me down to my station, sir. I know it's only in my head, but I see 'em plain, all round. You'll give me a drink, cappen, please; I know you'll give me a drink."

He brushed his knees gingerly, and stepped suddenly away from an isolated speaking-tube. Captain Blake's stern face softened. His mind went back to his midshipman days, to a stormy night and a heavy sea, an icy foot-rope, a fall, a plunge, and a cold, hopeless swim toward a shadowy ship hove to against the dark background, until this man's face, young, strong, and cheery then, appeared behind a white life-buoy; and he heard again the panting voice of his rescuer: "Here ye are, Mr. Blake; boat's comin'."

He whistled down the speaking-tube, and when answered, called: "Send an opened bottle of whisky into the conning-tower—no glasses."

"Thankee, sir."

The captain resumed his position at the peep-hole, and Finnegan busied himself with his troubles until a Japanese servant appeared with a quart bottle. The captain received it, and the Jap withdrew.

"Help yourself, Finnegan," said the captain, extending the bottle; "take a good drink—a last one." Finnegan took the equivalent of three. "Now, up with you." The captain stood the bottle under the binnacle. "Upper top. Report to Mr. Bates."

"Cappen, please send me down to the turret where I b'long, sir. I'm all right now. I don't want to go up there wi' the sogers. I'm not good at machine guns."

"No arguments. Up with you at once. You are

good for nothing but to work a lever under the eye
of an officer."

Finnegan saluted silently and turned toward the
stairs.

"Finnegan!"

He turned. The captain extended his hand.
"Finnegan," he said, "I don't forget that night,
but you must go; the eternal fitness of things de-
mands it. Perhaps I'll go, too. Good-by."

The two extremes of the ship's company shook
hands, and Finnegan ascended. When past the
quartermasters and out of hearing, he grumbled and
whined: "No good, hey? Thirty years in the service, and sent up here to think of my sins like a sick
monkey. Good for nothin' but to turn a crank with
the sogers. Nice job for an able seaman. What's
the blasted service a-comin' to?"

The two fleets were approaching in similar formation, double column, at about a twelve-knot speed.
Leading the left column was the *Lancaster*, and following came the *Argyll*, *Beaufort*, and *Atholl*, the
last two, like the *Lancaster*, armored cruisers of the
first class. On the *Lancaster's* starboard bow was the
flag-ship *Cumberland*, a large unarmored cruiser, and
after her came the *Marlborough*, *Montrose*, and
Sutherland, unarmored craft like the flag-ship,
equally vulnerable to fire, the two columns making a
zigzag line, with the heaviest ships to the left, nearest the enemy.

Heading as they were, the fleets would pass about
a mile apart. Led by a black, high-sided monster,
the left column of the enemy was made up of four
battle-ships of uncouth, foreign design and murderous appearance, while the right column contained

the flag-ship and three others, all heavily armored cruisers. Flanking each fleet, far to the rear, were torpedo-boats and destroyers.

"We're outclassed, Dalrymple," said Captain Blake. "There are the ships we expected—*Warsaw, Riga, Kharkov,* and *Moscow,* all of fighting weight, and the *Obdorsk, Tobolsk, Saratov,* and *Orenburg.* Leaving out the *Argyll,* we haven't a ship equal to the weakest one there. This fight is the *Argyll's.*"

"And the *Argyll* is equal to it, captain. All I fear is torpedoes. Of course our ends and superstructure will catch it, and I suppose we'll lose men—all the quick-fire men, perhaps."

"Those in the tops surely," said the captain. "Dalrymple, what do you think? I don't feel right about Finnegan. He belongs in the turret, and I've sentenced him. Have I the right? I've half a mind to call him down." He pushed a button marked "Forward turret," and listened at a telephone.

"Mr. Clarkson!" he called. "I've put your man Finnegan in the upper top; but he seems all right now. Can you use him?"

The answer came:

"No, sir; I've filled his place."

"Die, then. On my soul be it, Finnegan, poor devil," muttered the captain, gloomily.

His foot struck the bottle under the binnacle, and, on an impulse due to his mood, he picked it up and uncorked it. Mr. Dalrymple observed the action and stepped toward him.

"Captain, pardon me," he said, "if I protest unofficially. We are going into action—not to dinner."

The captain's eyes opened wide and shone brighter,

while his lip curled. He extended the bottle to the lieutenant.

"The apologies are mine, Mr. Dalrymple," he said. "I forgot your presence. Take a drink."

The officer forced a smile to his face, and stepped back, shaking his head. Captain Blake swallowed a generous portion of the whisky.

"The fool!" mused the navigator, as he looked through the peep-hole. "The whole world is watching him to-day, and he turns to whisky. That's it, dammit; that's the bond of sympathy: Blake and Finnegan, Finnegan and Blake—dipsomaniacs. Lord, I never thought. I've seen him drunker than Finnegan, and if it wasn't for his position and obligations, he'd see spiders, too."

Mr. Dalrymple was not the only one on board who disapproved of "Dutch courage" for captains. The Japanese servant, whose station was at the forward-turret ammunition-hoist, reported the service of the whisky to his mates, and from here the news spread—as news will in a cellular hull—up to turrets and gun-rooms, through speaking-tubes and water-tight bulkheads, down to stoke-hold, engine-rooms, and steering-room; and long before Captain Blake had thought of taking a drink the whole ship's company was commenting, mentally and openly, and more or less profanely, on the story that "the old man was getting drunk in the conning-tower."

And another piece of news traveled as fast and as far—the whereabouts of Finnegan. Mr. Clarkson had incidentally informed his gun-captain, who told the gun-crew; and from them the news went down the hoist and spread. Men swore louder over this; for though they did not want Finnegan around and in the way, they did not want him to die. Strong natures love those which may be teased; and not a heart was there but contained a soft spot for the helpless, harmless, ever good-natured, drunk, and ridiculous Finnegan.

The bark of an eight-inch gun was heard. Captain Blake saw, through the slits of the conning-tower, a cloud of thinning smoke drifting away from the flag-ship. Stepping back, he rang up the forward turret.

" Mr. Clarkson," he said to the telephone when it answered him, " remember: aim for the nearest water-line, load and fire, and expect no orders after the first shot."

Calling up the officer in the after-turret, he repeated the injunction, substituting turrets as the object of assault. He called to the officers at the eight-inch guns that conning-towers and superstructure were to receive their attention; to those at the six-inch guns to aim solely at turret apertures; to ensigns and officers of marine in charge of the quick-fire batteries to aim at all holes and men showing, to watch for torpedo-boats, and, like the others, to expect no orders after the first shot. Then, ringing up the round of gun-stations, one after another, he sang out, in a voice to be heard by all: " Fire away! "

The initial gun had been fired from the flag-ship when the leading ships of the two fleets were nearly abreast. It was followed by broadsides from all, and the action began. The *Argyll*, rolling slightly from the recoil of her guns, smoked down the line like a thing alive, voicing her message, dealing out death and receiving it. In this first round of the battle the fire of the eight opposing vessels was directed at her alone.   Shells punctured her vulnerable parts, and, exploding inside, killed men and dismounted guns. The groans of the stricken, the crash of steel against steel, the roar of the turret-guns, the rattling chorus of quick-fire rifles, and the drumming of heavy shells against the armor and turrets made an uproarious riot of sound over which no man above the water-line could lift his voice.   But there were some there, besides the dead,—men who worked through and sur-vived the action,—who, after the first impact of sound, did not hear it, nor anything else while they lived.   They were the men who had neglected stuffing their ears with cotton.

A fundamental canon of naval tactics is to main-tain formation.   Another is to keep moving, at the full speed of the slowest ship, not only to disconcert the enemy's fire, but to obtain and hold the most advantageous position—if possible, to flank him.   As these rules apply equally well to both sides, it is obvious that two fleets, passing in opposite directions, and each trying to flank the rear of the other, will eventually circle around a common center; and if the effort to improve position dominates the effort to evade fire, this circle will narrow until the battle be-comes a mêlée.

The two lines, a mile apart and each about a mile in length, were squarely abreast in less than five minutes from the time of firing the first gun; and by now the furious bombardment of the *Argyll* by eight ships had ceased, for each one found it more profitable to deal with its vis-à-vis.   But there was yet a deafening racket in the *Argyll's* conning-tower as small projectiles from the rear battle-ship abreast impinged on its steel walls; and Captain Blake, his ears ringing, his eyes streaming, half stunned by the noise, almost blinded and suffocated by the smoke from his forward guns, did not know that his ship had dropped back in the line until the signal-officer descended and shouted in his ear an order signaled from the admiral: "Move ahead to position."

"Hang the man who invented conning-towers," he muttered angrily. "Keep a lookout up there, Mr. Wright," he shouted; "I can see very little."

The officer half saluted, half nodded, and ran up the stair, while Captain Blake rang "full speed" to the engines. The indicators on the wall showed increased revolution, and he resumed his place at the peep-hole. In a few moments Mr. Wright reappeared with a message from the flag-ship to "starboard helm; follow ship ahead."

"All right. Watch out up there; report all you see," he answered. Peeping out, he saw the *Lancaster* and the *Cumberland* sheering to port, and he moved the lever of the steering-telegraph. There was no answering ring. "Shot away, by George," he growled. He yelled into a supplementary voice-tube to "starboard your wheel—slowly." This was not answered, and with his own hands he coupled up the steering-wheel on the binnacle and gave it a turn. It was merely a governor, which admitted steam to the steering-engine, and there was no resisting pressure to guide him; but a helm indicator showed him the changed position of the rudder, and, on looking ahead, he found that she answered the wheel; also, on looking to starboard, he found that he had barely escaped collision with the *Montrose*, whose fire he had been masking, to the scandal of the admiral and the *Montrose's* officers.

A little unnerved, Captain Blake called down a seven-inch tube to an apartment in the depths,—a central station of pipes and wires, to be used as a last resort,—directing the officer on post to notify the chief engineer of the damage, and to order the quartermasters in the steering-room to disconnect their wheel and stand by. This was answered, and the captain resumed his lookout, one hand on the wheel.

" Reduces the captain of the ship to a helmsman," he muttered.

The navigating officer approached, indicating by gesture and expression his intention of relieving him, but was waved away.

" I want the wheel myself," shouted the captain. " Devil take a conning-tower, anyway! Keep a lookout to port. But say, Dalrymple, send up for Finnegan. I'll not have him killed. Get him down, if he's alive."

Mr. Dalrymple ascended the stair to pass the word for Finnegan, but did not come down. He had reached the signal-platform, where one quartermaster lay dead, and was transmitting the order to Mr. Wright, when a heavy shell struck the mast, above their heads and below the lower top, exploded inside, killed the three men on the platform, and hurled the upper part of the mast, with both tops full of dead men and living, high in air. The conning-tower was filled with gas and smoke; but Captain Blake, though burned and nearly stripped of clothing by the blast of flame, was uninjured by the flying fragments of the shell. Smarting, gasping, and choking, fully aware of the complete destruction above, his mind dwelt for an instant on the man who had once saved his life, whom he had sentenced to death. He looked up the hollow within the wrecked staircase, but saw nothing.

Mr. Clarkson, however, happened to be looking through an upper peep-hole in the sighting-hood at this moment, and saw the upper half of the mast lift and turn; also, dimly through the smoke, he noticed, among the dozen of men hurled from the tops, the blue-shirted figure of one whom he knew to be Finnegan, clinging at arm's-length in mid-air to a Gatling gun, which had been torn from its fastenings. Then the smoke thickened and shut out the view; but a moment later he heard the rattling crash of the mast as it fell upon the superstructure beneath.

" The whole mast's gone, boys," he shouted to his crew—" both tops. Finnegan's done for."

And the story of Finnegan's finish went down the hoist and through the ship, everywhere received with momentary sorrow, and increased malediction on the drunken captain, who thought no more—and knew no more—of a blue-jacket than to masthead him with the marines.

The tactics of both admirals being the same, and the speed of both fleets—that of their slowest ships—being equal, they turned, and, like two serpents pursuing each other's tails, charged around in a circle, each ship firing at the nearest or most important enemy. This fire was destructive. A ship a mile distant is a point-blank target for modern guns and gunners, and everything protected by less than eight inches of steel suffered. The *Argyll* had lost her military mast and most of her secondary guns. The flag-ship *Cumberland*, raked and riddled by nine- and eleven-inch shells, surrounded herself with steam from punctured boilers shortly after the signal to turn, and swung drunkenly out of line, her boilers roaring, her heavy guns barking. A long, black thing, low down behind the wave created by its rush, darted by her, unstruck by the shells sent by the flag-ship and the *Marlborough*. A larger thing, mouse-colored and nearly hidden by a larger wave, was coming from the opposite direction, spitting one-pound shot at the rate of sixty a minute, but without present avail; for a spindle-shaped object left the deck of the first when squarely abreast of the helpless flag-ship, diving beneath the surface, and the existence and position of this object were hence-forth indicated only by a line of bubbles, a darting streak of froth, traveling toward the *Cumberland*. In less than a minute it had reached her. The sea alongside arose in a mound, and she semed to lean away from it; then the mound burst, and out of it, and spouting from funnels, ventilators, and ports, came a dense cloud of smoke, which mingled with the steam and hid her from view, while a dull, booming roar, barely distinguishable in the noise of battle, came across the water. When the cloud thinned there was nothing to be seen but heads of swimming men, who swam for a time and sank. The flag-ship had been torpedoed.

But the torpedo-boat followed her. Pursued by the mouse-colored destroyer, she circled around and headed back in the endeavor to reach her con-sorts; but she had not time. Little by little the avenger crept up, pounding her with small shot and shell, until, leaking from a hundred wounds, she settled beneath the surface. She had fulfilled her mission; she was designed to strike once and die.

No armored cruiser may withstand the fire of a battle-ship. The *Lancaster*, leading the *Argyll*, received through her eight-inch water-line belt the heavy shot and shell of the *Moscow* and *Orenburg*. Nine- and eleven-inch shell fire, sent by Canet and Hontoria guns, makes short work of eight-inch armor, and the doomed *Lancaster* settled and disappeared, her crew yelling, her screws turning, and her guns firing until the water swamped her. The following *Argyll* scraped her funnels and masts as she passed over.

Eight hundred feet back in the line was the *Beaufort*, armored like the *Lancaster*. Her ending was dramatic and suicidal. Drilled through and through by the fire of the *Riga*, she fought and suffered until the *Lancaster* foundered; then, with all guns out of action, but with still intact engine-power, she left the line, not to run, but to ram. The circle was narrowing, but she had fully four minutes to steam before she could reach the opposite side and intercept her slayer. And in this short time she was reduced to scrap-iron by the concentrated fire of the *Warsaw*, *Riga*, and *Kharkov*. Every shot from every gun on the three battle-ships struck the unlucky cruiser; but in the face of the storm of flame and steel she went on, exhaling through fissures and ports smoke from bursting shells and steam from broken pipes. Halfway across, an almost solid belching upward and outward of white steam indicated a stricken boiler, and from now on her progress was slow. She was visibly lower in the water and rolled heavily. Soon another cloud arose from her, her headway decreased, and she came to a stop, two hundred yards on the port bow of the onrushing *Riga*, whose crew yelled derisively—whose quick-fire guns still punished her.

But the yells suddenly ceased and the gunners

changed their aim.   A small thing had left the nearly
submerged tube in the cruiser's stem, and the gunners were now firing at a darting line of bubbles,
obliterating the target for a moment with the churning of the water, only to see the frothy streak within
their range, coming on at locomotive speed.   They
aimed ahead; two five-inch guns added their clamor,
and even a Hontoria turret-gun voiced its roar and
sent its messenger.   But the bubbles would not stop;
they entered the bow wave of the battle-ship, and a
second later the great floating fort separated into
two parts, with a crackling thunder of sound and an
outburst of flame and smoke which came of nothing
less than an exploded magazine.   The two halves
rolled far to starboard, then to port, shivered, settled, turned completely over, and sank in a turmoil
of bursting steam and air-bubbles.   Three minutes
later the *Beaufort* lifted her stern and dived gently
after her victim, still groaning hoarsely from her
punctured iron lungs.   In her death-agony she had
given birth to a child more terrible than a battle-
ship.

The rear ship of the inner column, the *Atholl*, was
officially an armored cruiser, but possessed none of
the attributes of the cruiser class.   She was the
laggard of the fleet, and her heaviest guns were of
six-inch caliber; but, being designed for a battle-
ship, she carried this temporary battery behind sixteen inches of steel, and had maintained her integrity,
taking harder blows than she could give.   With the
going down of the *Beaufort* she took a position astern
of the *Sutherland*, and the double line of battle was
reduced to a single line; for the *Argyll* had left the
column when the flag-ship sank.

And this is why the overmatched, battered, and all but demoralized cruisers received no more attention from the enemy; it were wiser to deal with the *Argyll*. The *Saratov*, blazing fiercely from the effects of a well-planted shell, had drawn out of line, the better to deal with her trouble. Her place in the line and that of the sunken *Riga* were filled by the following ships drawing ahead; but the fleet still held to double column, and into the lane between the lines the *Argyll* was coming at sixteen knots, breathing flame, vomiting steel—delivering destruction and death.

She had rounded the *Moscow's* stern, raking her as she came, and sending armor-piercing shells through her citadel. Some exploded on impact, some inside; all did work. An eight-inch projectile entered the after turret-port, and silenced the gun and gun-crew forever. Before the *Argyll* was abeam the *Moscow* had ceased firing. Rolling and smoking, her crew decimated, her guns disabled and steering-gear carried away, she swung out of line; and the appearance in his field of vision of several rushing waves with short smoke-stacks behind, and the supplementary pelting his ship was now receiving from the *Marlborough*, decided her commander to lower his flag.

On the starboard bow of the *Argyll* was the armored cruiser *Orenburg*. Her fire, hot and true, ceased on the explosion of a large shell at her waterline, and she swung out of the fight, silent but for the roar of escaping steam, heeled heavily to port, and sank in ten minutes, her ensigns flying to the last. Mr. Clarkson rejoiced with his gun-crew. He had sent the shell.

On stormed the *Argyll*. Her next adversary was the *Kharkov*, a battle-ship nearly equal in guns and armor to herself, but not quite—by an inch. And that inch cost her the fight. With her main turrets damaged, her superstructure, secondary guns, and torpedo-tubes shot away, she yielded to fate, and, while the *Argyll* passed on, hauled down her ensigns at the request of a torpedo-boat.

Ahead and to starboard was the cruiser *Tobolsk,* leaving the neighborhood as fast as her twin screws could push her. Her end was in sight; in her wake were two gray destroyers, and behind, charging across the broken formation, was the fleet *Marlborough.* The *Argyll* ignored the *Tobolsk;* for slowing down to await her coming was the black and high-sided *Warsaw,* the monster of the fleet, bristling with guns, somber and ominous in her silence.

Ahead of her, and turning to port, was the flagship *Obdorsk,* also slowed down; but she promised to be fully occupied with the *Atholl, Sutherland,* and *Montrose,* who had wheeled in their tracks, no longer obliged to traverse a circle to reach an enemy.

On rushed the *Argyll,* and when nearly up to the *Warsaw,* the latter gave steam to her engines. Breast to breast the gladiators charged across the sea, roaring, flaming, and smoking. A torpedo left the side of the *Warsaw,* pointed diagonally ahead, to intercept the *Argyll.* But it was badly aimed, and the hissing bubbles passed under her stern. Before another could be discharged, the torpedo-room, located by the *Argyll's* officers, was enlarged to the size of three by the succeeding bombardment and the explosion of the remaining torpedoes.

Twelve-inch armor cannot keep out thirteen-inch armor-piercing shell, and torpedoes cannot explode on board without damage to machinery, steering-gear, and vital connections. The *Warsaw* yawed, slackened speed, and came to a stop, her turret-guns still speaking, but the secondary guns silent. The *Argyll* circled around her, sending her thirteen-, eight-, and six-inch shells into her victim with almost muzzle energy. The two military masts of the *Warsaw* sank, and dead men in the fighting-tops were flung overboard. The forward turret seemed to explode; smoke and flame shot out of the ports, and its top lifted and fell. Then the *Argyll* turned and headed straight for her side.

There was little need of gun fire now; but the forward-turret guns belched once during the charge, and the more quickly handled eight- and six-inch rifles stormed away while there was time to reload. Smoking, rolling, and barking,—ten thousand tons of inertia behind a solid steel knife,—she pounced on her now silent enemy. There was a crunching sound, muffled and continuous. The speed of the *Argyll* seemed hardly checked. In went the ram farther and farther, until the slanting edge began cutting above the water. Then the *Warsaw*, heeled far over by the impact, rolled back, and the knife cut upward. The smooth plates at the *Argyll's* water-line wrinkled like paper, and the pile of shattered steel which had once been her forward deck and bulkheads was shaken up and adjusted to new positions; but not until her nose was actually buried in the wound—until the *Warsaw* was cut half in two— did the reversed engines begin to work. The *Argyll* backed out, exposing for a moment a hole like a cavern's mouth; then the stricken ship rolled heavily toward her, burying the sore, and, humming and buzzing with exhausting steam and rushing air, settled rapidly and sank, while out from ports, doors, and nearly vertical hatches came her crew, as many as could. They sprang overboard and swam, and those that reached the now stationary *Argyll* were rescued; for a cry had gone through the latter from the central station in her depths: "All hands on deck to save life! Bring ladders, life-buoys, and ropes' ends!"

The battle was ended; for, with the ramming of the *Warsaw*, the *Obdorsk* struck to the three ships circling around her. They had suffered, but the battleship *Argyll* was reduced to a monitor. Her superstructure and the bow and stern above the water-line were shattered to a shapeless tangle of steel. What was left of her funnels and ventilators resembled nutmeg-graters, and she was perceptibly down by the head; for her bow leaked through its wrinkled plates, and the forward compartment below the protective deck was filled. Yet she could still fight in smooth water. Her box-like citadel was intact, and standing naked out of the wreck, scarred and dented, but uninjured, were the turrets, ammunition-hoists, and conning-tower. In the latter was the brain of the ship, that had fought her to victory and then sent the call to her crew to save the lives of their enemies.

Two men met on a level spot amidships and clasped hands. Both were bare-waisted and grimy, and one showed red as a lobster under the stains. He was the chief engineer.

"We've won, Clarkson," he said. "We've won the hottest fight that history can tell of—won it ourselves; but he'll get the credit."

"And he's drunk as a lord—drunk through it all. What did he ram for? Why did he send two millions of prize-money to the bottom?   O Lord! O Lord! it's enough to make a man swear at his mother. We had her licked. Why did he ram? "

" Because he was drunk, that's why. He rang seven bells to me along at the first of the muss, and then sent word through young Felton that he wanted full speed. Dammit, he already had it, every pound of it. And he gave me no signal to reverse when we struck; if it wasn't for luck and a kind Providence we'd have followed the *Warsaw*. I barely got her over. Here, Mr. Felton; you were in the central, were you not? How'd the old man appear to be making it? Were his orders intelligible? "

A young man had joined them, hot, breathing hard, and unclothed.

" Not always, sir; I had to ask him often to repeat, and then I sometimes got another order. He kept me busy from the first, when he sent the torpedoes overboard."

" The torpedoes! " exclaimed Mr. Clarkson. " Did we use them? I didn't know it."

" He was afraid they'd explode on board, sir," he said. " That was just after we took full speed."

" And just before he got too full to be afraid of anything," muttered the lieutenant. " Why don't he come out of that? " He glanced toward the conning-tower. Other officers had joined them.

" We'll investigate," said Mr. Clarkson.

The door on the level of the main-deck leading into the mast was found to be wedged fast by the blow of a projectile. Men, naked and black, sprawled about the wreckage breathing fresh air, were ordered to get up and to rig a ladder outside. They did so, and Mr. Clarkson ascended to the ragged end of the

hollow stump and looked down.   Standing at the
wheel, steering the drifting ship with one hand and
holding an empty bottle in the other, was a man
with torn clothing and bloody face.   In spite of the
disfigurement Mr. Clarkson knew him.   Jammed into
the narrow staircase leading below was the body of a
man partly hidden by a Gatling gun, the lever of
which had pierced the forehead.

"Finnegan," yelled the officer, "how'd you get
there?"

The man at the wheel lifted a bleary eye and
blinked; then, unsteadily touching his forehead, answered: "Fe' dow'-shtairs, shir."

"Come out of that!   On deck there!   Take the
wheel, one hand, and stand by it!"   Mr. Clarkson
descended to the others with a serious look on his
grimy face, and a sailor climbed the ladder and went
down the mast.

"Gentlemen," said the first lieutenant, impressively, "we were mistaken, and we wronged Captain
Blake.   He is dead.   He died at the beginning.   He
lies under a Gatling gun in the bottom of the tower.
I saw Finnegan hanging to that gun, whirling around
it, when the mast blew up.   It is all plain now.   Finnegan and the gun fell into the tower.   Finnegan may
have struck the stairs and rolled down, but the gun
went down the hollow within and killed the captain.
We have been steered and commanded by a drunken
man—but it was Finnegan."

Finnegan scrambled painfully down the ladder.
He staggered, stumbled, and fell in a heap.

"Rise up," said Mr. Clarkson, as they surrounded
him; "rise up, Daniel Drake Nelson Farragut Finnegan.   You are small potatoes and few in the hill; you

are shamefully drunk, and your nose bleeds; you are stricken with Spanish mildew, and you smell vilely—but you are immortal. You have been a disgrace to the service, but Fate in her gentle irony has redeemed you, permitting you, in one brief moment of your misspent life, to save to your country the command of the seas—to guide, with your subconscious intelligence, the finest battle-ship the science of the world has constructed to glorious victory, through the fiercest sea-fight the world has known. Rise up, Daniel, and see the surgeon."

But Finnegan only snored.

THE WIGWAG MESSAGE

AS eight bells sounded, Captain Bacon and Mr. Knapp came up from breakfast, and Mr. Hansen, the squat and square-built second mate, immediately went down. The deck was still wet from the morning washing down, and forward the watch below were emerging from the forecastle to relieve the other half, who were coiling loosely over the top of the forward house a heavy, wet hawser used in towing out the evening before. They were doing it properly, and as no present supervision was necessary, the first mate remained on the poop for a few moments' further conversation with the captain.

" Poor crew, cap'n," he said, as, picking his teeth with the end of a match, he scanned the men forward. " It'll take me a month to lick 'em into shape."

To judge by his physique, a month was a generous limit for such an operation. He was a giant, with a giant's fist and foot; red-haired and bearded, and of sinister countenance. But he was no more formidable in appearance than his captain, who was equally big, but smooth-shaven, and showing the square jaw and beetling brows of a born fighter.

" Are the two drunks awake yet? " asked the latter.

" Not at four o'clock, sir," answered the mate. " Mr. Hansen couldn't get 'em out. I'll soon turn 'em to."

As he spoke, two men appeared from around the corner of the forward house, and came aft. They were young men, between twenty-five and thirty, with intelligent, sunburnt faces. One was slight of figure, with the refinement of thought and study in his features; the other, heavier of mold and muscular, though equally quick in his movements, had that in his dark eyes which said plainly that he was wont to supplement the work of his hands with the work of his brain. Both were dressed in the tar-stained and grimy rags of the merchant sailor at sea; and they walked the wet and unsteady deck with no absence of "sea-legs," climbed the poop steps to leeward, as was proper, and approached the captain and first mate at the weather rail. The heavier man touched his cap, but the other merely inclined his head, and smiling frankly and fearlessly from one face to the other, said, in a pleasant, evenly modulated voice:

"Good morning. I presume that one of you is the captain."

"I'm the captain. What do you want?" was the gruff response.

"Captain, I believe that the etiquette of the merchant service requires that when a man is shanghaied on board an outward-bound ship he remains silent, does what is told him cheerfully, and submits to fate until the passage ends; but we cannot bring ourselves to do so. We were struck down in a dark spot last night,—sandbagged, I should say,—and we do not know what happened afterward, though we must have been kept unconscious with chloroform or some such drug. We wakened this morning in your forecastle, dressed in these clothes, and robbed of everything we had with us."

"Where were you slugged?"

"In Cherry Street. The bridge cars were not

running, so we crossed from Brooklyn by the Catherine Ferry, and foolishly took a short cut to the elevated station."

"Well, what of it?"

"What—why—why, captain, that you will kindly put us aboard the first inbound craft we meet."

"Not much I won't," answered the captain, decidedly. "You belong to my crew. I paid for twenty men; and you two and two others skipped at the dock. I had to wait all day in the Horseshoe. You two were caught dead drunk last night, and came down with the tug. That's what the runners said, and that's all I know about it. Go forrard."

"Do you mean, captain—"

"Go forrard where you belong. Mr. Knapp, set these men to work."

Captain Bacon turned his back on them, and walked away.

"Get off the poop," snarled the mate. "Forrard wi' you both!"

"Captain, I advise you to reconsider—"

The words were stopped by a blow of the mate's fist, and the speaker fell to the deck. Then a hoarse growl of horror and rage came from his companion; and Captain Bacon turned to see him dancing around the first officer with the skill and agility of a professional boxer, planting vicious blows on his hairy face and neck.

"Stop this," roared the captain, as his right hand sought the pocket of his coat. "Stop it, I say. Mr. Hansen," he called down the skylight, "on deck, here."

The huge mate was getting the worst of the unexpected battle, and Captain Bacon approached cautiously. His right hand had come out of his pocket, armed with large brass knuckles; but before he could use them his dazed and astonished first officer went down under the rain of blows. It was then, while the victor waited for him to rise, that the brass knuckles impacted on his head, and he, too, went down, to lie quiet where he fell. The other young man had arisen by this time, somewhat shocked and unsteady in movement, and was coming bravely toward the captain; but before he could reach him his arms were pinioned from behind by Mr. Hansen, who had run up the poop steps.

"What is dis, onnyway?" he asked. "Mudiny, I dink?"

"Let go," said the other, furiously. "You shall suffer for this, you scoundrels. Let go of my arms." He struggled wildly; but Mr. Hansen was strong.

Mr. Knapp had regained his feet and a few of his faculties. His conqueror was senseless on the deck, but this other mutineer was still active in rebellion. So, while the approving captain looked on in brass-knuckled dignity, he sprang forward and struck, with strength born of his rage and humiliation, again and again at the man helpless in the arms of Mr. Hansen, until his battered head sank supinely back-ward, and he struggled no more. Then Mr. Hansen dropped him.

"Lay aft, here, a couple o' hands," thundered the captain from the break of the poop, and two awe-struck men obeyed him. The whole crew had watched the fracas from forward, and the man at the wheel had looked unspeakable things; but no hand or voice had been raised in protest. One at a time they car-ried the unconscious men to the forecastle; then the crew mustered aft at another thundering summons, and listened to a forceful speech by Captain Bacon, delivered in quick, incisive epigrams, to the effect that if a man aboard his ship—whether he believed himself shipped or shanghaied, a sailor, a priest, a policeman, or a dry-nurse—showed the slightest hesitation at obeying orders, or the slightest resentment at what was said to him, he would be punished with fists, brass knuckles, belaying-pins, or handspikes,—the officers were here for that purpose,—and if he persisted, he would be shot like a mad dog. They could go forward.

They went, and while the watch on deck, under the supervision of the second mate, finished coiling down the tow-line, the watch below finished their breakfast, and when the stricken ones had recovered consciousness, advised them, unsympathetically, to submit and make the best of it until the ship reached Hong-Kong, where they could all " jump her " and get better berths.

" For if ye don't," concluded an Irishman, " I take it ye'll die, an' take sam wan of us wid ye; fur this is an American ship, where the mates are hired fur the bigness o' their fists an' the hardness o' their hearts. Look pleasant, now, the pair o' ye; an' wan o' ye take this hash-kid back to the galley."

The larger of the two victims sprang to his feet. He was stained and disfigured from the effects of the brass knuckles, and he looked anything but " pleasant."

" Say, Irish," he said angrily, " do you know who you're talkin' to? Looks as though you don't. I'm used to all sorts of guff from all sorts of men, but Mr. Breen, here—"

" Johnson," interrupted the other, " wait—it's of no account now. This man's advice is sound. No one would believe us, and we can prove nothing. We are thoroughly helpless, and must submit until we reach a consular port, or something happens. Now, men," he said to the others, " my name is Breen. Call me by it. You, too, Johnson. I yield to the inevitable, and will do my share of the work as well as I can. If I make mistakes, don't hesitate to criticise, and post me, if you will. I'll be grateful."

" But I'll tell you one thing to start with," said Johnson, glaring around the forecastle: " we'll take turns at bringin' grub and cleanin' up the forecastle. Another thing: I've sailed in these wind-jammers enough to know my work; and that's more than you fellows know, by the looks of you. I don't want your instructions; but Mr. Breen, here—Breen, I mean " (a gesture from the other hand interrupted him)— " Breen's forgotten what you and I will never learn, though he might not be used to pullin' ropes and swabbin' paint-work. If I find one o' you pesterin' him, or puttin' up any jobs, I'll break that man's head; understand me? Any one want to put this thing to the test, now? " He scanned each man's face in turn; but none showed an inclination to respond. They had seen him fight the big first mate. " There's not the makin' of a whole man among you," he resumed. " You stand still while three men do up two, when, if you had any nerve, Mr.—Breen, here, might be aft, 'stead o' eatin' cracker-hash with a lot o' dock-rats and beach-combers. He's had better play-mates; so've I, for that matter, o' late years."

" Johnson, keep still," said the other. " It doesn't matter what we have had, who we were or might be.

We're before the mast, bound for Hong-Kong. We may find a consul at Anjer; I'm not sure. Meanwhile, I'm Breen, and you are Johnson, and it is no one's business what we have been. I'm not anxious for this matter to become public. I can explain to the department, and no one else need know."

"Very good, sir."

"No; not 'sir.' Keep that for our superiors."

Johnson grumbled a little; then Mr. Hansen's round Swedish face appeared at the door.

"Hi, you in dere—you big feller—you come out. You belong in der utter watch. You hear? You come out on deck," he called.

"Aye, aye, sir," said Johnson, rising sullenly.

"All the better, Johnson," whispered Breen. "One can keep a lookout all the time. Keep your eyes open and your mouth shut."

So for these two men the work of the voyage began. The hard-headed, aggressive Johnson, placed in the mate's watch, had no trouble in finding his place, and keeping it, at the top of the class. He ruled the assorted types of all nations, who worked and slept with him, with sound logic backed by a strong arm and hard fist, never trying to conceal his contempt for them.

"You mixed nest o' mongrels," he would say, at the end of some petty squabble which he had settled for them, "why don't you stay in your own country ships? Or, if you must sign in American craft, try to feel and act like Americans. It's just this same yawping at one another in the forecastles that makes it easy for the buckoes aft to hunt you. And that's why you get your berths. No skipper'll ship an American sailor while there's a Dutchman left in the

shippin'-office. He wouldn't think it safe to go to
sea with too many American sailors forward to call
him down and make him treat 'em decent. He picks
a Dago here, and a Dutchman there, and all the
Sou'wegians he sees, and fills in with the rakin's and
scrapin's o' Hell, Bedlam, and Newgate, knowin'
they'll hate one another worse than they hate him,
and never stand together."

To which they would respond in kind, though of
lesser degree, always yielding him the last word
when he spoke it loud enough.

But Breen, in the second mate's watch, had trouble
with his fellows at first. They could not understand
his quiet, gentlemanly demeanor, mistaking it for
fear of them; so, unknown to Johnson, for he would
not complain, they subjected him to all the petty
annoyances which ignorance may inflict upon intelligence. Though he showed a theoretical knowledge
of ships and the sea superior to any they had met
with, he was not their equal in the practical work of
a sailor. He was awkward at pulling ropes with
others, placing his hands in the wrong place and
mixing them up in what must be a concerted pull to
be effective. His hands, unused to labor, became
blistered and sore, and he often, unconsciously perhaps, held back from a task, to save himself from
pain. He was an indifferent helmsman, and off
Hatteras, in a blow, was sent from the wheel in disgrace. He did not know the ropes, and made sad
mistakes until he had mastered the lesson. He could
box the compass, in his own way; for instance, the
quarter-points between north-northeast and northeast by north he persisted in naming from the first
of these points instead of from the other, as was sea-

manlike and proper; and the same with the corresponding sectors in the other quadrants. Once, at the wheel, when the ship was heading southeast by south half-south, he had been asked the course, and answered: " South-southeast half-east, sir." For this he was profanely admonished by the captain and ridiculed by the men. Johnson had made the same mistake, but corrected himself in time, and nothing was said about it; but Breen was bullied and badgered in the watch below,—the lubberly nomenclature becoming a byword of derision and contempt,—until, patience leaving him, he doubled his sore fingers into fists one dog-watch, and thrashed the Irishman—his most unforgiving critic—so quickly, thoroughly, and scientifically that persecution ceased; for the Irishman had been the master spirit of the port forecastle.

But the captain and mates were not won over. Practical Johnson—an able seaman from crown to toe—knew how to avoid or forestall their abuse; but Breen did not. The very presence of such a man as he before the mast was a continuous menace,—an insult to their artificial superiority,—and they assailed him at each mistake with volleys of billingsgate that brought a flush to his fine face and tears to his eyes; later, a deadly paleness that would have been a warning to tyrants of better discrimination. Once again, while being rebuked in this manner, his self-control left him. With white face and blazing eyes he darted at Mr. Knapp, and had almost repeated Johnson's feat on the poop when an iron belaying-pin in the hands of the captain descended upon him and broke his left arm. Mr. Knapp's fists and boots completed his tutelage, and he was carried to his bunk with another lesson learned. Johnson, swearing the while, skilfully set the broken bones and made a sling; then, by tactful wheedling of the steward, secured certain necessaries from the medicine-chest, with hot water from the galley; but open assistance was refused by the captain.

Breen, scarcely able to move, held to his bunk for a few days; then, the first mild skirts of the trade-wind being reached, the mate drove him to the wheel, to steer one-handed through the day, while all hands (in the afternoon) worked in the rigging. But the trade-wind freshened, and his strength was not equal to the task set for it. With the men all aloft and the two mates forward, the ship nearly broached to one day, and only the opportune arrival of Captain Bacon on deck saved the spars. He seized the wheel, ground it up, and the ship paid off; then a whole man was called to relieve him, and the incompetent helmsman was promptly and properly punished. He was kicked off the poop, and his arm, as a consequence, needed resetting.

Johnson had been aloft, but there was murder in his dark eyes when he came down at supper-time. Yet he knew its futility, and while bandaging the broken arm earnestly explained, as Breen's groans would allow, that if he killed one the other two would kill him, and nothing would be gained. " For they've brass knuckles in their pockets, sir," he said, " and pistols under their pillows. We haven't even sheath-knives, and the crew wouldn't help."

Whereupon, an inspired Russian Finn of the watch remarked: " If a man know his work an' do his work, an' gif no back lip to te mates, he get no trupple mit te mates. In my country ships—" The dissertation was not finished. Johnson silently knocked him down, and the incident closed.

But they found work which the crippled man could do, after a short " lying up." With the steward's washboard, he could wash the captain's soiled linen, which the steward would afterward wring out and hang up. He refused at first, but was duly persuaded, and went to work in the lee scuppers amidships. Johnson made a detour on his way to the main-rigging, and muttered: " Say the word, sir, and I'll chance it. No jury'd convict."

" No, no; go aloft, Johnson. I'm all right," answered Breen, as he bent over the distasteful task.

Johnson climbed the rigging to the main-royalyard, which he was to scrape for reoiling, and had no sooner reached it than he sang out:

" Sail oh! Dead ahead, sir. Looks like an armored cruiser o' the first class."

" Armored cruiser o' the first class? " muttered the captain, as he carried his binoculars to the weather rail and looked ahead. " More'n I can make out with the glasses."

If three funnels, two masts, two bridges, and two sets of fighting-tops indicate an armored cruiser of the first class, Johnson was right. These the oncoming craft showed plainly even at seven miles' distance. Fifteen minutes later she was storming by, a half-mile to windward; a beautiful picture, long and white, with an incurving ram-bow, with buffcolored turrets and superstructure, and black guns bristling from all parts of her. The Stars and Stripes flew from the flagstaff at the stern; whiteclad men swarmed about her decks, and one of them, on the forward bridge, close to a group of officers, was waving by its staff a small red-and-white flag. Captain Bacon brought out the American ensign, and with his own hands hoisted it to the monkey-gaff on the mizzen, dipped it three times in respectful salute, and left it at the gaff-end. Then he looked at the cruiser, as every man on board was doing except the man washing clothes in the lee scuppers. His business was to wash clothes, not to cross a broad deck and climb a high rail to look at passing craft; but, as he washed away, he looked furtively aloft, with eyes that sparkled, at the man on the mainroyalyard. Johnson was standing erect on the small spar, holding on with his left hand to the royal-pole,—certainly the most conspicuous detail of the whole ship to the eyes of those on board the cruiser,—and with his right hand he was waving his cap to the right and left, and up and down. There was method in his motions, for when he would cease, the small red-and-white flag on the cruiser's bridge would answer, waving to the right and left, and up and down.

A secondary gun spoke from a midship sponson, and Captain Bacon exclaimed enthusiastically, " Salutin' the flag," and again dipped his ensign. Then, after an interval, during which it became apparent that the cruiser had altered her course to cross the ship's stern, there was seen another tongue of flame and cloud of smoke, and something seemed to rush through the air ahead of the ship. But it was a splash of water far off on the lee bow which really apprised them that the gun was shotted. At the same time a string of small flags arose to the signal-yard, and when Captain Bacon had found this combination in his code-book, he read with amazement: " Heave to or take the consequences." By this time the cruiser was squarely across his wake, most certainly rounding to for an interview.

"Heave to or take the consequences!" he exclaimed. "And he's firin' on us. Down from aloft, all hands!" he roared upward; then he seized the answering pennant from the flag-locker and displayed it from the rail, begrudging the time needful to hoist it. The men were sliding to the deck on backstays and running-gear, and the mates were throwing down coils of rope from the belaying-pins.

"Man both main clue-garnets, some o' you!" yelled the captain. "Clue up! Weather main-braces, the rest o' you! Slack away to looward! Round wi' the yards, you farmers—round wi' 'em! Down wi' the wheel, there! Bring her up three points and hold her. H—l an' blazes, what's he firin' on me for?"

Excitedly, the men obeyed him; they were not used to gun fire, and it is certainly exciting to be shot at. Conspicuous among them was Johnson, who pulled and hauled lustily, shouting exuberantly the formless calls which sailors use in pulling ropes, and smiling sardonically. In five minutes from the time of the second gun the yards were backed, and, with weather leeches trembling, the ship lay "hove to," drifting bodily to leeward. The cruiser had stopped her headway, and a boat had left her side. There were ten men at the oars, a coxswain at the yoke-ropes, and with him in the stern-sheets a young man in an ensign's uniform, who lifted his voice as the boat neared the lee quarter, and shouted: "Rig a side-ladder aboard that ship!"

He was hardly more than a boy, but he was obeyed; not only the side-ladder, but the gangway steps were rigged; and leaving the coxswain and bow oarsman to care for the boat, the young officer climbed aboard, followed by the rest—nine muscular man-of-war's-men, each armed with cutlass and pistol, one of them carrying a hand-bag, another a bundle. Captain Bacon, as became his position, remained upon the poop to receive his visitor, while the two mates stood at the main fife-rail, and the ship's crew clustered forward. Johnson, alert and attentive, stood a little in the van, and the man in the lee scuppers still washed clothes.

"What's the matter, young man?" asked the captain from the break of the poop, with as much of dignity as his recent agitation would permit. "Why do you stop my ship on the high seas and board her with an armed boat's crew?"

"You have an officer and seaman of the navy on board this ship," answered the ensign, who had been looking about irresolutely. "Produce them at once, if you please."

"What—what—" stuttered the captain, descending the poop steps; but before more was said there was a sound from forward as of something hard striking something heavy, and as they looked they saw Captain Bacon's bucket of clothes sailing diagonally over the lee rail, scattering a fountain of soapy water as it whirled; his late laundryman coming toward them with head erect, as though he might have owned the ship and himself; and Johnson, limping slightly, making for the crowd of blue-jackets at the gangway. With these he fraternized at once, telling them things in a low voice, and somewhat profanely, while the two mates at the fife-rail eyed him reprovingly, but did not interrupt.

Breen advanced to the ensign, and said, as he extended his hand: "I am Lieutenant Breen. Did you bring the clothing? This is an extremely fortunate meeting for me; but I can thank you—you and your brother officers—much more gracefully aboard the cruiser."

The officer took the extended hand gingerly, with suspicion in his eyes. Perhaps, if it had not been thoroughly clean from its late friction with soap and water, he might have declined taking it; for there was nothing in the appearance of the haggard, ragged wreck before him to indicate the naval officer.

"There is some mistake," he said, coldly. "I am well acquainted with Lieutenant Breen, and you are certainly not he."

Breen's face flushed hotly, but before he could reply, the captain broke in.

"Some mistake, hey?" said he, derisively. "I guess there is—another mistake—another bluff that don't go. Get out o' here; and I tell you now, blast yer hide, that if you make me any more trouble 'board my ship yer liable to go over the side feet first, with a shackle to yer heels. And you, young man," he stormed, turning to the ensign, "you look round, if you like. There's my crew. All the navy officers you find you can have, and welcome to 'em." He turned his back, stamped a few paces along the deck, and returned, working himself into a fury.

Breen had not moved, but, with a slight sparkle to his eyes, said to the young officer:

"I think, sir, that if you take the trouble to investigate, you will be satisfied. There are two Breens in the navy. You know one, evidently; I am the other. Lieutenant William Breen is on shore duty at

Washington, I think. Lieutenant John Breen, lately in command of the torpedo-boat *Wainwright*, with his signalman, Thomas Johnson, are shanghaied on board this ship. There is Johnson talking to your men."

The young man's face changed, and his hand went to his cap in salute; but the mischief was done. Captain Bacon's indignation was at bursting-pressure, and his mind in no condition to respond readily to new impressions. He was captain of the ship, and grossly affronted. Johnson, noting his purple face, wisely reached for a topsail-brace belaying-pin, and stepped toward him; for he now towered over Breen, cursing with volcanic energy.

"Didn't I tell you to go forrard?" he roared, drawing back his powerful fist.

Breen stood his ground; the officer raised his hand and half drew his sword, while the blue-jackets sprang forward; but it was Johnson's belaying-pin which stopped that mighty fist in mid-passage. It was an iron club, eighteen inches long by an inch and a half diameter; and Johnson, strong man though he was, used it two-handed. It struck the brawny forearm just above the wrist with a crashing sound, and seemed to sink in. Captain Bacon almost fell, but recovered his balance, and, holding the broken bones together, staggered toward the booby-hatch for support. He groaned in pain, but did not curse; for it requires a modicum of self-respect for this, and Captain Bacon's self-respect was completely shocked out of him.

But Mr. Knapp and Mr. Hansen still respected themselves, and were coming.

"You keep back, there—you two," yelled John-

son, excitedly. "Stand by here, mates. These
buckoes'll kill some one yet. Look out for their brass
knuckles and guns."

And the two officers halted. They had no desire
to assert themselves before nine scowling, armed men,
an angry and aggressive mutineer with a belaying-
pin, and a rather confused, but wakening, young
officer with drawn sword. Johnson backed toward
the latter.

"Don't you know me, Mr. Bronson," he said—
"Tom Johnson, cocks'n o' the gig on your practice-
cruise? 'Member me, sir? This is Lieutenant Breen
—take my word, sir."

"Yes—yes—I understand," said the ensign, with
a face redder than Breen's had been. "I really beg
your pardon, Mr. Breen. It was inexcusable in me,
I know—but—I had expected to see a different face,
and—and—we're three months out from Hong-Kong,
you see—"

Breen smiled, and interrupted with a gesture.

"No time for explanations, Mr. Bronson," said
he, kindly. "Did you bring the clothes? Thoughtful of Johnson to ask for them, wasn't it? It really
would be embarrassing to join your ship in this rig.
In the grip and bundle? All right. Form your men
across the deck, please, forward of the cabin. Keep
these brutes away from us while we change. Come,
Johnson."

Taking the hand-bag and the bundle, they brazenly
entered the cabin by the forward door. In ten
minutes they emerged, Johnson clad in the blue rig
of a man-of-war's-man, Breen in the undress uniform
of an officer, his crippled arm buttoned into the coat.
As they stepped toward the gangway, Captain Bacon,

pale and perspiring, wheezing painfully, entered the cabin and passed out of their lives. The steward followed at his heels, and the two mates, with curiously working faces, approached Breen.

"Excuse me, sir," said Mr. Knapp, "but I want to say that I had no notion o' this at all; and I hope you won't make no trouble for me ashore."

Breen, one foot on the steps while he waited for the blue-jackets to file over the side, eyed him thoughtfully.

"No," he said, slowly. "I hardly think, Mr. Knapp, that I shall exert myself to make trouble for you personally, or for the other two. There is a measure now before Congress which, if it passes, will legislate brutes like you and your captain off the American quarter-deck by its educational conditions. This, with a consideration for your owners, is what permits you to continue this voyage, instead of going back to the United States in irons. But if I had the power," he added, looking at the beautiful flag still flying at the gaff, "I would lower that ensign, and forbid you to hoist it. It is the flag of a free country, and should not float over slave-ships."

He mounted the steps, and, assisted by the young officer and Johnson, descended to the boat; but before Johnson went down, he peered over the rail at the two mates, grinning luridly.

"And I'll promise you," he said, "that I'm always willing to make trouble for you, ashore or afloat, and wish I had a little more time for it now. And you can tell your skipper, if you like, in case he don't know it, that he got smashed with the same club that he used on Mr. Breen, and I'm only d—d sorry I didn't bring it down on his head. So long, you bloody-minded hell-drivers.　See you again some day."

He descended, and Mr. Knapp gave the order to brace the yards.

" Give a good deal," he mused, as the men manned the braces, " to know just how they got news to that cruiser.　Homeward bound from Hong-Kong—three months out.　Couldn't ha' been sent after us."

But he never learned.

THE orgy was finished. The last sea-song had resounded over the smooth waters of the bay; the last drunken shout, oath, and challenge were voiced; the last fight ended in helplessness and maudlin amity, and the red-shirted men were sprawled around on the moonlit deck, snoring. Though the barrel of rum broached on the main-hatch was but slightly lowered, their sleep was heavy; scurvy-tainted men at the end of a Cape Horn passage may not drink long or deeply. Some lay as they fell—face upward; others on their sides for a while, then to roll over on their backs and so remain until the sleep was done; for in no other position may the human body rest easy on a hard bed with no pillow. And as they slept through the tropic night the full moon in the east rose higher and higher, passed overhead and disappeared behind a thickening haze in the western sky; but before it had crossed the meridian its cold, chemical rays had worked disastrously on the eyes of the sleeping men.

Captain Swarth, prone upon the poop-deck, was the first to waken. There was pain in his head, pain in his eyes,—which were swollen,—and a whistling tumult of sound in his ears coming from the Plutonian darkness surrounding him, while a jarring vibration of the deck beneath him apprised his awakening brain that the anchor was dragging. As he staggered to his feet a violent pressure of wind hurled him against the wheel, to which he clung, staring into the blackness to windward.

"All hands, there!" he roared. "Up with you all! Go forward and pay out on the chain!"

Shouts, oaths, and growls answered him, and he heard the nasal voice of his mate repeating his order. "Angel," he called, "get the other anchor over and give her all of both chains."

"Aye, aye, sir," answered the mate. "Send a lantern forrard, Bill. Can't see our noses."

"Steward," yelled the captain, "where are you? Light up a deck-lantern and the binnacle. Bear a hand."

He heard the steward's voice close to him, and the sound of the binnacle lights being removed from their places, then the opening and closing of the cabin companionway. He could see nothing, but knew that the steward had gone below to his store-room. In a minute more a shriek came from the cabin. It rang out again and again, and soon sounded from the companionway: "I'm blind, I'm blind, capt'n. I can't see. I lit the lantern and burned my fingers; but I can't see the light. I'm blind." The steward's voice ended in a howl.

"Shut up, you blasted fool," answered Captain Swarth; "get down there and light up."

"Where's that light?" came the mate's voice in a yell from amidships. "Shank-painter's jammed, Bill. Can't do a thing without a light."

"Come aft here and get it. Steward's drunk."

The doors in the forward part of the cabin slammed, and the mate's profanity mingled with the protest of the steward in the cabin. Then shouts came from forward, borne on the gale, and soon followed by the shuffling of feet as the men groped their way aft and climbed the poop steps.

"We're stone-blind, cappen," they wailed. "We lit the fo'c'sle lamp, an' it don't show up. We can't see it. Nobody can see it. We're all blind."

"Come down here, Bill," called the mate from below.

As Captain Swarth felt his way down the stairs a sudden shock stilled the vibrations caused by the dragging anchor, and he knew that the chain had parted.

"Stand by on deck, Angel; we're adrift," he said. "It's darker than ten thousand black cats. What's the matter with you?"

"Can you see the light, Bill? I can't. I'm blind as the steward, or I'm drunker."

"No. Is it lit? Where? The men say they're blind, too."

"Here, forrard end o' the table."

The captain reached this end, searched with his hands, and burned them on the hot glass of a lantern. He removed the bowl and singed the hair on his wrists. The smell came to his nostrils.

"I'm blind, too," he groaned. "Angel, it's the moon. We're moonstruck—moonblind. And we're adrift in a squall. Steward," he said as he made his way toward the stairs, "light the binnacle, and stop that whining. Maybe some one can see a little."

When he reached the deck he called to the men, growling, cursing, and complaining on the poop. "Down below with you all!" he ordered. "Pass through and out the forrard door. If any man sees the light on the cabin table, let that man sing out."

They obeyed him. Twenty men passed through the cabin and again climbed the poop stairs, their lamentations still troubling the night. But not one had seen the lantern. Some said that they could not open their eyes at all; some complained that their faces were swollen; others that their mouths were twisted up to where their ears should be; and one man averred that he could not breathe through his nose.

"It'll only last a few days, boys," said the captain, bravely; "we shouldn't have slept in the moonlight in these latitudes. Drop the lead over, one of you—weather side. The devil knows where we're drifting, and the small anchor won't hold now; we'll save it." Captain Swarth was himself again.

But not so his men. They had become children, with children's fear of the dark. Even the doughty Angel Todd was oppressed by the first horror of the situation, speaking only when spoken to. Above the rushing sound of wind and the smacking of short seas could be heard the voice of the steward in the cabin, while an occasional heart-borne malediction or groan—according to temperament—added to the distraction on deck. One man, more self-possessed than the rest, had dropped the lead over the side. An able seaman needs no eyes to heave the lead.

"A quarter six," he sang out, and then, plaintively: "We'll fetch up on the Barrier, capt'n. S'pose we try an' get the other hook over."

"Yes, yes," chorused some of the braver spirits. "It may hold. We don't want to drown on the reef. Let's get it over. Chain's overhauled."

"Let the anchor alone," roared the captain. "No anchor-chain'll hold in this. Keep that lead a-going, Tom Plate, if it's you. What bottom do you find?"

"Quarter less six," called the leadsman. "Soft bottom. We're shoaling."

"Angel," said the captain to his mate, who stood close to him, "we're blowing out the south channel. We've been drifting long enough to fetch up on the reef if it was in our way. There's hard bottom in the north channel, and the twenty-fathom lead wouldn't reach it half a length from the rocks."

The mate had nothing to say.

"And the south channel lay due southeast from our moorings," continued the captain. "Wind's nor'west, I should say, right down from the hilltops; and I've known these blasted West India squalls to last three days, blowing straight and hard. This has the smell of a gale in it already. Keep that lead a-going, there."

"No bottom," answered the leadsman.

"Good enough," said the captain, cheerfully.

"No bottom," was called repeatedly, until the captain sang out: "That'll do the lead." Then the leadsman coiled up the line, and they heard his rasping, unpleasant voice, cursing softly but fiercely to himself. Captain Swarth descended the stairs, silenced the steward with a blow, felt of the clock hands, secured his pistols, and returned to the deck.

"We're at sea," he said. "Two hands to the wheel. Loose and set the foretopmast-staysails and the foretopsail. Staysail first. Let a man stay in the slings to square the yard by the feel as it goes up."

"What for?" they answered, complainingly. "What ye goin' to do? We can't see. Why didn't you bring to when you had bottom under you?"

"No arguments!" yelled Swarth. "Forward with you. What are you doing on the poop, anyway? If you can't see, you can feel, and what more do you want? Jump, now. Set that head-sail and get her 'fore the wind—quick, or I'll drop some of you."

They knew their captain, and they knew the ropes —on the blackest of dark nights. Blind men climbed aloft, and felt for foot-ropes and gaskets. Blind men on deck felt for sheets, halyards, and braces, and in ten minutes the sails were set, and the brig was charging wildly along before the gale, with two blind men at the wheel endeavoring to keep her straight by the right and left pressure of the wind on their faces.

"Keep the wind as much on the port quarter as you can without broaching to," yelled the captain in their ears, and they answered and did their best. She was a clean-lined craft and steered easily; yet the off-shore sea which was rising often threw her around until nearly in the trough. The captain remained by them, advising and encouraging.

"Where're ye goin', Bill?" asked the mate, weakly, as he scrambled up to him.

"Right out to sea, and, unless we get our eyes back soon, right across to the Bight of Benin, three thousand miles from here. We've no business on this coast in this condition. What ails you, Angel? Lost your nerve?"

"Mebbe, Bill." The mate's voice was hoarse and strained. "This is new to me. I'm falling—falling —all the time."

"So am I. Brace up. We'll get used to it. Get a couple of hands aft and heave the log. We take our departure from Kittredge Point, Barbados Island, at six o'clock this morning of the 10th October. We'll keep a Geordie's log-book—with a jack-knife and a stick."

They hove the log for him. It was marked for a

now useless 28-second sand-glass, which Captain Swarth replaced by a spare chronometer, held to his ear in the companionway. It ticked even seconds, and when twenty-eight of them had passed he called, "Stop." The markings on the line that had slipped through the mate's fingers indicated an eight-knot speed.

"Seven, allowing for wild steering," said the captain when he had stowed away his chronometer and returned to the deck. "Angel, we know we're going about sou'east by east, seven knots. There's practically no variation o' the compass in these seas, and that course'll take us clear of Cape St. Roque. Just as fast as the men can stand it at the wheel, we'll pile on canvas and get all we can out o' this good wind. If it takes us into the southeast trades, well and good. We can feel our way across on the trade-wind—unless we hit something, of course. You see, it blows almost out of the east on this side, and'll haul more to the sou'east and south'ard as we get over. By the wind first, then we'll square away as we need to. We'll know the smell o' the trades—nothing like it on earth—and the smell o' the Gold Coast, Ivory Coast, Slave Coast, and the Kameruns. And I'll lay odds we can feel the heat o' the sun in the east and west enough to make a fair guess at the course. But it won't come to that. Some of us'll be able to see pretty soon."

It was wild talk, but the demoralized mate needed encouraging. He answered with a steadier voice: "Lucky we got in grub and water yesterday."

"Right you are, Angel. Now, in case this holds on to us, why, we'll find some of our friends over in the Bight, and they'll know by our rig that something's wrong. Flanders is somewhere on the track, —you know he went back to the nigger business,— and Chink put a slave-deck in his hold down Rio way last spring. And old man Slack—I did him a service when I crippled the corvette that was after him, and he's grateful. Hope we'll meet him. I'd rather meet Chink than Flanders in the dark, and I'd trust a Javanese trader before either. If either of them come aboard we'll be ready to use their eyes for our benefit, not let 'em use ours for theirs. Flanders once said he liked the looks of this brig."

" S'pose we run foul of a bulldog? "

" We'll have to chance it. This coast's full o' them, too. Great guns, man! Would you drift around and do nothing? Anywhere east of due south there's no land nearer than Cape Orange, and that's three hundred and fifty miles from here. Beginning to-morrow noon, we'll take deep-sea soundings until we strike the trade-wind."

The negro cook felt his way through the preparing of meals and served them on time. The watches were set, and sail was put on the brig as fast as the men became accustomed to the new way of steering, those relieved always imparting what they had learned to their successors. Before nightfall on that first day they were scudding under foresail, topsail and topgallantsail and maintopsail, with the spanker furled as useless, and the jib adding its aid to the foretopmast-staysail in keeping the brig before the quartering seas which occasionally climbed aboard. The bowsprit light was rigged nightly; they hove the log every two hours; and Captain Swarth made scratches and notches on the sliding-hood of the companionway, while careful to wind his chronometer daily.

But, in spite of the cheer of his indomitable courage and confidence, his men, with the exception of a few, dropped into a querulous, whining discontent. Mr. Todd, spurred by his responsibility, gradually came around to something like his old arbitrary self. Yank Tate, the carpenter, maintained through it all a patient faith in the captain, and, in so far as his influence could be felt, acted as a foil to the irascible, fault-finding Tom Plate, the forecastle lawyer, the man who had been at the lead-line at Barbados. But the rest of them were dazed and nerveless, too shaken in brain and body to consider seriously Tom's proposition to toss the afterguard overboard and beach the brig on the South American coast, where they could get fresh liver of shark, goat, sheep, or bullock, which even a "nigger" knew was the only cure for moonblindness.

They had not yet recovered from the unaccustomed debauch; their clouded brains seemed too large for their skulls, and their eyeballs ached in their sockets, while they groped tremblingly from rope to rope at the behest of the captain or mate.

So Tom marked himself for future attention by insolent and disapproving comments on the orders of his superiors, and a habit of moving swiftly to another part of the deck directly he had spoken, which prevented the blind and angry captain from finding him in the crowd.

Dim as must have been the light of day through the pelting rain and storm-cloud, it caused increased pain in their eyes, and they bound them with their neckerchiefs, applying meanwhile such remedies as forecastle lore could suggest. The captain derided these remedies, but frankly confessed his ignorance of anything but time as a means of cure. And so they existed and suffered through a three days' damp gale and a fourth day's dead calm, when the brig rolled scuppers under with all sail set, ready for the next breeze. It came, cool, dry, and faint at first, then brisker—the unmistakable trade-wind. They boxed the brig about and braced sharp on the starboard tack, steering again by the feel of the wind and the rattling of shaking leeches aloft. The removal of bandages to ascertain the sun's position by sense of light or increase of pain brought agonized howls from the experimenters, and this deterred the rest. Not even by its warmth could they locate it. It was overhead at noon and useless as a guide. In the early morning, and late afternoon, when it might have indicated east and west, its warmth was overcome by the coolness of the breeze. So they steered on blindly, close-hauled on the starboard tack, nearly as straight a course as though they were whole men.

They took occasional deep-sea soundings with the brig shaking in the wind, but found no bottom, and at the end of fifteen days a longer heave to the ground-swell was evidence to Captain Swarth's mind that he was passing Cape St. Roque, and the soundings were discontinued.

"No use bothering about St. Paul Rocks or the Rocas, Angel," said he. "They rise out o' the deep sea, and if we're to hit, soundings won't warn us in time. I take it we'll pass between them and well north of Ascension." So he checked in the yards a little and brought the wind more abeam.

One day Yank Tate appeared at the captain's elbow, and suggested, in a low voice, that he examine the treasure-chests in the 'tween-deck. " I was down stowing away some oakum," he said, " an' I was sure I heard the lid close; but nobody answered me, an' I couldn't feel anybody."

Captain Swarth descended to his cabin and found his keys missing; then he and the carpenter visited the chests. They were locked tight, and as heavy as ever.

" Some one has the keys, Yank, and has very likely raided the diamonds. We can't do anything but wait. He can't get away. Keep still about it."

The air became cooler as they sailed on; and judging that the trade-wind was blowing more from the south than he had allowed for, the captain brought the wind squarely abeam, and the brig sailed faster. Still, it was too cool for the latitude, and it puzzled him, until a man came aft and groaned that he had lifted his bandage to bathe his eyes, and had unmistakably seen the sun four points off the port quarter; but his eyes were worse now, and he could not do it again.

" Four points off! " exclaimed Swarth. " Four o'clock in the afternoon. That's just about where the sun ought to be heading due east, and far enough south o' the line to bring this cool weather. We're not far from Ascension. Never knew the sou'east trade to act like this before. Must ha' been blowing out o' the sou'west half the time."

A week later they were hove to on the port tack under double-reefed topsails, with a cold gale of wind screaming through the rigging and cold green seas boarding their weather bow. It was the first break in the friendly trade-wind, and Swarth confessed to

himself—though not to his men—that he was out of
his reckoning; but one thing he was sure of—that
this was a cyclone with a dangerous center.

The brig. labored heavily during the lulls as the
seas rose, and when the squalls came, flattening them
to a level, she would lie down like a tired animal,
while the æolian song aloft prevented orders being
heard unless shouted near by. Captain Swarth went
below and smashed the glass of an aneroid barometer (newly invented and lately acquired from an out-
ward-bound Englishman), in which he had not much
confidence, but which might tell him roughly of the
air-density. Feeling of the indicator, and judging
by the angle it made with the center,—marked by a
ring at the top,—he found a measurement which
startled him. Setting the adjustable hand over the
indicator for future reference, he returned to the
deck, ill at ease, and ordered the topsails goose-
winged. By the time the drenched and despairing
blind men had accomplished this, a further lowering
of the barometer induced him to furl topsails and
foretopmast-staysail, and allow the brig to ride under
a storm-spanker. Then the increasing wind required
that this also should be taken in, and its place filled
by a tarpaulin lashed to the weather main-rigging.

" Angel," said the captain, shouting into the mate's
ear, " there's only one thing to account for this.
We're on the right tack for the Southern Ocean; but
the storm-center is overtaking us faster than we can
drift away from it. We must scud out of its way."

So they took in the tarpaulin and set the foretopmast-staysail again, and, with the best two helmsmen
at the wheel, they sped before the tempest for four
hours, during which there was no increase of the

wind and no change in the barometer; it still remained at its lowest reading.

"Keep the wind as much on the port quarter as you dare," ordered Swarth. "We're simply sailing around the center, and perhaps in with the vortex."

They obeyed him as they could, and in a few hours more there was less fury in the blast and a slight rise in the barometer.

"I was right," said the captain. "The center will pass us now. We're out of its way."

They brought the brig around amid a crashing of seas over the port rail, and stowing the staysail, pinned her again on the port tack with the tarpaulin. But a few hours of it brought an increase of wind and a fall of the barometer.

"What in d—nation does it mean, Angel?" cried the captain, desperately. "By all laws of storms we ought to drift away from the center."

The mate could not tell; but a voice out of the night, barely distinguishable above the shrieking wind, answered him.

"You — all-fired — fool — don't — you — know — any — more — than — to — heave — to — in — the — Gulf — Stream?"

Then there was the faintest disturbance in the sounds of the sea, indicating the rushing by of a large craft.

"What!" roared Swarth. "The Gulf Stream? I've lost my reckoning. Where am I? Ship ahoy! Where am I?"

There was no answer, and he stumbled down to the main-deck among his men, followed by the mate.

"Draw a bucket of water, one of you," he ordered.

This was done, and he immersed his hand. The water was warm.

"Gulf Stream," he yelled frantically, "Gulf Stream—how in h—l did we get up here? We ought to be down near St. Helena. Angel, come here. Let's think. We sailed by the wind on the southeast trade for—no, we didn't. It was the northeast trade. We caught the northeast trade, and we've circled all over the Western Ocean."

"You're a bully full-rigged navigator, you are," came the sneering, rasping voice of Tom Plate from the crowd. · "Why didn't you drop your hook at Barbados, and give us a chance for our eyes?"

The captain lunged toward him on the reeling deck; but Tom moved on.

"Your time is coming, Tom Plate," he shouted, insanely; then he climbed to the poop, and when he had studied the situation awhile, called his bewildered mate up to him.

"We were blown out of the north entrance o' the bay, Angel, instead of the south, as we thought. I was fooled by the soundings. At this time o' the year Barbados is about on the thermal equator— half-way between the trades. This is a West India cyclone, and we're somewhere around Hatteras. No wonder the port tack drifted us into the center. Storms revolve against the sun north o' the line, and with the sun south of it. Oh, I'm the two ends and the bight of a d—d fool! Wear ship!" he added in a thundering roar.

They put the brig on the starboard tack, and took hourly soundings with the deep-sea lead. As they hauled it in for the fourth time, the men called that the water was cold; and on the next sounding the lead reached bottom at ninety fathoms.

"We're inside the Stream and the hundred-fathom curve, Angel. The barometer's rising now. The storm-center's leaving us, and we're drifting ashore," said the captain. "I know pretty well where I am. These storms follow an invariable track, and I judge the center is to the east of us, moving north. That's why we didn't run into it when we thought we were dodging it. We'll square away with the wind on the starboard quarter now, and if we pick up the Stream and the glass don't rise, I'll be satisfied to turn in. I'm about fagged out."

"It's too much for me, Bill," answered Mr. Todd, wearily. "I can navigate; but this ain't navigation. This is blindman's-buff."

But he set the head-sail for his captain, and again the brig fled before the wind. Only once did they round to for soundings, and this time found no bottom; so they squared away, and when, a few hours later, the seas came aboard warm, Swarth was confident enough of his position to allow his mind to dwell on pettier details of his business.

It was nearly breakfast-time now, and the men would soon be eating. With his pistols in his coat pockets he stationed himself beside the scuttle of the fore-hatch,—the entrance to the forecastle,—and waited long and patiently, listening to occasional comments on his folly and bad seamanship which ascended from below, until the harsh voice of Tom Plate on the stairs indicated his coming up. He reached toward Tom with one hand, holding a cocked pistol with the other; but Tom slid easily out of his wavering grasp and fled along the deck. He followed his footsteps until he lost them, and picked up instead the angry plaint of the negro cook in the galley amidships.

"I do' know who you are, but you want to git right out o' my galley, now. You heah me? I'se had enough o' dis comin' inter my galley. Gwan, now! Is you de man dat's all time stealin' my coffee? I'll gib you coffee, you trash! Take dat!"

Captain Swarth reached the galley door in time to receive on the left side of his face a generous share of a pot of scalding coffee. It brought an involuntary shriek of agony from him; then he clung to the galley-lashings and spoke his mind. Still in torment, he felt his way through the galley; but the cook and the intruder had escaped by the other door and made no sound.

All that day and the night following he chose to lie in his darkened state-room, with his face bandaged in oily cloths, while Yank Tate stood his watch. In the morning he removed the bandages and took in the sight of his state-room fittings: the bulkhead, his desk, chronometer, cutlass, and clothing hanging on the hooks. It was a joyous sight, and he shouted in gladness. He could not see with his right eye and but dimly with his left, but a scrutiny of his face in a mirror disclosed deep lines that had not been there, distorted eyelids, and the left side where the coffee had scalded puffed to a large, angry blister. He tied up his face, leaving his left eye free, and went on deck.

The wind had moderated, but on all sides was a wild gray waste of heaving, white-crested combers, before which the brig was still scudding under the staysail. Three miles off on the port bow was a large, square-bowed, square-yarded ship, hove to and heading away from them, which might be a frigate or a subsidized Englishman with painted ports; but in either case she could not be investigated now. He looked at the compass. The brig was heading about southeast, and his judgment was confirmed. Two haggard-faced men with bandaged eyes were grinding the wheel to starboard and port, and keeping the brig's yaws within two points each way—good work for blind men. Angel Todd stood near, his chin resting in his hand and his elbow on the companion-way. Forward the watch sat about in coils of rope and sheltered nooks or walked the deck unsteadily, and a glance aloft showed the captain his rigging hanging in bights and yards pointed every way. She was unkempt as a wreck. The same glance apprised him of an English ensign, union down, tattered and frayed to half its size, at the end of the standing spanker-gaff, with the halyards made fast high on the royal-backstay, above the reach of bungling blind fingers. Tom Plate was coming aft with none of the hesitancy of the blind, and squinting aloft at the damaged distress-signal. He secured another ensign—American—from the flag-locker in the booby-hatch, mounted the rail, and hoisted it, union down, in place of the other. Then he dropped to the deck and looked into the glaring left eye and pepper-box pistol of Captain Swarth, who had descended on him.

"Hands up, Tom Plate, over your head—quick, or I'll blow your brains out!"

White in the face and open-mouthed, Tom obeyed.

"Mr. Todd," called the captain, "come down here—port main-rigging."

The mate came quickly, as he always did when he heard the prefix to his name. It was used only in emergencies.

"What soundings did you get at the lead when we were blowing out?" asked the captain. "What water did you have when you sang out 'a quarter six' and 'a quarter less six'?"

"N-n-one, capt'n. There warn't any bottom. I jess wanted to get you to drop the other anchor and hold her off the reef."

"Got him tight, cappen?" asked the mate. "Shall I help you hold 'im?"

"I've got my sight back. I've got Tom Plate under my gun. How long have you been flying signals of distress, Tom Plate?"

"Ever since I could see, capt'n," answered the trembling sailor.

"How long is that?"

"Second day out, sir."

"What's your idea in keeping still about it? What could you gain by being taken aboard a man-of-war?"

"I didn't want to have all the work piled on me jess 'cause I could see, capt'n. I never thought anybody could ever see again. I slept partly under No. 2 gun that night, and didn't get it so bad."

"You sneaked into my room, got my keys, and raided the treasure-chests. You know what the rules say about that? Death without trial."

"No, I didn't, capt'n; I didn't."

"Search him, Mr. Todd."

The search brought to light a tobacco-pouch in which were about fifty unset diamonds and a few well-jeweled solid-gold ornaments, which the captain pocketed.

"Not much of a haul, considering what you left behind," he said, calmly. "I suppose you only took what you could safely hide and swim with."

"I only took my share, sir; I did no harm; I didn't want to be driftin' round wi' blind men. How'd I know anybody could ever see any more?"

"Sad mistake, Tom. All we wanted, it seems, was a good scalding with hot coffee." He mused a few moments, then continued: "There must be some medical virtue in hot coffee which the doctors haven't learned, and—well—Tom, you've earned your finish."

"You won't do it, capt'n; you can't do it. The men won't have it; they're with me," stuttered the man.

"Possibly they are. I heard you all growling down the hatch yesterday morning. You're a pack of small-minded curs. I'll get another crew. Mr. Todd," he said to the listening mate, "steward told me he was out of coffee, so we'll break a bag out o' the lazarette. It's a heavy lift—two hundred pounds and over—'bout the weight of a man; so we'll hoist it up. Let Tom, here, rig a whip to the spanker-gaff. He can see."

"Aye, aye, sir," answered the mate. "Get a single block and a strap and a gant-line out o' the bo's'n's locker, Tom."

"Is it all right, capt'n?" asked Tom, lowering his hands with a deep sigh of relief. "I did what seemed right, you know."

"Rig that whip," said Swarth, turning his back and ascending the poop.

Tom secured the gear, and climbing aloft and out

the gaff, fastened the block directly over the laza-rette-hatch, just forward of the binnacle. Then he overhauled the rope until it reached the deck, and descended.

"Come up here on the poop," called the captain; and he came.

"Shall I go down and hook on, sir?" he asked zealously.

"Make a hangman's noose in the end of the rope," said Swarth.

"Eh—what—a runnin' bowline—a timber-hitch? No, no," he yelled, as he read the captain's face. "You can't do it. The men—"

"Make a hangman's knot in the end of the rope," thundered the captain, his pistol at Tom's ear.

With a face like that of a death's-head he tied the knot.

"Pass it round your neck and draw it tight."

Hoarse, inarticulate screams burst from the throat of the man, ended by a blow on the side of his face by the captain's iron-hard fist. He fell, and lay quiet, while Swarth himself adjusted the noose and bound the hands with his own handkerchief. The men at the wheel strained their necks this way and that, with tense waves of conflicting expressions flit-ting across their weary faces, and the men forward, aroused by the screams, stood about in anxious ex-pectancy until they heard Swarth's roar: "Lay aft here, the watch!"

They came, feeling their way along by rail and hatch.

"Clap on to that gant-line at the main fife-rail, and lift this bag of coffee out o' the lazarette," sang out the captain.

They found the loose rope, tautened it, hooked the bight into an open sheave in the stanchion, and listlessly walked forward with it. When they had hoisted the unconscious Tom to the gaff, Swarth ordered: "Belay, coil up the fall, and go forrard."

They obeyed, listlessly as ever, with no wondering voice raised to inquire why they had not lowered the coffee they had hoisted.

Captain Swarth looked at the square-rigged ship, now on the port quarter—an ill-defined blur to his imperfect vision. "Fine chance we'd have had," he muttered, "if that happened to be a bulldog. Angel," he said, as the mate drew near. "Hot coffee is good for moon-blindness, taken externally, as a blistering agent—a counter-irritant. We have no fly-blisters in the medicine chest, but smoking hot grease must be just as good, if not better than either. Have the cook heat up a potful, and you get me out a nice small paint-brush."

Forty-eight hours later, when the last wakening vision among the twenty men had taken cognizance of the grisly object aloft, the gaff was guyed outboard, the rope cut at the fife-rail, and the body of Tom Plate dropped, feet first, to the sea.

Then when Captain Swarth's eyes permitted he took an observation or two, and, after a short lecture to his crew on the danger of sleeping in tropic moonlight, shaped his course for Barbados Island, to take up the burden of his battle with fate where the blindness had forced him to lay it down; to scheme and to plan, to dare and to do, to war and to destroy, against the inevitable coming of the time when fate should prove the stronger—when he would lose in a game where one must always win or die.

SALVAGE

SHE had a large crew, abnormally large hawse-pipes, and a bad reputation—the last attribute born of the first. Registered as the *Rosebud*, this innocent name was painted on her stern and on her sixteen dories; but she was known among the fishing-fleet as the *Ishmaelite*, and the name fitted her. Secretive and unfriendly, she fished alone, avoided company, answered few hails, and, seldom filling her hold, disposed of her catch as her needs required, in out-of-the-way ports, often as far south as Charleston. And she usually left behind her such bitter memories of her visit as placed the last port at the bottom of her list of markets.

No ship-chandler or provision-dealer ever showed her receipted bills, and not a few of them openly averred that certain burglaries of their goods had plausible connection with her presence in port. Be this as it may, the fact stood that farmers on the coast who saw her high bow and unmistakable hawse-pipes when she ran in for bait invariably double-locked their barns and chicken-coops, and turned loose all tied dogs when night descended, often to find both dogs and chickens gone in the morning.

Once, too, three small schooners had come home with empty holds, and complained of the appearance, while anchored in the fog, of a flotilla of dories manned by masked men, who overpowered and locked all hands in cabin or forecastle, and then removed the cargoes of fish to their own craft, hidden in the

112

fog. Shortly after this, the *Ishmaelite* disposed of
a large catch in Baltimore, and the piracy was believed of her, but never proved.

Her luck at finding things was remarkable. Drifting dories, spars, oars, and trawl-tubs sought her unsavory company, as though impelled by the inanimate
perversity which had sent them drifting. They were
sold in port, or returned to their owners, when paid
for. In the early part of her career she had towed
a whistling buoy into Boston and claimed salvage
of the government, showing her log-book to prove
that she had picked it up far at sea. The salvage
was paid; but, as her reputation spread, there were
those who declared that she herself had sent the
buoy adrift.

As poets and sailors believe that ships have souls,
it may be that she gloried in her shame, like other
fallen creatures; for her large, slanting oval hawse-
pipes and boot-top stripe gave a fine, Oriental sneer
to her face-like bow, and there was slur and insult to
respectable craft in the lazy dignity with which she
would swash through the fleet on the port tack, com-
pelling vessels on the starboard tack to give up their
right of way or be rammed; for she was a large craft,
and there was menace in her solid, one-piece jib-
boom, thick as an ordinary mainmast. An outward-
bound coasting-schooner, resenting this lawlessness
on one occasion, attempted to assert her rights, and
being on the lawful starboard tack, bore steadily
down on the *Ishmaelite*,—who budged not a quarter-
point,—and, losing heart at the last moment, luffed
up, all shaking, in just the position to allow the ring
of her port anchor to catch on the bill of the *Ishmaelite's* starboard anchor. As her own ring-stopper

and shank-painter were weak, the patent windlass
unlocked, and the end of the cable not secured in
the chain-locker, the *Ishmaelite* walked calmly away
with the anchor and a hundred fathoms of chain,
which, at the next port, she sold as legitimate spoil
of the sea.

As her reputation increased, so did the hatred
of men, while the number of ports on the coast
which she could safely enter became painfully small.
To avoid conflict with local authority, she had hurried to sea without clearing at the custom-house
from Boston, Bangor, Portland, and Gloucester. She
had carried local authority in the persons of distressed United States marshals to sea with her from
three other ports, and landed it on some outlying
point before the next meal-hour. With her blunt
jib-boom she had prodded a hole in the side of a
lighthouse supply-boat, and sailed away without
answering questions. The government was taking
cognizance, and her description was written on the
fly-leaves of several revenue cutters' log-books, while
Sunday newspapers in the large cities began a series
of special articles about the mysterious schooner-
rigged pirate of the fishing-fleet.

The future looked dark for her, and when the
time came that she was chased away from Plymouth
harbor—which she had entered for provisions—by a
police launch, it seemed that the end was at hand;
for she had done no wrong in Plymouth, and the
police boat was evidently acting on general principles
and instructions, which were vital enough to extend
the pursuit to the three-mile limit. Her trips had
become necessarily longer, and there was but two
weeks' supply of food in the lazarette. The New

England coast was an enemy's country, but in the crowded harbor of New York was a chance to lie unobserved at anchor long enough to secure the stores she needed, which only a large city can supply. So Cape Cod was doubled on the way to New York; but the brisk offshore wind, which had helped her in escaping the police boat, developed to a gale that blew her to sea, and increased in force as the hours passed by.

Hard-headed, reckless fellows were these men who owned the *Rosebud* and ran her on shares and under laws of their own making. Had they been of larger, broader minds, with no change of ethics they would have acquired a larger, faster craft with guns, hoisted the black flag, and sailed southward to more fruitful fields. Being what they were,—fishermen gone wrong,—they labored within their limitations and gleaned upon known ground.

They were eighteen in number, and they typified the maritime nations of the world. Americans predominated, of course, but English, French, German, Portuguese, Scandinavian, and Russian were among them. The cook was a West India negro, and the captain—or their nearest approach to a captain— a Portland Yankee. Both were large men, and held their positions by reason of special knowledge and a certain magnetic mastery of soul which dominated the others against their rules; for in this social democracy captains and bosses were forbidden. The cook was an expert in the galley and a thorough seaman; the other as able a seaman, and a navigator past the criticism of the rest.

His navigation had its limits, however, and this gale defined them. He could find his latitude by

meridian observation, and his longitude by morning
sights and chronometer time; his dead-reckoning was
trustworthy, and he possessed a fair working conception of the set and force of the Atlantic cur-
rents and the heave of the sea in a blow.   But his
studies had not given him more than a rudimentary
knowledge of meteorology and the laws of storms.
A gale was a gale to him, and he knew that it would
usually change its direction as a clock's hands will in
moving over the dial; and if, by chance, it should
back around to its former point, he prepared for
heavier trouble, with no reference to the fluctuations
of the barometer, which instrument to him was
merely a weather-glass—about as valuable as a rheu-
matic big toe.

So, in the case we are considering, not knowing
that he was caught by the southern fringe of a St.
Lawrence valley storm, with its center of low
barometer to the northwest and coming toward him,
he hove to on the port tack to avoid Cape Cod, and
drifted to sea, shortening sail as the wind increased,
until, with nothing set but a small storm-mainsail, he
found himself in the sudden calm of the storm-center,
which had overtaken him.   Here, in a tumultuous
cross-sea, fifty miles off the shore, deceived by the
light, shifty airs and the patches of blue sky showing between the rushing clouds, he made all sail and
headed west, only to have the masts whipped out as
the whistling fury of wind on the opposite side of
the vortex caught and jibed the canvas.

It was manifestly a judgment of a displeased
Providence; and, glad that the hull was still tight,
they cut away the wreck and rode out the gale,—
now blowing out of the north,—hanging to the

tangle of spar and cordage which had once been the foremast and its gear. It made a fairly good sea-anchor, with the forestay—strong as any chain—for a cable, and she lay snug under the haphazard break-water and benefited by the protection, as the seas must first break their heads over the wreckage be-fore reaching her. The mainmast was far away, with all that pertained to it; but the solid, hard-pine jib-boom was still intact, and not one of the sixteen dories piled spoon-fashion in the four nests had been injured when the spars went by the board. So they were content to smoke, sleep, and kill time as they could, until the gale and sea should moderate, and they could rig a jury-foremast of the wreck.

But before they could begin,—while there was still wind enough to curl the head of an occasional sea into foam,—a speck which had been showing on the shortened horizon to windward, when the schooner lifted out of the hollows, took form and identity—a two-masted steamer, with English colors, union down, at the gaff. High out of water, her broadside drift was faster than that of the dismasted craft rid-ing to her wreckage, and in a few hours she was dangerously near, directly ahead, rolling heavily in the trough of the sea. They could see shreds of canvas hanging from masts and gaffs.

"Wunner what's wrong wid her," said the cook, as he relinquished the glasses to the next man. "Amos," he called to another, "you've been in the ingine-room, you say. Is her ingine bus' down?"

"Dunno," answered Amos. "Steam's all right; see the jet comin' out o' the stack? There! she's turnin' over—kickin' ahead. 'Bout time if she wants

to clear us. She's signalin'. What's that say,
Elisha?"

The ensign was fluttering down, and a string of
small flags going aloft on the other part of the signal-halyards, while the steamer, heading west, pushed
ahead about a length under the impulse of her pro-
peller. Elisha, the navigator, went below, and returned with a couple of books, which he consulted.

"Her number," he said. "She's the *Afghan
Prince* o' London." As the schooner carried no signal-flags, he waved his sou'wester in answer, and the
flags came down, to be replaced by others.

"Rudder carried away," he read, and then looked
with the glasses. "Rudder seems all right; must
mean his steerin'-gear. Why don't they rig up
suthin', or a drag over the stern?"

"Don't know enough," said an expatriated Englishman of the crew. "She's one o' them bloomin',
undermanned tramps, run by apprentices an' Thames
watermen. They're drivin' sailors an' sailin'-ships off
the sea, blarst 'em!"

"Martin," said Elisha to the cook, "what's the
matter with our bein' a drag for her?"

"Dead easy, if we kin git his line an' he knows
how to rig a bridle."

"We can show him, if it comes to it. What ye
say, boys? If we steer her into port we're entitled
to salvage. She's helpless; we're not, for we've got a
jury-rig under the bows. Hello! what's he sayin'
now?" Other flags had gone aloft on the steamer,
which asked for the longitude. Then followed others
which said that the chronometer was broken.

"Better'n ever!" exclaimed Elisha, excitedly.
"Can't navigate. Our chronometer's all right; we

never needed it, an' don't know, but it's a big help in a salvage claim. What ye say? Can't we get our hemp cable to him with a dory?"

Why not? They were fishermen, accustomed to dory work. A short confab settled this point; a dory was thrown over, and Elisha and Amos pulled to the steamer, which was now abreast, near enough for the name which Elisha had read to be seen plainly on the stern, but not near enough for the men shouting from her taffrail to make themselves heard on the schooner. Elisha and Amos, in the dory, conferred with these men and then returned.

"Badly rattled," they reported. "Tiller-ropes parted, an' not a man aboard can put a long splice in a wire rope, an' o' course we said we couldn't. They'll take our line, an' we're to chalk up the position an' the course to New York. Clear case o' salvage. We furnish everything, an' sacrifice our jury-material to aid 'em."

"What'll be our chance in court, I'm thinkin'," said one, doubtfully. "Hadn't we better keep out o' the courts? It's been takin' most of our time lately."

"What's the matter wi' ye?" yelled Elisha. "We owe a few hundreds, an' mebbe a fine or two; an' there's anywhere from one to two hundred thousand —hull an' cargo—that we save. We'll get no less than a third, mebbe more. Go lay down, Bill."

Bill subsided. They knotted four or five dory rodings together, coiled the long length of rope in the dory, unbent the end of their water-laid cable from the anchor, and waited until the wallowing steamer had drifted far enough to leeward to come within the steering-arc of a craft with no canvas;

then they cut away the wreck, crowded forward, all hands spreading coats to the breeze, and when the schooner had paid off, steered her down with the wind on the quarter until almost near enough to hail the steamer, where they rounded to, safe in the knowledge that she could not drift as fast as the other.

Away went the dory, paying out on the roding, the end of which was fastened to the disconnected cable, and when it had reached the steamer, a heaving-line was thrown, by which the roding was hauled aboard. Then the dory returned, while the steamer's men hauled the cable to their stern. The bridle, two heavy ropes leading from the after-winch out the opposite quarter-chocks to the end of the cable, was quickly rigged by the steamer's crew.

With a warning toot of the whistle, she went ahead, and the long tow-line swept the sea-tops, tautened, strained, and creaked on the windlass-bitts, and settled down to its work, while the schooner, dropping into her wake, was dragged westward at a ten-knot rate.

"This is bully," said Elisha, gleefully. "Now I'll chalk out the position an' give her the course—magnetic, to make sure."

He did so, and they held up in full view of the steamer's bridge a large blackboard showing in six-inch letters the formula: "Lat. 41–20. Lon. 69–10. Mag. Co. W. half S."

A toot of the whistle thanked them, and they watched the steamer, which had been heading a little to the south of this course, painfully swing her head up to it by hanging the schooner to the starboard leg of the bridle; but she did not stop at west-half-south, and when she pointed unmistakably as high as northwest, still dragging her tow by the starboard bridle, a light broke on them.

"She's goin' on her way with us," said Elisha. "No, no; she can't. She's bound for London," he added. "Halifax, mebbe."

They waved their hats to port, and shouted in chorus at the steamer. They were answered by caps flourished to starboard from the bridge, and out-stretched arms which pointed across the Atlantic Ocean, while the course changed slowly to north, then faster as wind and sea bore on the other bow, until the steamer steadied and remained at east-by-north.

"The rhumb course to the Channel," groaned Elisha, wildly. "The nerve of it! An' I'm sup-posed to give the longitude every noon. Why, dammit, boys, they'll claim they rescued us, an' like as not the English courts'll allow them salvage on our little tub."

"Let go the tow-line! Let 'em go to h—l!" they shouted angrily, and some started forward, but were stopped by the cook. His eyes gleamed in his black face, and his voice was a little higher pitched than usual; otherwise he was the steadiest man there.

"We'll hang right on to our bran-new cable, men," he said. "It's ours, not theirs. 'Course we kin turn her adrif' ag'in, an' be wuss off, too; we can't find de foremast now. But dat ain't de bes' way. John," he called to the Englishman of the crew, "how many men do you' country tramp steamers carry?"

John computed mentally, then muttered: "Two mates, six ash-cats,[1] two flunkies, two quartermasters,

---

[1] Ash-cats: engineers and firemen.

watchman, deck-hands—oh, 'bout sixteen or seventeen, Martin."

"Boys, le' 's man de win-lass. We'll heave in on our cable, an' if we kin git close enough to climb aboard, we'll reason it out wid dat English cappen, who can't fin' his way roun' alone widout stealin' little fishin'-schooners."

"Right!" they yelled. "Man the windlass. We'll show the lime-juice thief who's doin' this."

"Amos," said Martin to the ex-engineer, "you try an' 'member all you forgot 'bout ingines in case anything happens to de crew o' dat steamer; an', Elisha, you want to keep good track o' where we go, so's you kin find you' way back."

"I'll get the chronometer on deck now. I can take sights alone."

They took the cable to the windlass-barrel and began to heave. It was hard work,—equal to heaving an anchor against a strong head wind and ten-knot tideway,—and only half the crew could find room on the windlass-brakes; so, while the first shift labored and swore and encouraged one another, the rest watched the approach of a small tug towing a couple of scows, which seemed to have arisen out of the sea ahead of them. When the steamer was nearly upon her, she let go her tow-line and ranged up alongside, while a man leaning out of the pilot-house gesticulated to the steamer's bridge and finally shook his fist. Then the tug dropped back abreast of the schooner. She was a dingy little boat, the biggest and brightest of her fittings being the name-board on her pilot-house, which spelled in large gilt letters the appellation *J. C. Hawks.*

"Say," yelled her captain from his door, "I'm

blown out wi' my barges, short o' grub an' water. Can you gi' me some? That lime-juice sucker ahead won't."

"Can you tow us to New York?" asked Elisha, who had brought up the chronometer and placed it on the house, ready to take morning sights for his longitude if the sun should appear.

"No; not unless I sacrifice the barges an' lose my contract wi' the city. They're garbage-scows, an' I haven't power enough to hook on to another. Just got coal enough to get in."

"An' what do you call this—a garbage-scow?" answered Elisha, ill-naturedly. "We've got no grub or water to spare. We've got troubles of our own."

"Dammit, man, we're thirsty here. Give us a breaker o' water. Throw it overboard; I'll get it."

"No; told you we have none to spare; an' we're bein' yanked out to sea."

"Well, gi' me a bottleful; that won't hurt you."

"No; sheer off. Git out o' this. We're not in the Samaritan business."

A forceful malediction came from the tug captain, and a whirling monkey-wrench from the hand of the engineer, who had listened from the engine-room door. It struck Elisha's chronometer and knocked it off the house, box and all, into the sea. He answered the profanity in kind, and sent an iron belaying-pin at the engineer; but it only dented the tug's rail, and with these compliments the two craft separated, the tug steaming back to her scows.

"That lessens our chance just so much," growled Elisha, as he joined the rest. "Now we can't do all we agreed to."

"Keep dead-reckonin', 'Lisha," said Martin;

" dat's good 'nough for us; an', say, can't you take sights by a watch—jess for a bluff, to show in de log-book? "

" Might; 'twouldn't be reliable. Good enough, though, for log-book testimony. That's what I'll do."

Inch by inch they gathered in their cable and coiled it down, unmoved by the protesting toots of the steamer's whistle. When half of it lay on the deck, the steamer slowed down, while her crew worked at their end of the rope; then she went ahead, the schooner dropped back to nearly the original distance, and they saw a long stretch of new Manila hawser leading out from the bridle and knotted to their cable. They cursed and shook their fists, but pumped manfully on the windlass, and by nightfall had brought the knot over their bows by means of a " messenger," and were heaving on the new hawser.

" Weakens our case just that much more," growled Elisha. " We were to furnish the tow-line."

" Heave away, my boys!" said Martin. " Dey's only so many ropes aboard her, an' when we get 'em all we've got dat boat an' dem men."

So they warped their craft across the Western Ocean. Knot after knot, hawser after hawser, came over the bows and cumbered the deck.

They would have passed them over the stern as fast as they came in, were they not salvors with litigation ahead; for their hands must be clean when they entered their claim, and to this end Elisha chalked out the longitude daily at noon and showed it to the steamer, always receiving a thankful acknowledgment on the whistle. He secured the figures by his dead-reckoning; but the carefully kept log-book also showed longitude by chronometer sights, taken when the sun shone, with his old quadrant and older watch, and corrected to bring a result plausibly near to that of the reckoning by log and compass. But the log-book contained no reference to the loss of the chronometer. That was to happen at the last.

On stormy days, when the sea rose, they dared not shorten their tow-line, and the steamer-folk made sure that it was long enough to eliminate the risk of its parting. So these days were passed in idleness and profanity; and when the sea went down they would go to work, hoping that the last tow-line was in their hands. But it was not until the steamer had given them three Manila and two steel hawsers, four weak—too weak—mooring chains, and a couple of old and frayed warping-lines, that the coming up to the bow of an anchor-chain of six-inch link told them that the end was near, that the steamer had exhausted her supply of tow-lines, and that her presumably sane skipper would not give them his last means of anchoring—the other chain.

They were right. Either for this reason or because of the proximity to English bottom, the steamer ceased her coyness, and her crew watched from the taffrail, while those implacable, purposeful men behind crept up to them. It was slow, laborious work; for the small windlass would not grip the heavy links of the chain, and they must needs climb out a few fathoms, making fast messengers to heave on, while the idle half of them gathered in the slackened links by hand.

On a calm, still night they finally unshipped the windlass-brakes and looked up at the round, black stern of the steamer not fifty feet ahead. They were surrounded by lights of outgoing and incoming craft, and they knew by soundings taken that day, when the steamer had slowed down for the same purpose, that they were within the hundred-fathom curve, close to the mouth of the Channel, but not within the three-mile limit. Rejoicing at the latter fact, they armed themselves to a man with belaying-pins from their still intact pin-rails, and climbed out on the cable, the whole eighteen of them, man following man, in close climbing order.

"Now, look here," said a portly man with a gilt-bound cap to the leader of the line, as he threw a leg over the taffrail, "what's the meaning, may I ask, of this unreasonable conduct?"

"You may ask, of course," said the man,—it was Elisha,—"but we'd like to ask something, too," (he was sparring for time until more should arrive); "we'd like to ask why you drag us across the Atlantic Ocean against our will?"

Another man climbed aboard, and said:

"Yes; we 'gree to steer you into New York. You's adrif' in de trough of de sea, an' you got no chronometer, an' you can't navigate, an' we come 'long—under command, mind you—an' give you our tow-line, an' tell you de road to port. Wha' you mean by dis?"

"Tut, tut, my colored friend!" answered the man of gilt. "You were dismasted and helpless, and I gave you a tow. It was on the high seas, and I chose the port, as I had the right."

Another climbed on board.

"We were not helpless," rejoined Elisha. "We had a good jury-rig under the bows, and we let it go to assist you. Are you the skipper here?"

" I am."

Martin's big fist smote him heavily in the face, and the blow was followed by the crash of Elisha's belaying-pin on his head. The captain fell, and for a while lay quiet. There were four big, strong men over the rail now, and others coming. Opposing them were a second mate, an engineer, a fireman, coal-passer, watchman, steward, and cook—easy victims to these big-limbed fishermen. The rest of the crew were on duty below decks or at the steering-winch. It was a short, sharp battle; a few pistols exploded, but no one was hurt, and the firearms were captured and their owners well hammered with belaying-pins; then, binding all victims as they overcame them, the whole party raided the steering-winch and engine-room, and the piracy was complete.

But from their standpoint it was not piracy—it was resistance to piracy; and when Amos, the ex-engineer, had stopped the engines and banked the fires, they announced to the captives bound to the rail that, with all due respect for the law, national and international, they would take that distressed steamboat into New York and deliver her to the authorities, with a claim for salvage. The bargain had been made on the American coast, and their log-book not only attested this, but the well-doing of their part of the contract.

When the infuriated English captain, now recovered, had exhausted his stock of adjectives and epithets, he informed them (and he was backed by his steward and engineer) that there was neither food nor coal for the run to New York; to which Elisha replied that, if so, the foolish and destructive waste would be properly entered in the log-book, and might form the basis of a charge of barratry by the underwriters, if it turned out that any underwriters had taken a risk on a craft with such an " all-fired lunatic " for a skipper as this. But they would go back; they might be forced to burn some of the woodwork fittings (her decks were of iron) for fuel, and as for food, though their own supply of groceries was about exhausted, there were several cubic yards of salt codfish in the schooner's hold, and this they would eat: they were used to it themselves, and science had declared that it was good brain-food—good for feeble-minded Englishmen who couldn't splice wire nor take care of a chronometer.

Before starting back they made some preliminary and precautionary preparations. While Martin inventoried the stores and Amos the coal-supply, the others towed the schooner alongside and moored her. Then they shackled the schooner's end of the chain cable around the inner barrel of the windlass and riveted the key of the shackle. They transhipped their clothing and what was left of the provisions. They also took the log-book and charts, compass, empty outer chronometer-case,—which Elisha handled tenderly and officiously by its strap in full view of the captives,—windlass-brakes, tool-chest, deck-tools, axes, handspikes, heavers, boat-hooks, belaying-pins, and everything in the shape of weapon or missile by which disgruntled Englishmen could do harm to the schooner or their rescuers.

Then they passed the rescued ones down to the schooner, and Martin told them where they would find the iron kettle for boiling codfish, with the additional information that with skill and ingenuity they could make fish-balls in the same kettle.

Martin had reported a plenitude of provisions, and anathematized the lying captain and steward; and Amos had declared his belief that with careful economy in the use of coal they could steam to the American coast with the supply in the bunkers: so they did not take any of the codfish, and the hawsers, valuable as fuel in case of a shortage, were left where they would be more valuable as evidence against the lawless, incompetent Englishmen. And they also left the dories, all but one, for reasons in Elisha's mind which he did not state at the time.

They removed the bonds of one man—who could release the others—and cast off the fastenings; then, with Amos and a picked crew of pupils in the boat's vitals, they went ahead and dropped the prison-hulk back to the full length of the chain, while the furious curses of the prisoners troubled the air. They found a little difficulty in steering by the winch and deck-compass (they would have mended the tiller-ropes with a section of backstay had they not bargained otherwise), but finally mastered the knack, and headed westerly.

You cannot take an Englishman's ship from under him—homeward bound and close to port—and drag him to sea again on a diet of salt codfish without impinging on his sanity. When day broke they looked and saw the hawsers slipping over the schooner's rail, and afterward a fountain of fish arising from her hatches to follow the hawsers overboard.

"What's de game, I wunner?" asked Martin. "Tryin' to starve deyselves?"

"Dunno," answered Elisha, with a serious expression. "They're not doin' it for nothin'. They're wavin' their hats at us. Somethin' on their minds."

"We'll jes let 'em wave. We'll go 'long 'bout our business."

So they went at eight knots an hour; for, try as they might, Amos could get no more out of the engine. "She's a divil to chew up coal," he explained; "we may have to burn the boat yet."

"Hope not," said Elisha. "'Tween you an' me, Amos, this is a desperate bluff we're makin', an' if we go to destroyin' property we may get no credit for savin' it. We'd have no chance in the English courts at all, but it's likely an American judge 'ud recognize our original position—our bargain to steer her in."

"Too bad 'bout that tarred cable of ours," rejoined Amos; "three days' good fuel in that, I calculate."

"Well, it's gone with the codfish, and the fact is properly entered in the log as barratrous conduct on the part of the skipper. Enough to prove him insane."

And further to strengthen this possible aspect of the case, Elisha found a blank space on the leaf of the log-book which recorded the first meeting and bargain to tow, and filled it with the potential sentence, "Steamer's commander acts strangely." For a well-kept log-book is excellent testimony in court.

Elisha's knowledge of navigation did not enable him to project a course on the great circle—the shortest track between two points on the earth's surface, and the route taken by steamers. But he possessed a fairly practical and ingenious mind, and with a flexible steel straight-edge rule, and a classroom globe in the skipper's room, laid out his course

between the lane-routes of the liners,—which he
would need to vary daily,—as it was not wise to court
investigation. But he signaled to two passing steam-
ships for Greenwich time, and set his watch, obtain-
ing its rate of correction by the second favor; and
with this, and his surely correct latitude by meridian
observation, he hoped to make an accurate landfall
in home waters.

And so the hours went by, with their captives
waving caps ceaselessly, until the third day's sun
arose to show them an empty deck on the schooner,
over a dozen specks far astern and to the southward,
and an east-bound steamship on their port bow. The
specks could be nothing but the dories, and they were
evidently trying to intercept the steamship. Elisha
yelled in delight.

" They've abandoned ship—just what I hoped for
—in the dories. They've no case at all now."

" But what for, Elisha? " asked Martin. " Mus'
be hungry, I t'ink."

" Mebbe, or else they think that liner, who can
stop only to save life,—carries the mails, you see,—
will turn round and put 'em in charge here. Why,
nothin' but an English man-o'-war could do that
now."

They saw the steamship slow down, while the
black specks flocked up to her, and then go on her
way. And they went on theirs; but three days later
they had reasoned out a better explanation of the
Englishmen's conduct. Martin came on deck with a
worried face, and announced that, running short of
salt meat in the harness-cask, he had broken out the
barrels of beef, pork, and hard bread that he had
counted upon, and found their contents absolutely un-

eatable, far gone in putrescence, alive with crawling things.

" Must ha' thought he was fitting out a Yankee hell-ship when he bought this," said Elisha, in disgust, as he looked into the ill-smelling barrels. " Overboard with it, boys ! "

Overboard went the provisions, for starving animals could not eat of them, and the odor permeated the ship. They resigned themselves to a gloomy outlook—gloomier when Amos reported that the coal in the bunkers would last but two days longer. He had been mistaken, he said; he had calculated to run compound engines with Scotch boilers, not a full-powered blast-furnace with six inches of scale on the crown-sheets.

" And they knew this," groaned Elisha. " That's why they chucked the stuff overboard—to bring us to terms, and never thinkin' they'd starve first. They were dead luny, but we're lunier."

They stopped the engines and visited the schooner in the dory. Not a scrap of food was there, and the fish-kettle was scraped bright. They returned and went on. With plenty of coal there was still six days' run ahead to New York. How many with wood fuel, chopped on empty stomachs and burned in coal-furnaces, they could not guess. But they went to work. There were three axes, two top-mauls, and several handspikes and pinch-bars aboard, and with these they attacked bulkheads and spare woodwork, and fed the fires with the fragments; for a glance down the hatches had shown them nothing more combustible and detachable in the cargo than a few layers of railroad iron, which covered and blocked the openings to the lower hold.

With the tools at hand they could not supply the rapacious fires fast enough to keep up steam, and the engines slowed to a five-knot rate. As this would not maintain a sufficient tension on the dragging schooner to steer by, they were forced to sacrifice the best item in their claim for salvage: they spliced the tiller-ropes and steered from the pilot-house. They would have sacrificed the schooner, too, for Amos complained bitterly of the load on the engines; but Elisha would not hear of it. She was the last evidence in their favor now, their last connection with respectability.

"She and the pavement o' h—l," he growled fiercely, "are all we've got to back us up. Without proof we're pirates under the law."

However, he made no entry in the log of the splicing, trusting that a chance would come in port to remove the section of wire rope with which they had joined the broken ends.

And, indeed, it seemed that their claim was dwindling. The chronometer which they were to use for the steamer's benefit was lost; the tow-line which they were to furnish had been given back to them; the course to New York which they chalked out had not been accepted; the abandoning of their ship by the Englishmen was clearly enforced by the pressure of their own presence; and now they themselves had been forced to cancel from the claim the schooner's value as a necessary drag behind the steamer, by substituting a three hours' splicing-job, worth five dollars in a rigging-loft, and possibly fifty if bargained for at sea. Nothing was left them now but their good intentions, duly entered in the log-book.

But fate, and the stupid understanding of some

one or two of them, decreed that their good intentions also should be taken from them. The log-book disappeared, and the strictest search failing to bring it to light, the conclusion was reached that it had been fed to the fires among the wreckage of the skipper's room and furniture. They blasphemed to the extent that the occasion required, and there was civil war for a time, while the suspected ones were being punished; then they drew what remaining comfort they could from burning the steamer's log-book and track-chart, which contained data conflicting with their position in the case, and resumed their labors.

Martin had raked and scraped together enough of food to give them two scant meals; but these eaten, starvation began. The details of their suffering need not be given. They chopped, hammered, and pried in hunger and anxiety, and with lessening strength, while the days passed by—fortunately spared the torture of thirst, for there was plenty of water in the tanks. Upheld by the dominating influence of Elisha, Martin, and Amos, they stripped the upper works and fed to the fires every door and sash, every bulkhead and wooden partition, all chairs, stools, and tables, cabin berths and forecastle bunks. Then they attempted sending down the topmasts, but gave it up for lack of strength to get mast-ropes aloft, and attacked instead the boats on the chocks, of which there were four.

It was no part of the plan to ask help of passing craft and have their distressed condition taken advantage of; but when the hopelessness of the fight at last appealed to the master spirits, they consented to the signaling of an east-bound steamer, far to the northward, in the hope of getting food. So the

English ensign, union down, was again flown from the gaff. It was at a time when Elisha could not stand up at the wheel, when Amos at the engines could not have reversed them, when Martin—man of iron—staggered weakly around among the rest and struck them with a pump-brake, keeping them at work. (They would strive under the blows, and sit down when he had passed.) But the flag was not seen; a haze arose between the two craft and thickened to fog.

By Elisha's reckoning they were on the Banks now, about a hundred miles due south from Cape Sable, and nearer to Boston than to Halifax; otherwise he might have made for the latter port and defied alien prejudice. But the fog continued, and it was not port they were looking for now; it was help, food: they were working for life, not salvage; and, wasting no steam, they listened for whistles or foghorns, but heard none near enough to be answered by their weak voices.

And so the boat, dragging the dismal mockery behind her, plodded and groped her way on the course which Elisha had shaped for Boston, while man after man dropped in his tracks, refusing to rise; and those that were left nourished the fires as they could, until the afternoon of the third day of fog, when the thumping, struggling engines halted, started, made a half-revolution, and came to a dead stop. Amos crawled on deck and forward to the bridge, where, with Elisha's help, he dragged on the whistle rope and dissipated the remaining steam in a wheezy, gasping howl, which lasted about a half-minute. It was answered by a furious siren-blast from directly astern; and out of the fog, at twenty

knots an hour, came a mammoth black steamer.
Seeming to heave the small tramp out of the way
with her bow wave, she roared by at six feet distance,
and in ten seconds they were looking at her vanishing
stern. But ten minutes later the stern appeared in
view, as the liner backed toward them. The reversed
English ensign still hung at the gaff; and the starving men, some prostrate on the deck, some clinging
to the rails, unable to shout, had pointed to the flag
of distress and beckoned as the big ship rushed by.

"THERE's a chance," said the captain of this liner
to the pilot, as he rejoined him on the bridge an hour
later, " of international complications over this case,
and I may have to lose a trip to testify. That's the
Afghan Prince and consort that I was telling you
about. Strange, isn't it, that I should pick up these
fellows after picking up the legitimate crew going
east? I don't know which crew was the hungriest.
The real crew charge this crowd with piracy. By
George, it's rather funny!"

"And these men," said the pilot, with a laugh,
" would have claimed salvage?"

"Yes, and had a good claim, too, for effort expended; but they've offset it by their violence. Their
chance was good in the English courts, if they'd
only allowed the steamer to go on; and then, too,
they abandoned her in a more dangerous position
than where they found her. You see, they met her
off Nantucket with sea-room, and nothing wrong
with her but broken tiller-ropes; and they quit her
here close to Sandy Hook, in a fog, more than likely
to hit the beach before morning. Then, in that case,
she belongs to the owners or underwriters."

" Why didn't they make Boston? " asked the pilot.

" Tried to, but overran their distance. Chronometer must have been 'way out. I talked to the one who navigated, and found that he'd never thought of allowing for local attraction,—didn't happen to run against the boat's deviation table,—and so, with all that railway iron below hatches, he fetched clear o' Nantucket, and 'way in here."

" That's tough. The salvage of that steamer would make them rich, wouldn't it? And I think they might have got it if they could have held out."

" Yes; think they might. But here's another funny thing about it. They needn't have starved. They needn't have chopped her to pieces for fuel. I just remember, now. Her skipper told me there was good anthracite coal in her hold, and Chicago canned meats, Minnesota flour, beef, pork, and all sorts of good grub. He carried some of the rails in the 'tween-deck for steadying ballast, and I suppose it prevented them looking farther. And now they'll lose their salvage, and perhaps have to pay it on their own schooner if anything comes along and picks them up. That's the craft that'll get the salvage."

" Not likely," said the pilot; " not in this fog, and the wind and sea rising. I'll give 'em six hours to fetch up on the Jersey coast. A mail contract with the government is sometimes a nuisance, isn't it, captain? How many years would it take you to save money to equal your share of the salvage if you had yanked that tramp and the schooner into New York? "

" It would take more than one lifetime," answered

the captain, a little sadly. " A skipper on a mail-boat is the biggest fool that goes to sea."

The liner did not reach quarantine until after sundown, hence remained there through the night. As she was lifting her anchor in the morning, preparatory to steaming up to her dock, the crew of the *Rosebud*, refreshed by food and sleep, but still weak and nerveless, came on deck to witness a harrowing sight. The *Afghan Prince* was coming toward the anchorage before a brisk southeast wind. Astern of her, held by the heavy iron chain, was their schooner. Moored to her, one on each side, were two garbage-scows; and at the head of the parade, pretending to tow them all,—puffing, rolling, and smoking in the effort to keep a strain on the tow-line,—and tooting joyously with her whistle, was a little, dingy tugboat, with a large gilt name on her pilot-house—*J. C. Hawks.*

BETWEEN THE MILLSTONES

HE stood before the recruiting officer, trembling with nervousness, anxious of face, and clothed in rags; but he was clean, for, knowing the moral effect of cleanliness, he had lately sought the beach and taken a swim.

"Want to enlist?" asked the officer, taking his measure with trained eye.

"Yes, sir; I read you wanted men in the navy."

"Want seamen, firemen, and landsmen. What's your occupation? You look like a tramp."

"Yes," he answered bitterly, "I'm a tramp. That's all they'd let me be. I used to be a locomotive engineer—before the big strike. Then they blacklisted me, and I've never had a job above laborin' work since. It's easy to take to the road and stay at it when you find you can't make over a dollar a day at back-breakin' work after earnin' three and four at the throttle. An engineer knows nothin' but his trade, sir. Take it away, and he's a laborin' man.

"I'd ha' worked and learned another, but they jailed me—put me in choky, 'cause I had no visible means o' support. I had no money, and was a criminal under the law. And they kept at it,—jailed me again and again as a vagrant,—when all I wanted was work. After a while I didn't care. But now's my chance, sir, if you'll take me on. I don't know much about boats and the sea, but I can fire an engine, and know something about steam."

"A fireman's work on board a war-vessel is very different from that of a locomotive fireman," said the officer, leaning back in his chair.

"I know, sir; that may be," the tramp replied eagerly; "but I can shovel coal, and I can learn, and I can work. I'm not very strong now, 'cause I haven't had much to eat o' late years; but I'm not a drinkin' man—why, that costs more than grub. Give me a chance, sir; I'm an American; I'm sick o' bein' hunted from jail to jail, like a wild animal, just 'cause I can't be satisfied with pick-and-shovel work. I've spent half o' the last five years in jail as a vagrant. I put in a month at Fernandina, and then I was chased out o' town. They gave me two months at Cedar Keys, and I came here, only to get a month more in this jail. I got out this mornin', and was told by the copper who pinched me to get out o' Pensacola or he'd run me in again. And he's outside now waitin' for me. I dodged past 'im to get in."

"Pass this man in to the surgeon," said the officer, with something like a sympathetic snort in the tone of his voice; for he also was an American.

An orderly escorted him to the surgeon, who examined him and passed him. Then the recruit signed his name to a paper.

"Emaciated," wrote the surgeon in his daily report; "body badly nourished, and susceptible to any infection. Shows slight febrile symptoms, which should be attended to. An intelligent man; with good food and care will become valuable."

The tramp marched to the receiving-ship with a squad of other recruits, and on the way smiled triumphantly into the face of a mulatto policeman, who glared at him. He had signed his name on a piece of paper, and the act had changed his status. From a hunted fugitive and habitual criminal he had become a defender of his country's honor—a potential hero.

On board the receiving-ship he was given an outfit of clothes and bedding; but before he had learned more than the correct way to lash his hammock and tie his silk neckerchief he was detailed for sea duty, and with a draft of men went to Key West in a navy-yard tug; for war was on, and the fleet blockading Havana needed men.

At Key West he was appointed fireman on a torpedo-boat, where his work—which he soon learned—was to keep up steam in a tubular boiler. But he learned nothing of the rest of the boat, her business, or the reason of her construction. Seasickness prevented any assertion of curiosity at first, and later the febrile symptoms which the examining surgeon had noted developed in him until he could think of nothing else. There being no doctor aboard to diagnose his case, he was jeered by his fellows, and kept at work until he dropped; then he took to his hammock. Shooting pains darted through him, centering in his head, while his throat was dry and his thirst tormenting.

Life on a torpedo-boat engaged in despatch duty and rushing through a Gulf Stream sea at thirty knots is torture to a healthy, nervous system. It sent this sick man into speedy delirium. He could eat very little, but he drank all the water that was given him. Moaning and muttering, tossing about in his hammock, never asleep, but sometimes unconscious, at other times raving, and occasionally lucid, he presented a problem which demanded solution.

His emaciated face, flushed at first, had taken on a peculiar bronzed appearance, and there were some who declared that it was Yellow Jack. But nothing could be done until they reached the fleet and could interview a cruiser with a surgeon.

The sick man solved the problem. He scrambled out of his hammock at daylight in the morning and dressed himself in his blue uniform, carefully tying his black neckerchief in the regulation knot. Then, muttering the while, he gained the deck.

The boat was charging along at full speed, throwing aside a bow wave nearly as high as herself. Three miles astern, just discernible in the half-light, was a pursuing ram-bowed gunboat, spitting shot and shell; and forward near the conning-tower were two blue-coated, brass-buttoned officers, watching the pursuer through binoculars.

The crazed brain of the sick man took cognizance of nothing but the blue coats and brass buttons. He did not look for locust clubs and silver shields. These were policemen—his deadliest enemies; but he would escape them this time.

With a yell he went overboard, and, being no swimmer, would have drowned had not one of the blue-coated officers flung a life-buoy. He came to the surface somewhat saner, and seized the white ring, which supported him, while the torpedo-boat rushed on. She could not stop for one man in time of war, with a heavily armed enemy so near.

A twenty-knot gunboat cannot chase a thirty-knot torpedo-boat very long without losing her below the horizon; but this pursuit lasted ten minutes from the time the sick man went overboard before the gunboat ceased firing and slackened speed. The quarry was five miles away, out of Spanish range, and the floating man directly under her bow. He was seen and taken on board, with Spanish profanity sounding in his unregarding ears.

He lay on the deck, a bedraggled heap, gibbering and shivering, while a surgeon, with cotton in his nostrils and smelling-salts in his hand, diagnosed his case. Then the gunboat headed north and dropped anchor in the bight of a small, crescent-shaped sand-key of the Florida Reef. For the diagnosis was such as to suggest prompt action. Two brave men bundled him into the dinghy, lowered it, pulled ashore, and laid him on the sand.

Returning, they stripped and threw away their clothing, sank the boat with a buoy on the painter, took a swim, and climbed aboard to be further disinfected. Then the gunboat lifted her anchor and steamed eastward, her officers watching through glasses a small, low torpedo-boat, far to the southeast,—too far to be reached by gun fire,—which was steering a parallel course, and presumably watching the gunboat.

An idiot, a lunatic, with bloodshot eyes glaring from a yellow face, raved, rolled, and staggered bareheaded under the sun about the sandy crescent until sundown, then fell prostrate and unconscious into the water on the beach, luckily turning over so that his nostrils were not immersed. The tide went down, leaving him damp and still on the sands. In about an hour a sigh, followed by a deep, gasping breath, escaped him; another long inhalation succeeded, and another; then came steady, healthy breathing and childlike sleep, with perspiration oozing from every pore. He had passed a crisis.

About midnight the cloudy sky cleared and the tropic stars came out, while the tide climbed the beach again, and lapped at the sleeping man's feet; but he did not waken, even when the Spanish gun-boat stole slowly into the bay from the sea and dropped anchor with a loud rattling of chain in the hawse-pipe. A boat was lowered, and a single man sculled it ashore; then lifting out a small cask and bag, he placed them high on the sands and looked around.

Spying the sleeping man, half immersed now, he approached and felt of the damp clothing and equally damp face. Not noticing that he breathed softly, the man crossed himself, then moved quickly and nervously toward his boat, muttering, " Muerto, muerto!" Pushing out, he sculled rapidly toward the anchored craft, and disposed of the boat and his clothing as had been done before; then he swam to the gangway and climbed aboard.

Shortly after, the sleeping man, roused by the chill of the water, crawled aimlessly up the sand and slept again—safe beyond the tide-line. In three hours he sat up and rubbed his eyes, half awake, but sane.

Strange sights and sounds puzzled him. He knew nothing of this starlit beach and stretch of sparkling water—nothing of that long black craft at anchor, with the longer beam of white light reaching over the sea from her pilot-house. He could only surmise that she was a war-vessel from the ram-bow,—a feature of the government model which had impressed him at Key West,—and from the noise she was making. She quivered in a maze of flickering red flashes, and the rattling din of her rapid-fire and machine guns transcended in volume all the roadside blastings he had heard in his wanderings.   Dazed and astonished, he rose to his feet, but, too weak to stand, sat down again and looked.

Half a mile seaward, where the beam of light ended, a small craft, low down between two crested waves, was speeding toward the gunboat in the face of her fire.   The water about her was lashed into turmoil by the hail of projectiles; but she kept on, at locomotive speed, until within a thousand feet of the gunboat, when she turned sharply to starboard, doubled on her track, and raced off to sea, still covered by the search-light and followed by shot and shell while the gunners could see her.

When the gun fire ceased, a hissing of steam could be heard in the distance, and a triumphant Spanish yell answered.   The small enemy had been struck, and the gunboat slipped her cable and followed.

The tired brain could not cope with the problem, and again the man slept, to awaken at sunrise with ravenous hunger and thirst, and a memory of what seemed to be horrible dreams,—vague recollections of painful experiences,—torturing labor with aching muscles and blistered hands; harsh words and ridicule from strong, bearded men; and running through and between, the shadowy figures of blue-coated, brass-buttoned men, continually ordering him on, and threatening arrest.   The spectacle of the night was as dream-like as the rest; for he remembered nothing of the gunboat which had rescued and marooned him.

His face had lost its yellowish-bronze color, but was pale and emaciated as ever, while his sunken eyes held the soft light which always comes of extreme physical suffering.   He was too weak to remain on

his feet, but in the effort to do so he spied the cask
and bag higher up on the beach and crawled to them.
Prying a plug from the bunghole with his knife, he
found water, sweet and delicious, which he drank by
rolling the cask carefully and burying his lips in the
overflow.   Evidently some one in authority on the
gunboat had decreed that he should not die of hunger
or thirst, for the bag contained hard bread.

Stronger after a meal, he climbed the highest
sand-dune and studied the situation.   An outcrop-
ping of coral formed the backbone of the thin
crescent which held him, and which was about half a
mile between the points.   To the south, opening out
from the bay, was a clear stretch of sea, green in
the sunlight, deep blue in the shadows of the clouds,
and on the horizon were a few sails and smoke
columns.   West and east were other sandy islets and
coral reefs, and to the north a continuous line of
larger islands which might be inhabited, but gave
no indication of it.

Out in the bay, bobbing to the heave of the slight
ground-swell, were the three white buoys left by the
Spaniards to mark the sunken boats and slipped
cable; and far away on the beach, just within the
western point, was something long and round, which
rolled in the gentle surf and glistened in the sunlight.
He knew nothing of buoys, but they relieved his
loneliness; they were signs of human beings, who
must have placed him there with the bread and water,
and who might come for him.

"Wonder if I got pinched again, and this is some
new kind of a choky," he mused.   "Been blamed
sick and silly, and must ha' lost the job and got
jailed again.   Just my luck!   S'pose the jug was

crowded and they run me out here. Wish they'd left me a hat. Wonder how long I'm in for this time."

He descended to the beach and found that repeated wettings of his hair relieved him from the headache that the sun's heat was bringing on; and satisfied that the strong hand of local law had again closed over him, he resigned himself to the situation, resenting only the absence of a shade-tree or a hat. " Much better'n the calaboose in El Paso," he muttered, " or the brickyard in Chicago."

As he lolled on the sand, the glistening thing over at the western point again caught his eye. After a moment's scrutiny he rose and limped toward it, following the concave of the beach, and often pausing to rest and bathe his head. It was a long journey for him, and the tide, at half-ebb when he started, was rising again when he came abreast of the object and sat down to look at it. It was of metal, long and round, rolling nearly submerged, and held by the alternate surf and undertow parallel with the beach, about twenty feet out.

He waded in, grasped it by a T-shaped projection in the middle, and headed it toward the shore. Then he launched it forward with all his strength—not much, but enough to lift a bluntly pointed end out of water as it grounded and exposed a small, four-bladed steel wheel, shaped something like a windmill. He examined this, but could not understand it, as it whirled freely either way and seemed to have no internal connection. The strange cylinder was about sixteen feet long and about eighteen inches in diameter.

"Boat o' some kind," he muttered; "but what

kind? That screw's too small to make it go. Let's see the other end."

He launched it with difficulty, and noticed that when floating end on to the surf it ceased to roll and kept the T-shaped projection uppermost, proving that it was ballasted. Swinging it, he grounded the other end, which was radically different in appearance. It was long and finely pointed, with four steel blades or vanes, two horizontal and two vertical, —like the double tails of an ideal fish,—and in hollowed parts of these vanes were hung a pair of unmistakable propellers, one behind the other, and of opposite pitch and motion.

"One works on the shaft, t'other on a sleeve," he mused, as he turned them. "A roundhouse wiper could see that. Bevel-gearin' inside, I guess. It's a boat, sure enough, and this reverse action must be to keep her from rolling."

On each of the four vanes he found a small blade, showing by its connection that it possessed range of action, yet immovable as the vane itself, as though held firmly by inner leverage. Those on the horizontal vanes were tilted upward. Just abaft the T-shaped projection—which, fastened firmly to the hull, told him nothing of its purpose—were numerous brass posts buried flush with the surface, in each of which was a square hole, as though intended to be turned with a key or crank. Some were marked with radiating lines and numbers, and they evidently controlled the inner mechanism, part of which he could see—little brass cog-wheels, worms, and levers —through a fore-and-aft slot near the keyholes.

Rising from the forward end of this slot, and lying close to the metal hull in front of it, was a strong lever of brass, L-shaped, connected internally, and indicating to his trained mechanical mind that its only sphere of action was to lift up and sink back into the slot. He fingered it, but did not yet try to move it. A little to the left of this lever was a small blade of steel, curved to fit the convex hull,—which it hugged closely,—and hinged at its forward edge. This, too, must have a purpose,—an internal connection,—and he did not disturb it until he had learned more.

To the right of the brass lever was an oblong hatch about eight inches long, flush with the hull, and held in place by screws. Three seams, with lines of screws, encircled the round hull, showing that it was constructed in four sections; and these screws, with those in the hatch, were strong and numerous —placed there to stay.

Fatigued from his exertion, he moistened his hair, sat down, and watched the incoming tide swing the craft round parallel with the beach. As the submerged bow raised to a level with the stern, he noticed that the small blades on the horizontal vanes dropped from their upward slant to a straight line with the vanes.

" Rudders," he said, " horizontal rudders. Can't be anything else." With his chin in his hand and his wrinkled brow creased with deeper corrugations, he put his mind through a process of inductive reasoning.

" Horizontal rudders," he mused, " must be to keep her from diving, or to make her dive. They work automatically, and I s'pose the vertical rudders are the same. There's nothing outside to turn 'em with. That boat isn't made to ride in,—no way to get into her,—and she isn't big enough, anyhow. And as you can't get into her, that brass lever must be what starts and stops her. Wonder what the steel blade's for. 'Tisn't a handy shape for a lever, —to be handled with fingers,—too sharp; but it has work to do, or it wouldn't be there. That section o' railroad iron on top must be to hang the boat by,— a traveler,—when she's out o' water.

" And the fan-wheel on the nose—what's that for? If it's a speed or distance indicator, the dial's inside, out o' sight. There's no exhaust, so the motive power can't be steam. Clockwork or electricity, maybe. Mighty fine workmanship all through! That square door is fitted in for keeps, and she must ha' cost a heap. Now, as she has horizontal rudders, she's intended to steer up and down; and as there's no way to get into her or to stay on her, and as she can't be started from the inside or steered from the outside, I take it she's a model o' one o' those submarine boats I've heard of—some fellow's invention that's got away from him. Guess I'll try that lever and see what happens. I'll bury the propellers, though; no engine ought to race."

He pushed the craft into deeper water, pointed it shoreward, and cautiously lifted the curved blade to a perpendicular position, as high as it would go. Nothing happened. He lowered it, raised it again,— it worked very easily,—then, leaving it upright, he threw the long brass lever back into the slot. A slight humming came from within, the propellers revolved slowly, and the craft moved ahead until the bow grounded. Then he followed and lifted the lever out of the slot to its first position, shutting off the power.

Delighted with his success, he backed it out farther than before and again threw back the brass lever, this time with the curved blade down flat on the hull. With the sinking of the lever into the slot the mechanism within gave forth a rushing sound, the propellers at the stern threw up a mound of foam, and the craft shot past him, dived until it glanced on the sandy bottom, then slid a third of its length out of water on the beach and stopped, the propellers still churning, and the small wheel on the nose still spinning with the motion given it by the water.

"Air-pressure!" he exclaimed, as he shut it off. He had seen a line of bubbles rise as the thing dived. "An air-engine, and the whole thing must be full o' compressed air. The brass lever turns it on, and if the steel blade's up it gives it the slow motion; if it's down, she gets full speed at once. Now I know why it's blade-shaped. It's so the water itself can push it down—after she starts."

He did not try to launch it; he waited until the tide floated it, then pushed it along the beach toward his store of food, arriving at high water too exhausted to do more that day than ground his capture and break hard bread. And as the afternoon drew to a close the fatigue in his limbs became racking pain; either as a result of his exposure, or as a later symptom of the fever, he was now in the clutch of a new enemy—rheumatism.

Then, with the coming of night came a return of his first violent symptoms; he was hot, shivery, and feverish by turns, with dry tongue and throat, and a splitting headache; but in this condition he could still take cognizance of a black, ram-bowed gunboat, which stole into the bay from the east and dropped anchor near the buoys.

A half-moon shone in the western sky, and by its light the steamer presented an unkempt, broken appearance, even to the untrained eye of this cast-away. Her after-funnel was but half as high as the other; there were gaps in her iron rail, and vacancies below the twisted davits where boats should be; and her pilot-house was wrecked—the starboard door and nearest window merged in a large, ragged hole.

Officers on the bridge gave orders in foreign speech, in tones which came shoreward faintly. Men sprang overboard with ropes, which they fastened to the buoys; then they swam back, and for an hour or two the whole crew was busy getting the boats to the davits and the end of the cable into the hawse-pipe.

The man on the beach recognized the craft he had seen when he wakened.

He felt that she must in some way be connected with his being there, and he waited, expecting to see a boat put off; but when both boats were hoisted and he heard the humming of a steam-windlass, he gave up this expectation and tried to hail.

His voice could not rise above a hoarse whisper. The anchor was fished, and after an interval he heard the windlass again, heaving in the other chain. They were going away—going to leave him there to die.

He crawled and stumbled down to the water's edge. The tide was up again, rippling around the strange thing he had resolved to navigate. It was not a boat, but it would go ahead, and it would float —it would possibly float him.

With strength born of desperation and fear, he

pushed it, inch by inch, into the water until it was clear of the sand, and tried the engine on the slow motion. The propellers turned and satisfied him. He shut off the power, swung the thing round until it pointed toward the steamer, and seated himself astride of it, just abaft the T-shaped projection in the middle. The long cylinder sank with him, and when it had steadied to a balance between his weight and its buoyancy he found that it bore him, shoulders out; and the position he had taken—within reach of the levers behind him—lifted the blunt nose higher than the stern, but not out of water. This was practicable.

He reached behind, raised the blade lever, threw back the large brass lever, and the craft went ahead, at about the speed of a healthy man's walk. He kept his left hand on the blade lever to hold it up, and by skillful paddling with his right maintained his balance and assisted his legs in steering. He had never learned to swim, but he felt less fear of drowning than of slow death on the island.

In five minutes he was near enough to the steamer to read her name. He pulled the starting-lever forward, stopping his headway; for he must be sure of his welcome.

"Say, boss," he called, faintly and hoarsely, "take me along, can't you? Or else gi' me some medicine. I'm blamed sick—I'll die if I stay here."

The noise of the windlass and chain prevented this being heard, but at last, after repeated calls on his part, a Spanish howl went up from amidships, and a sailor sprang from one of the boats to the deck, crossed himself, and pointing to the man in the water, ran forward.

"Madre de Dios!" he yelled. "El aparecido del muerto."

Work stopped, and a call down a hatchway stopped the windlass. In ports and dead-lights appeared faces; and those on deck, officers and men, crowded to the rail, some to cross themselves, some to sink on their knees, others to grip the rail tightly, while they stared in silence at the torso and livid face in the moonlight on the sea—the ghastly face of the man they had marooned to die alone, who had been seen later dead on the beach.

"Take me with you, boss," he pleaded with his weak voice. "I'm sick; I can't hold on much longer."

It was not the dead man's body washed out from the beach, for it moved, it spoke. And it was not a living man; no man may recover from advanced yellow fever, and this man had been found afterward, dead—cold and still. And no living man may swim in this manner—high out of water, patting and splashing with one hand. It was a ghost. It had come to punish them.

"Por qué nos atormentan así, hombre, deja?" cried a white-faced officer.

"Can't you hear me?" asked the apparition. "I'll come closer."

He threw back the starting lever, and the thing began moving. Then a rifle-barrel protruded from a dead-light. There was a report and a flash, and a bullet passed through his hair. The shock startled him, and he lost his balance. In the effort to recover it his leg knocked down the blade lever, and the steel cylinder sprang forward, leaving him floundering in the water. Pointed upward, it appeared for a moment on the surface, then dived like a porpoise and disappeared. In five seconds something happened to the gunboat.

Coincident with a sound like near-by thunder, the black craft lifted amidships like a bending jack-knife, and up from the shattered deck, and out from ports, doors, and dead-lights, came a volcano of flame and smoke. The sea beneath followed in a mound, which burst like a great bubble, sending a cloud of steam and spray and whitish-yellow smoke aloft to mingle with the first and meet the falling fragments. These fell for several seconds—hatches, gratings, buckets, ladders, splinters of wood, parts of men, and men whole, but limp.

A side-ladder fell near the choking and half-stunned sick man, and he seized it. Before he could crawl on top the two halves of the gunboat had sunk in a swirl of bubbles and whirlpools.

A few broken and bleeding swimmers approached to share his support, saw his awful face in the moonlight, and swam away.

A few hours later a gray cruiser loomed up close by and directed a search-light at him. Then a gray cutter full of white-clad men approached and took him off the ladder. He was delirious again, and bleeding from mouth, nose, and ears.

THE surgeon and the torpedo-lieutenant came up from the sick-bay, the latter with enthusiasm on his face,—for he was young,—and joined a group of officers on the quarter-deck.

"He'll pull through, gentlemen," said the surgeon. "He is the man Mosher lost overboard, though he doesn't know anything about it, nor how he got on that sand-key. I suppose the *Destructor* picked him

up and landed him. He found bread and water, he
says. You see, the first symptoms are similar in
Yellow Jack and relapsing bilious fever. I don't
wonder that Mosher was nervous."

" Then it *was* the *Destructor?* " asked an ensign,
pulling out a note-book and a pencil. " And Lieutenant Mosher was right, after all? "

" Yes; this man read her name before she blew up;
and a Spanish sailor has waked up and confirmed it.
She was the *Destructor*, just over, and trying to get
into Havana. Instead of blowing up in Algeciras
Bay, as they thought, she had left with despatches
for Havana, only to blow up on the Florida Reef."

" The *Destructor*," said the ensign, as he pocketed
his note-book and pencil, " carried fifty-five men.
Don't we get the bounty as the nearest craft? "

" Not much," said the young and enthusiastic torpedo-lieutenant. " We were not even within signal
distance, and came along by accident. Listen, all
of you. When an American war-craft sinks or de-
stroys a larger enemy, there is a bounty due her
crew of two hundred dollars for every man on board
the enemy. That is law, isn't it? " They nodded.
" If a submarine boat can be a war-craft, so may a
Whitehead torpedo, and certainly is one, being built
for war. A war-craft abandoned is a derelict, and
the man who finds her becomes her lawful commander
for the time. If he belongs to the navy his position
is strengthened, and if he is alone he is not only
commander, but the whole crew, and consequently
he is entitled to all the bounty she may earn. That
is law.

" Now, listen hard. Lieutenant Mosher sent one
torpedo at the gunboat; it missed and became derelict,

while Mosher escaped under one boiler. This man found the derelict adrift, puzzled out the action, waited until the gunboat came back for her anchor, then straddled his craft, and rode out with the water-tripper up. They shot at him. He turned his dog loose and destroyed the enemy. If the *Destructor* carried fifty-five men he is entitled to eleven thousand dollars, and the government must pay, for that is law."

THE BATTLE OF THE MONSTERS

EXTRACT from hospital record of the case of John Anderson, patient of Dr. Brown, Ward 3, Room 6:

August 3. Arrived at hospital in extreme mental distress, having been bitten on wrist three hours previously by dog known to have been rabid. Large, strong man, full-blooded and well nourished. Sanguine temperament. Pulse and temperature higher than normal, due to excitement. Cauterized wound at once (2 P.M.) and inoculated with antitoxin.

As patient admits having recently escaped, by swimming ashore, from lately arrived cholera ship, now at quarantine, he has been isolated and clothing disinfected. Watch for symptoms of cholera.

August 3, 6 P.M. Microscopic examination of blood corroborative of Metchnikoff's theory of fighting leucocytes. White corpuscles gorged with bacteria.

He was an amphibian, and, as such, undeniably beautiful; for the sunlight, refracted and diffused in the water, gave his translucent, pearl-blue body all the shifting colors of the spectrum. Vigorous and graceful of movement, in shape he resembled a comma of three dimensions, twisted, when at rest, to a slight spiral curve; but in traveling he straightened out with quick successive jerks, each one sending him ahead a couple of lengths. Supplemented by the undulatory movement of a long continuation of his tail, it was his way of swimming, good enough to enable him to escape his enemies; this, and riding at anchor in a current by his cable-like appendage, constituting his main occupation in life. The

158

pleasure of eating was denied him; nature had given him a mouth, but he used it only for purposes of offense and defense, absorbing his food in a most unheard-of manner—through the soft walls of his body.

Yet he enjoyed a few social pleasures. Though the organs of the five senses were missing in his economy, he possessed an inner sixth sense which answered for all and also gave him power of speech. He would converse, swap news and views, with creatures of his own and other species, provided that they were of equal size and prowess; but he wasted no time on any but his social peers. Smaller creatures he pursued when they annoyed him; larger ones pursued him.

The sunlight, which made him so beautiful to look at, was distasteful to him; it also made him too visible. He preferred a half-darkness and less fervor to life's battle—time to judge of chances, to figure on an enemy's speed and turning-circle, before beginning flight or pursuit. But his dislike of it really came of a stronger animus—a shuddering recollection of three hours once passed on dry land in a comatose condition, which had followed a particularly long and intense period of bright sunlight. He had never been able to explain the connection, but the awful memory still saddened his life.

And now it seemed, as he swam about, that this experience might be repeated. The light was strong and long-continued, the water uncomfortably warm, and the crowd about him denser—so much so as to prevent him from attending properly to a social inferior who had crossed his bow. But just as his mind grasped the full imminence of the danger, there

came a sudden darkness, a crash and vibration of
the water, then a terrible, rattling roar of sound.
The social inferior slipped from his mouth, and
with his crowding neighbors was washed far away,
while he felt himself slipping along, bounding and
rebounding against the projections of a corrugated
wall which showed white in the gloom.   There was an
unpleasant taste to the water, and he became aware
of creatures in his vicinity unlike any he had
known,—quickly darting little monsters about a
tenth as large as himself,—thousands of them, black
and horrid to see, each with short, fish-like body and
square head like that of a dog; with wicked mouth
that opened and shut nervously; with hooked flippers on the middle part, and a bunch of tentacles on
the fore that spread out ahead and around.   A
dozen of them surrounded him menacingly; but he
was young and strong, much larger than they, and
a little frightened.   A blow of his tail killed two, and
the rest drew off.

The current bore them on until the white wall
rounded off and was lost to sight beyond the mass
of darting creatures.   Here was slack water, and
with desperate effort he swam back, pushing the
small enemies out of his path, meeting some resistance and receiving a few bites, until, in a hollow
in the wall, he found temporary refuge and time to
think.   But he could not solve the problem.   He
had not the slightest idea where he was or what
had happened—who and what were the strange
black creatures, or why they had threatened him.

His thoughts were interrupted.   Another vibrant
roar sounded, and there was pitch-black darkness;
then he was pushed and washed away from his shelter,

jostled, bumped, and squeezed, until he found himself in a dimly lighted tunnel, which, crowded as it was with swimmers, was narrow enough to enable him to see both sides at once. The walls were dark brown and blue, broken up everywhere into depressions or caves, some of them so deep as to be almost like blind tunnels. The dog-faced creatures were there—as far as he could see; but besides them, now, were others, of stranger shape—of species unknown to him.

A slow current carried them on, and soon they entered a larger tunnel. He swam to the opposite wall, gripped a projection, and watched in wonder and awe the procession gliding by. He soon noticed the source of the dim light. A small creature with barrel-like body and innumerable legs or tentacles, wavering and reaching, floated past. Its body swelled and shrank alternately, with every swelling giving out a phosphorescent glow, with every contraction darkening to a faint red color. Then came a group of others; then a second living lamp; later another and another: they were evenly distributed, and illumined the tunnel.

There were monstrous shapes, living but inert, barely pulsing with dormant life, as much larger than himself as the dog-headed kind were smaller—huge, unwieldy, disk-shaped masses of tissue, light gray at the margins, dark red in the middle. They were in the majority, and blocked the view. Darting and wriggling between and about them were horrible forms, some larger than himself, others smaller. There were serpents, who swam with a serpent's motion. Some were serpents in form, but were curled rigidly into living corkscrews, and by sculling with their tails screwed their way through the water with surprising rapidity. Others were barrel- or globe-shaped, with swarming tentacles. With these they pulled themselves along, in and out through the crowd, or, bringing their squirming appendages rearward,—each an individual snake,—used them as propellers, and swam. There were creatures in the form of long cylinders, some with tentacles by which they rolled along like a log in a tideway; others, without appendages, were as inert and helpless as the huge red-and-gray disks. He saw four ball-shaped creatures float by, clinging together; then a group of eight, then one of twelve. All these, to the extent of their volition, seemed to be in a state of extreme agitation and excitement.

The cause was apparent. The tunnel from which he had come was still discharging the dog-faced animals by the thousand, and he knew now the business they were on. It was war—war to the death. They flung themselves with furious energy into the parade, fighting and biting all they could reach. A hundred at a time would pounce on one of the large red-and-gray creatures, almost hiding it from view; then, and before they had passed out of sight, they would fall off and disperse, and the once living victim would come with them, in parts. The smaller, active swimmers fled, but if one was caught, he suffered; a quick dart, a tangle of tentacles, an embrace of the wicked flippers, a bite—and a dead body floated on.

And now into the battle came a ponderous engine of vengeance and defense. A gigantic, lumbering, pulsating creature, white and translucent but for the dark, active brain showing through its walls, horrible in the slow, implacable deliberation of its movements, floated down with the current. It was larger than the huge red-and-gray creatures. It was formless, in the full irony of the definition—for it assumed all forms. It was long—barrel-shaped; it shrank to a sphere, then broadened laterally, and again extended above and below. In turn it was a sphere, a disk, a pyramid, a pentahedron, a polyhedron. It possessed neither legs, flippers, nor tentacles; but out from its heaving, shrinking body it would send, now from one spot, now from another, an active arm, or feeler, with which it swam, pulled, or pushed. An unlucky invader which one of them touched made few more voluntary movements; for instantly the whole side of the whitish mass bristled with arms. They seized, crushed, killed it, and then pushed it bodily through the living walls to the animal's interior to serve for food. And the gaping fissure healed at once, like the wounds of Milton's warring angels.

The first white monster floated down, killing as he went; then came another, pushing eagerly into the fray; then came two, then three, then dozens. It seemed that the word had been passed, and the army of defense was mustering.

Sick with horror, he watched the grim spectacle from the shelter of the projection, until roused to an active sense of danger to himself—but not from the fighters. He was anchored by his tail, swinging easily in the eddy, and now felt himself touched from beneath, again from above. A projection downstream was extending outward and toward him. The cave in which he had taken refuge was closing on him like a great mouth—as though directed by an intelligence behind the wall. With a terrified flirt of his tail he flung himself out, and as he drifted down with the combat the walls of the cave crunched together.   It was well for him that he was not there.

The current was clogged with fragments of once living creatures, and everywhere, darting, dodging, and biting, were the fierce black invaders.   But they paid no present attention to him or to the small tentacled animals.   They killed the large, helpless red-and-gray kind, and were killed by the larger white monsters, each moment marking the death and rending to fragments of a victim, and the horrid interment of fully half his slayers.   The tunnel grew larger, as mouth after mouth of tributary tunnels was passed; but as each one discharged its quota of swimming and drifting creatures, there was no thinning of the crowd.

As he drifted on with the inharmonious throng, he noticed what seemed the objective of the war. This was the caves which lined the tunnel.   Some were apparently rigid, others were mobile.   A large red-and-gray animal was pushed into the mouth of one of the latter, and the walls instantly closed; then they opened, and the creature drifted out, limp and colorless, but alive; and with him came fragments of the wall, broken off by the pressure.   This happened again and again, but the large creature was never quite killed—merely squeezed.   The tentacled non-combatants and the large white fighters seemed to know the danger of these tunnel mouths, possibly from bitter experiences, for they avoided the walls; but the dog-faced invaders sought this death, and only fought on their way to the caves.   Sometimes two, often four or more, would launch themselves together into a hollow, but to no avail; their united strength could not prevent the closing in of the mechanical maw, and they were crushed and flung out, to drift on with other débris.

Soon the walls could not be seen for the pushing, jostling crowd, but everywhere the terrible, silent war went on until there came a time when fighting ceased; for each must look out for himself. They seemed to be in an immense cave, and the tide was broken into cross-currents rushing violently to the accompaniment of rhythmical thunder. They were shaken, jostled, pushed about and pushed together, hundreds of the smaller creatures dying from the pressure. Then there was a moment of comparative quiet, during which fighting was resumed, and there could be seen the swiftly flying walls of a large tunnel. Next they were rushed through a labyrinth of small caves with walls of curious, branching formation, sponge-like and intricate. It required energetic effort to prevent being caught in the meshes, and the large red-and-gray creatures were sadly torn and crushed, while the white ones fought their way through by main strength. Again the flying walls of a tunnel, again a mighty cave, and the cross-currents, and the rhythmical thunder, and now a wild charge down an immense tunnel, the wall of which surged outward and inward, in unison with the roaring of the thunder.

The thunder died away in the distance, though the walls still surged—even those of a smaller tunnel which divided the current and received them. Downstream the tunnel branched again and again, and with the lessening of the diameter was a lessening of the current's velocity, until, in a maze of small, short passages, the invaders, content to fight and kill in the swifter tide, again attacked the caves.

But to the never-changing result: they were
crushed, mangled, and cast out, the number of sui-
cides, in this neighborhood, largely exceeding those
killed by the white warriors. And yet, in spite of
the large mortality among them, the attacking force
was increasing. Where one died two took his place;
and the reason was soon made plain—they were re-
producing. A black fighter, longer than his fellows,
a little sluggish of movement, as though from the
restrictive pressure of a large, round protuberance
in his middle, which made him resemble a snake which
had swallowed an egg, was caught by a white monster
and instantly embraced by a multitude of feelers.
He struggled, bit, and broke in two; then the two
parts escaped the grip of the astonished captor, and
wriggled away, the protuberance becoming the head
of the rear portion, which immediately joined the
fight, snapping and biting with unmistakable jaws.
This phenomenon was repeated.

And on went the battle. Illumined by the living
lamps, and watched by terrified non-combatants, the
horrid carnival continued with never-slacking fury
and ever-changing background—past the mouths of
tributary tunnels which increased the volume and
velocity of the current and added to the fighting
strength, on through widening archways to a repetition of the cross-currents, the thunder, and the
sponge-like maze, down past the heaving walls of
larger tunnels to branched passages, where, in comparative slack water, the siege of the caves was resumed. For hour after hour this went on, the invaders dying by hundreds, but increasing by thousands and ten thousands, as the geometrical progres-
sion advanced, until, with swimming-spaces nearly

choked by their bodies, living and dead, there came the inevitable turn in the tide of battle. A white monster was killed.

Glutted with victims, exhausted and sluggish, he was pounced upon by hundreds, hidden from view by a living envelop of black, which pulsed and throbbed with his death-throes. A feeler reached out, to be bitten off; then another, to no avail. His strength was gone, and the assailants bit and burrowed until they reached a vital part, when the great mass assumed a spherical form and throbbed no more. They dropped off, and, as the mangled ball floated on, charged on the next enemy with renewed fury and courage born of their victory. This one died as quickly.

And as though it had been foreseen, and a policy arranged to meet it, the white army no longer fought in the open, but lined up along the walls to defend the immovable caves. They avoided the working jaws of the other kind, which certainly needed no garrison, and drifting slowly in the eddies, fought as they could, with decreasing strength and increasing death-rate. And thus it happened that our conservative non-combatant, out in midstream, found himself surrounded by a horde of black enemies who had nothing better to do than attack him.

And they did. As many as could crowd about him closed their wicked jaws in his flesh. Squirming with pain, rendered trebly strong by his terror, he killed them by twos and threes as he could reach them with his tail. He shook them off with nervous contortions, only to make room for more. He plunged, rolled, launched himself forward and back, up and down, out and in, bending himself nearly double, then with lightning rapidity throwing himself far into the reverse curve. He was fighting for his life, and knew it. When he could, he used his jaws, only once to an enemy. He saw dimly at intervals that the white monsters were watching him; but none offered to help, and he had not time to call.

He thought that he must have become the object of the war; for from all sides they swarmed, crowding about him, seeking a place on which to fasten their jaws. Little by little the large red-and-gray creatures, the non-combatants, and the phosphorescent animals were pushed aside, and he, the center of an almost solid black mass, fought, in utter darkness, with the fury of extreme fright. He had no appreciation of the passing of time, no knowledge of his distance from the wall, or the destination of this never-pausing current. But finally, after an apparently interminable period, he heard dimly, with failing consciousness, the reverberations of the thunder, and knew momentary respite as the violent cross-currents tore his assailants away. Then, still in darkness, he felt the crashing and tearing of flesh against obstructing walls and sharp corners, the repetition of thunder and the roar of the current which told him he was once more in a large tunnel. An instant of light from a venturesome torch showed him to his enemies, and again he fought, like a whale in his last flurry, slowly dying from exhaustion and pain, but still potential to kill—terrible in his agony. There was no counting of scalps in that day's work; but perhaps no devouring white monster in all the defensive army could have shown a death-list equal to this. From the surging black cloud there was a steady outflow of the dead, pushed back by the living.

Weaker and weaker, while they mangled his flesh, and still in darkness, he fought them down through branching passages to another network of small tunnels, where he caught a momentary view of the walls and the stolid white guard, thence on to what he knew was open space. And here he felt that he could fight no more. They had covered him completely, and try as he might with his failing strength, he could not dislodge them. So he ceased his struggles; and numb with pain, dazed with despair, he awaited the end.

But it did not come. He was too exhausted to feel surprise or joy when they suddenly dropped away from him; but the instinct of self-preservation was still in force, and he swam toward the wall. The small creatures paid him no attention; they scurried this way and that, busy with troubles of their own, while he crept stupidly and painfully between two white sentries floating in the eddies,—one of whom considerately made room for him,—and anchored to a projection, luckily choosing a harbor that was not hostile.

"Any port in a storm, eh, neighbor?" said the one who had given him room, and who seemed to notice his dazed condition. "You'll feel better soon. My, but you put up a good fight, that's what you did!"

He could not answer, and the friendly guard resumed his vigil. In a few moments, however, he could take cognizance of what was going on in the stream. There was a new army in the fight, and reinforcements were still coming. A short distance above him was a huge rent in the wall, and the caves around it, crushed and distorted, were grinding fiercely. Protruding through the rent and extending half-way across the tunnel was a huge mass of some strange substance, roughly shaped to a cylindrical form. It was hollow, and out of it, by thousands and hundred thousands, was pouring the auxiliary army, from which the black fighters were now fleeing for dear life.

The newcomers, though resembling in general form the creatures they pursued, were much larger and of two distinct types. Both were light brown in color; but while one showed huge development of head and jaw, with small flippers, the other kind reversed these attributes, their heads being small, but their flippers long and powerful. They ran their quarry down in the open, and seized them with outreaching tentacles. No mistakes were made—no feints or false motions; and there was no resistance by the victims. Where one was noticed he was doomed. The tentacles gathered him in—to a murderous bite or a murderous embrace.

At last, when the inflow had ceased,—when there must have been millions of the brown killers in the tunnel,—the great hollow cylinder turned slowly on its axis and backed out through the rent in the wall, which immediately closed, with a crushing and scattering of fragments. Though the allies were far down-stream now, the war was practically ended; for the white defenders remained near the walls, and the black invaders were in wildest panic, each one, as the resistless current rushed him past, swimming against the stream, to put distance between himself and the destroyer below. But before long an advance-guard of the brown enemy shot out from the tributaries above, and the tide of retreat swung backward. Then came thousands of them, and the massacre was resumed.

"Hot stuff, eh?" said the friendly neighbor to him.

"Y-y-y-es—I guess so," he answered, rather vacantly; "I don't know. I don't know anything about it. I never saw such doings. What is it all for? What does it mean?"

"Oh, this is nothing; it's all in a lifetime. Still, I admit it might ha' been serious for us—and you, too—if we hadn't got help."

"But who are they, and what? They all seem of a family, and are killing each other."

"Immortal shade of Darwin!" exclaimed the other sentry, who had not spoken before. "Where were you brought up? Don't you know that variations from type are the deadliest enemies of the parent stock? These two brown breeds are the hundredth or two-hundredth cousins of the black kind. When they've killed off their common relative, and get to competing for grub, they'll exterminate each other, and we'll be rid of 'em all. Law of nature. Understand?"

"Oh, y-yes, I understand, of course; but what did the black kind attack me for? And what do they want, anyway?"

"To follow out their destiny, I s'pose. They're the kind of folks who have missions. Reformers, we call 'em—who want to enforce their peculiar ideas and habits on other people. Sometimes we call them expansionists—fond of colonizing territory that doesn't belong to them. They wanted to get through the cells to the lymph-passages, thence on to the brain and spinal marrow. Know what that means? Hydrophobia."

" What's that? "

" Oh, say, now! You're too easy."

" Come, come," said the other, good-naturedly; " don't guy him. He never had our advantages. You see, neighbor, we get these points from the sub-jective brain, which knows all things and gives us our instructions. We're the white corpuscles—phagocytes, the scientists call us,—and our work is to police the blood-vessels, and kill off invaders that make trouble. Those red-and-gray chumps can't take care of themselves, and we must protect 'em. Understand? But this invasion was too much for us, and we had to have help from outside. You must have come in with the first crowd—think I saw you—in at the bite. Second crowd came in through an inoculation tube, and just in time to pull you through."

" I don't know," answered our bewildered friend. " In at the bite? What bite? I was swimming round comfortable-like, and there was a big noise, and then I was alongside of a big white wall, and then—"

" Exactly; the dog's tooth. You got into bad company, friend, and you're well out of it. That first gang is the microbe of rabies, not very well known yet, because a little too small to be seen by most microscopes. All the scientists seem to have learned about 'em is that a colony of a few hundred generations old—which they call a culture, or serum —is death on the original bird; and that's what they sent in to help out. Pasteur's dead, worse luck, but sometime old Koch'll find out what we've known all along—that it's only variation from type."

"Koch!" he answered, eagerly and proudly. "Oh, I know Koch; I've met him. And I know about microscopes, too. Why, Koch had me under his microscope once. He discovered my family, and named us—the comma bacilli—the Spirilli of Asiatic Cholera."

In silent horror they drew away from him, and then conversed together. Other white warriors drifting along stopped and joined the conference, and when a hundred or more were massed before him, they spread out to a semi-spherical formation and closed in.

"What's the matter?" he asked, nervously. "What's wrong? What are you going to do? I haven't done anything, have I?"

"It's not what you've done, stranger," said his quondam friend, "or what we're going to do. It's what you're going to do. You're going to die. Don't see how you got past quarantine, anyhow."

"What—why—I don't want to die. I've done nothing. All I want is peace and quiet, and a place to swim where it isn't too light nor too dark. I mind my own affairs. Let me alone—you hear me—let me alone!"

They answered him not. Slowly and irresistibly the hollow formation contracted—individuals slipping out when necessary—until he was pushed, still protesting, into the nearest movable cave. The walls crashed together and his life went out. When he was cast forth he was in five pieces.

And so our gentle, conservative, non-combative cholera microbe, who only wanted to be left alone to mind his own affairs, met this violent death, a martyr to prejudice and an unsympathetic environment.

Extract from hospital record of the case of John Anderson:

August 18.   As period of incubation for both cholera and hydrophobia has passed and no initial symptoms of either disease have been noticed, patient is this day discharged, cured.

FROM THE ROYAL-YARD DOWN

AS night descended, cold and damp, the wind hauled, and by nine o'clock the ship was charging along before a half-gale and a rising sea from the port quarter. When the watch had braced the yards, the mate ordered the spanker brailed in and the mizzen-royal clued up, as the ship steered hard. This was done, and the men coiled up the gear.

"Let the spanker hang in the brails; tie up the royal," ordered the mate from his position at the break of the poop.

"Aye, aye, sir," answered a voice from the group, and an active figure sprang into the rigging. Another figure—slim and graceful, clad in long, yellow oilskin coat, and a sou'-wester which could not confine a tangled fringe of wind-blown hair—left the shelter of the after-companionway and sped along the alley to the mate's side.

"The foot-rope, Mr. Adams," she said, hurriedly. "The seizing was chafed, you remember."

"By George, Miss Freda!" said the officer. "Forgot all about it. Glad you spoke. Come down from aloft," he added, in a roar.

The sailor answered and descended.

"Get a piece of spun yarn out o' the booby-hatch and take it up wi' you," continued the mate. "Pass a temporary seizing on the lee royal foot-rope. Make sure it's all right 'fore you get on it, now."

"Aye, aye, sir."

The man passed down the poop steps, secured the

spun yarn, and while rolling it into a ball to put
in his pocket, stood for a moment in the light shining
from the second mate's room. The girl on the poop
looked down at him. He was a trim-built, well-
favored young fellow, with more refinement in his
face than most sailors can show; yet there was no
lack of seamanly deftness in the fingers which balled
up the spun yarn and threw a half-hitch with the
bight of the lanyard over the point of the marlinespike which hung to his neck. As he climbed the
steps, the girl faced him, looking squarely into his
eyes.

" Be careful, John—Mr. Owen," she said. " The
seizing is chafed through. I heard the man report
it—it was Dutch George of the other watch. Do be
careful."

" Er, why—why, yes, Miss Folsom. Thank you.
But you startled me. I've been Jack for three years
—not John, nor Mister. Yes, it's all right; I—"

" Get aloft to that mizzenroyal," thundered the
mate, now near the wheel.

" Aye, aye, sir." He touched his sou'-wester to
the girl and mounted the weather mizzen-rigging,
running up the ratlines as a fireman goes up a ladder.
It was a black night with cold rain, and having
thrown off his oiled jacket, he was already drenched
to the skin; but no environment of sunshine, green
fields and woodland, and flower-scented air ever
made life brighter to him than had the incident of
the last few moments; and with every nerve in his
body rejoicing in his victory, and her bitter words
of four years back crowding his mind as a con-
trasting background, he danced up and .over the
futtock-shrouds, up the topmast-rigging, through

the crosstrees, and up the topgallant-rigging to where
the ratlines ended and he must climb on the runner
of the royal-halyards.   As the yard was lowered,
this was a short climb, and he swung himself upward
to the weather yard-arm, where he rolled up one side
of the sail with extravagant waste of muscular
effort; for she had said he was not a man, and he
had proved her wrong: he had conquered himself,
and he had conquered her.

He hitched the gasket, and crossed over to the
lee side, forgetting, in his exhilaration, the object of
the spun yarn in his pocket and the marlinespike
hung from his neck, stepped out on the foot-rope,
passed his hands along the jack-stay to pull himself
farther, and felt the foot-rope sink to the sound of
snapping strands.   The jack-stay was torn from
his grasp, and he fell, face downward, into the black
void beneath.

An involuntary shriek began on his lips, but was
not finished.   He felt that the last atom of air was
jarred from his lungs by what he knew was the
topgallant-yard, four feet below the royal; and, unable to hold on, with a freezing cold in his veins and
at the hair-roots, he experienced in its fullness the
terrible sensation of falling,—whirling downward,—
clutching wildly at vacancy with stiffened fingers.

The first horror past, his mind took on a strange
contemplativeness; fear of death gave way to mild
curiosity as to the manner of it.   Would he strike
on the lee quarter, or would he go overboard?   And
might he not catch something?   There was rigging
below him—the lee royal-backstay stretched farthest
out from the mast, and if he brushed it, there was a
possible chance.   He was now face upward, and with

the utmost difficulty moved his eyes,—he could not yet, by any exercise of will or muscle, move his head,— and there, almost within reach, was a dark line, which he knew was the royal-backstay; farther in toward the spars was another—the topgallant-backstay; and within this, two other ropes which he knew for the topgallant-rigging, though he could see no ratlines, nor could he distinguish the lay of the strands; the ropes appeared like solid bars. This, with the fact that he was still but a few feet below the topgallant-yard, surprised him, until it came to him that falling bodies travel over sixteen feet in the first second of descent, which is at a rate too fast for distinct vision, and that the apparent slowness of his falling was but relative—because of the quickness of his mind, which could not wait on a sluggish optic nerve and more sluggish retina.

Yet he wondered why he could not reach out and grasp the backstay. It seemed as though invisible fetters bound every muscle and joint, though not completely. An intense effort of will resulted in the slow extension of all the fingers of his right hand, and a little straightening of the arm toward the back-stay; but not until he had fallen to the level of the upper topsail-yard was this result reached. It did no good; the backstay was now farther away. As it led in a straight line from the royal-masthead to the rail, this meant that he would fall overboard, and the thought comforted him. The concussion would kill him, of course; but no self-pity afflicted him now. He merely considered that she, who had relented, would be spared the sight of him crushed to a pulp on the deck.

As he drifted slowly down past the expanse of

upper topsail, he noticed that his head was sinking and his body turning so that he would ultimately face forward; but still his arms and legs held their extended position, like those of a speared frog, and the thought recalled to him an incident of his infancy—a frog-hunt with an older playmate, his prowess, success, wet feet, and consequent illness. It had been forgotten for years, but the chain was started, and led to other memories, long dead, which rose before him. His childhood passed in review, with its pleasures and griefs; his school-days, with their sports, conflicts, friends and enemies; college, where he had acquired the polish to make him petted of all but one—and abhorrent to her. Almost every person, man or woman, boy or girl, with whom he had conversed in his whole life, came back and repeated the scene; and as he passed the lower topsail-yard, nearly head downward, he was muttering commonplaces to a brown-faced, gray-eyed girl, who listened, and looked him through and through, and seemed to be wondering why he existed.

And as he traversed the depth of the lower topsail, turning gradually on his axis, he lived it over—next to his first voyage, the most harrowing period of his life: the short two months during which he had striven vainly to impress this simple-natured sailor-girl with his good qualities, ending at last with his frantic declaration of a love that she did not want.

" But it's not the least use, John," she said to him. " I do not love you, and I cannot. You are a gentleman, as they say, and as such I like you well enough; but I never can love you, nor any one like you. I've been among men, real men, all my life, and perhaps have ideals that are strange to you.

John,"—her eyes were wide open in earnestness,—
" you are not a man."

Writhing under her words, which would have been
brutal spoken by another, he cursed, not her, nor
himself, but his luck and the fates that had shaped
his life. And next she was showing him the opened
door, saying that she could tolerate profanity in
a man, but not in a gentleman, and that under no
circumstances was he to claim her acquaintance
again. Then followed the snubbing in the street,
when, like a lately whipped dog, he had placed himself in her way, hoping she would notice him; and
the long agony of humiliation and despair as his
heart and soul followed her over the seas in her
father's ship, until the seed she had planted—the
small suspicion that her words were true—developed
into a wholesome conviction that she had measured
him by a higher standard than any he had known,
and found him wanting. So he would go to her
school, and learn what she knew.

With lightning-like rapidity his mind rehearsed the
details of his tuition: the four long voyages; the
brutality of the officers until he had learned his work;
their consideration and rough kindness when he had
become useful and valuable; the curious, incongruous feeling of self-respect that none but able seamen
feel; the growth in him of an aggressive physical
courage; the triumphant satisfaction with which he
finally knew himself as a complete man, clean in
morals and mind, able to look men in the face. And
then came the moment when, mustering at the capstan
with the new crew of her father's ship, he had met
her surprised eyes with a steady glance, and received
no recognition.

And so he pleaded his cause, dumbly, by the life that he lived. Asking nothing by word or look, he proved himself under her eyes—first on deck; first in the rigging; the best man at a weather-earing; the best at the wheel; quick, obedient, intelligent, and respectful, winning the admiration of his mates, the jealous ill will of the officers, but no sign of interest or approval from her until to-night—the ninety-second day of the passage. She had surrendered; he had reached her level, only to die; and he thought this strange.

Facing downward, head inboard now, and nearly horizontal, he was passing the cross-jack yard. Below him was the sea—black and crisp—motionless as though carved in ebony. Neither was there movement of the ship and its rigging; the hanging bights of ropes were rigid, while a breaking sea just abaft the main chains remained poised, curled, its white crest a frozen pillow of foam. "The rapidity of thought," he mused, dreamily; "but I'm falling fast enough— fast enough to kill me when I strike."

He could not move an eyelid now, nor was he conscious that he breathed; but, being nearly upright, facing aft and inboard, the quarter-deck and its fittings were before his eyes, and he saw what brought him out of eternity to a moment of finite time and emotion. The helmsman stood at the motionless wheel with his right hand poised six inches above a spoke, as though some sudden paralysis gripped him, and his face, illumined by the binnacle light, turned aloft inquiringly. But it was not this. Standing at the taffrail, one hand on a life-buoy, was a girl in yellow looking at him,—unspeakable horror in the look,—and around her waist the arm of the mate, on whose rather handsome face was an evil grin.

A pang of earthly rage and jealousy shot through him, and he wished to live. By a supreme effort of will he brought his legs close together and his arms straight above his head; then the picture before him shot upward, and he was immersed in cold salt water, with blackness all about him. How long he remained under he could not guess. He had struck feet first and suffered no harm, but had gone down like a deep-sea lead. He felt the aching sensation in his lungs coming from suppressed breathing, and swam blindly in the darkness, not knowing in which direction was the surface, until he felt the marlinespike— still fastened to his neck—extending off to the right. Sure that it must hang downward, he turned the other way, and, keeping it parallel with his body, swam with bursting lungs until he felt air upon his face and knew that he could breathe. In choking sobs and gasps his breath came and went, while he paddled with hands and feet, glad of his reprieve; and when his lungs worked normally, he struck out for a white, circular life-buoy, not six feet away. "Bless her for this," he prayed, as he slipped it under his arms. His oilskin trousers were cumbersome, and with a little trouble he shed them.

He was alive, and his world was again in motion. Seas lifted and dropped him, occasionally breaking over his head. In the calm of the hollows, he listened for voices of possible rescuers. On the tops of the seas,—ears filled with the roar of the gale,—he shouted, facing to leeward, and searching with strained eyes for sign of the ship or one of her boats. At last he saw a pin-point of light far away, and around it and above it blacker darkness, which was faintly shaped to the outline of a ship and canvas—hove to in the trough, with maintopsail aback, as he knew by its fore-shortening. And even as he looked and shouted it faded away. He screamed and cursed, for he wanted to live. He had survived that terrible fall, and it was his right.

Something white showed on the top of a sea to leeward and sank in a hollow. He sank with it, and when he rose again it was nearer.

"Boat ahoy!" he sang out. "Boat ahoy!—this way—port a little—steady."

He swam as he could, cumbered by the life-buoy, and with every heaving sea the boat came nearer. At last he recognized it—the ship's dinghy; and it was being pulled into the teeth of that forceful wind and sea by a single rower—a slight figure in yellow.

"It's Freda," he exclaimed; and then, in a shout: "This way, Miss Folsom—a little farther."

She turned, nodded, and pulled the boat up to him. He seized the gunwale, and she took in the oars.

"Can you climb in alone, John?" she asked in an even voice—as even as though she were asking him to have more tea. "Wait a little,—I am tired, —and I will help you."

She was ever calm and dispassionate, but he wondered at her now; yet he would not be outdone.

"I'll climb over the stern, Freda, so as not to capsize you. Better go forward to balance my weight."

She did so. He pulled himself to the stern, slipped the life-buoy over his head and into the boat, then, by a mighty exercise of all his strength, vaulted

aboard with seeming ease and sat down on a thwart.
He felt a strong inclination to laughter and tears,
but repressed himself; for masculine hysterics would
not do before this young woman. She came aft to
the next thwart, and when he felt steadier he said:

"You have saved my life, Freda; but thanks are
idle now, for your own is in danger. Give me the
oars. We must get back to the ship."

She changed places with him, facing forward, and
said, wearily, as he shipped the oars: "So you want
to get back?"

"Why, yes; don't you? We are adrift in an
open boat."

"The wind is going down, and the seas do not
break," she answered, in the same weary voice. "It
does not rain any more, and we will have the
moon."

A glance around told him that she spoke truly.
There was less pressure to the wind, and the seas
rose and fell, sweeping past them like moving hills
of oil. Moonlight shining through thinning clouds
faintly illumined her face, and he saw the expres-
sionless weariness of her voice, and a sad, dreamy
look in her gray eyes.

"How did you get the dinghy down, Freda?" he
asked. "And why did no one come with you?"

"Father was asleep, and the mate was incompetent. I had my revolver, and they backed the yards
for me and threw the dinghy over. I had loosened
the gripes as you went aloft. I thought you would
fall. Still—no one would come."

"And you came alone," he said in a broken voice,
"and pulled this boat to windward in this sea. You
are a wonder."

"I saw you catch the life-buoy. Why did you fall? You were cautioned."

"I forgot the foot-rope. I was thinking of you."

"You are like the mate. He forgot the foot-rope all day because he was thinking of me. I should have gone aloft and seized it myself."

There was no reproof or sarcasm in the tired voice. She had simply made an assertion.

"Why are you at sea, before the mast—a man of your talents?"

It was foolish, he knew; but the word "man" sent a thrill through him.

"To please you if I may; to cultivate what you did not find in me."

"Yes, I knew; when you came on board I knew it. But you might have spoken to me."

There was petulance in the tone now, and the soul of the man rejoiced. The woman in her was asserting itself.

"Miss Folsom," he answered warmly, "I could not. You had made it impossible. It was your right, your duty, if you wished it. But you ignored my existence."

"I was testing you. I am glad now, Mr. Owen."

The petulance was gone, but there was something chilling in this answer.

"Can you see the ship?" he asked after a moment's silence. "The moonlight is stronger."

"We will not reach her. They have squared away. The mate had the deck, and father is asleep."

"And left you in an open boat," he answered angrily.

"He knew I was with you."

What was irrelevant in this explanation of the

mate's conduct escaped him at the time. The full moon had emerged from behind the racing clouds, and it brightened her face, fringed by the tangled hair and yellow sou'-wester, to an unearthly beauty that he had never seen before. He wondered at it, and for a moment a grisly thought crossed his mind that this was not life, but death; that he had died in the fall, and in some manner the girl had followed.

She was standing erect, her lithe figure swaying to the boat's motion, and pointing to leeward, while the moonlit face was now sweetened by the smile of a happy child. He stood up, and looked where she pointed, but saw nothing, and seated himself to look at her.

"See!" she exclaimed gleefully. "They have hauled out the spanker and are sheeting home the royal. I will never be married! I will never be married! He knew I was with you."

Again he stood up and searched the sea to leeward. There was nothing in sight.

"Unhinged," he thought, "by this night's trouble. Freda," he said gently, "please sit down. You may fall overboard."

"I am not insane," she said, as though reading his thought; and, smiling radiantly in his face, she obeyed him.

"Do you know where we are?" he asked tentatively. "Are we in the track of ships?"

"No," she answered, while her face took on the dreamy look again. "We are out of all the tracks. We will not be picked up. We are due west from Ilio Island. I saw it at sundown broad on the starboard bow. The wind is due south. If you will pull in the trough of the sea we can reach it before daylight. I am tired—so tired—and sleepy. Will you watch out?"

"Why, certainly. Lie down in the stern-sheets and sleep if you can."

She curled up in her yellow oil-coat and slumbered through the night, while he pulled easily on the oars—not that he had full faith in her navigation, but to keep himself warm. The sea became smoother, and as the moon rose higher, it attained a brightness almost equal to that of the sun, casting over the clear sky a deep-blue tint that shaded indefinitely into the darkness extending from itself to the horizon. Late in the night he remembered the danger of sleeping in strong moonlight, and arising softly to cover her face with his damp handkerchief, he found her looking at him.

"We are almost there, John. Wake me when we arrive," she said, and closed her eyes.

He covered her face, and marveling at her words, looked ahead. He was within a half-mile of a sandy beach which bordered a wooded island. The sea was now like glass in its level smoothness and the air was warm and fragrant with the smell of flowers and foliage. He shipped the oars, and pulled to the beach. As the boat grounded she arose, and he helped her ashore.

The beach shone white under the moonlight, and dotting it were large shellfish and moving crabs that scuttled away from them. Bordering the beach were forest and undergrowth with interlacery of flowering vines. A ridge of rocks near by disclosed caves and hollows, some filled by the water of tinkling cascades. Oranges showed in the branches of trees, and cocoa-palms lifted their heads high in the distance. A small deer arose, looked at them, and lay down, while a rabbit inspected them from another direction and began nibbling.

"An earthly paradise, I should say," he observed, as he hauled the boat up the beach. "Plenty of food and water, at any rate."

"It is Ilio Island," she answered, with that same dreamy voice. "It is uninhabited and never visited."

"But surely, Freda, something will come along and take us off."

"No; if I am taken off I must be married, of course; and I will never be married."

"Who to, Freda? Whom must you marry if we are rescued?"

"The mate—Mr. Adams. Not you, John Owen —not you. I do not like you."

She was unbalanced, of course; but the speech pained him immeasurably, and he made no answer. He searched the clean-cut horizon for a moment, and when he looked back she was close to him, with the infantile smile on her face, candor and sanity in her gray eyes. Involuntarily he extended his arms, and she nestled within them.

"You *will* be married, Freda," he said; "you *will* be married, and to me."

He held her tightly and kissed her lips; but the kiss ended in a crashing sound, and a shock of pain in his whole body which expelled the breath from his lungs. The moonlit island, sandy beach, blue sea and sky were swallowed in a blaze of light, which gave way to pitchy darkness, with rain on his face and whistling wind in his ears, while he clung with both arms, not to a girl, but to a hard wet, and cold mizzentopgallant-yard whose iron jack-stay had

bumped him severely between the eyes.   Below him
in the darkness a scream rang out followed by the
roar of the mate: "Are you all right up there?
Want any help?"

He had fallen four feet.

When he could speak he answered: "I'm all right,
sir."   And catching the royal foot-rope dangling
from the end of the yard above him, he brought it
to its place, passed the seizing, and finished furling
the royal.   But it was a long job; his movements
were uncertain, for every nerve in his body was jump-
ing in its own inharmonious key.

"What's the matter wi' you up there?" demanded
the mate when he reached the deck; and a yellow-
clad figure drew near to listen.

"It was nothing, sir; I forgot about the foot-
rope."

"You're a bigger lunkhead than I thought.   Go
forrard."

He went, and when he came aft at four bells to
take his trick at the wheel, the girl was still on
deck, standing near the companionway, facing forward.   The mate stood at the other side of the binnacle, looking at her, with one elbow resting on the
house.   There was just light enough from the cabin
skylight for Owen to see the expression which came
over his face as he watched the graceful figure bal-
ancing to the heave of the ship.   It took on the same
evil look which he had seen in his fall, while there
was no mistaking the thought behind the gleam in
his eyes.   The mate looked up,—into Owen's face,—
and saw something there which he must have understood; for he dropped his glance to the compass,
snarled out, "Keep her on the course," and stepped

into the lee alleyway, where the dinghy, lashed up-
side down on the house, hid him from view.

The girl approached the man at the wheel.

"I saw you fall, Mr. Owen," she said in a trembling voice, "and I could not help screaming. Were
you hurt much?"

"No, Miss Folsom," he answered in a low though
not a steady tone; "but I was sadly disappointed."

"I confess I was nervous—very nervous—when
you went aloft," she said; "and I cleared away the
life-buoy. Then, when you fell, it slipped out of
my hand and went overboard. Mr. Adams scolded
me. Wasn't it ridiculous?" There were tears and
laughter in the speech.

"Not at all," he said gravely; "it saved my life
—for which I thank you."

"How—why—"

"Who in Sam Hill's been casting off these gripe-
lashings?" growled the voice of the mate behind the
dinghy.

The girl tittered hysterically, and stepped beside
Owen at the wheel, where she patted the moving
spokes, pretending to assist him in steering.

"Miss Freda," said the officer, sternly, as he came
around the corner of the house, "I must ask you
plainly to let things alone; and another thing, please
don't talk to the man at the wheel."

"Will you please mind your own business?" she
almost screamed; and then, crying and laughing together: "If you paid as much attention to your
work as you do to—to—me, men wouldn't fall from
aloft on account of rotten foot-ropes."

The abashed officer went forward, grumbling about
"discipline" and "women aboard ship." When he

was well out of sight in the darkness, the girl turned
suddenly, passed both arms around Owen's neck, ex-
erted a very slight pressure, patted him playfully
on the shoulder as she withdrew them, and sped down
the companionway.

He steered a wild course during that trick, and
well deserved the profane criticism which he received
from the mate.

NEEDS MUST WHEN THE DEVIL DRIVES

HOGGED at bow and stern, her deck sloped at the ends like a truck's platform, while a slight twist in the old hull canted the foremast to port and the mizzen to starboard. It would be hard to know when she was on an even keel. The uneven planking, inboard and out, was scarred like a chopping-block, possibly from a former and intimate acquaintance with the coal trade. Aloft were dingy gray spars, slack hemp rigging, untarred for years, and tan-colored sails, mended with patch upon patch of lighter-hued canvas that seemed about to fall apart from their own weight. She was English-built, bark-rigged, bluff in the bow, square in the stern, unpainted and leaky—on the whole as unkempt and disreputable-looking a craft as ever flew the black flag; and with the clank of the pumps marking time to the wailing squeak of the tiller-ropes, she wallowed through the waves like a log in an eddying tideway.

Even the black flag at the gaff-end wore a makeshift, slovenly air. It was a square section of the bark's foreroyal, painted black around the skull-and-cross-bones design, which had been left the original hue of the canvas. The port-holes were equally slovenly in appearance, being cut through between stanchions with axes instead of saws; and the bulwarks were further disfigured by extra holes smashed through at the stanchions to take the lashings of the gun-breechings. But the guns were bright and cared for, as were the uniforms of the crew; for they had been lately transhipped. Far from home, with a general cargo, this ancient trader had been taken in a fog by Captain Swarth and his men an hour before their own well-found vessel had sunk alongside—which gave them just time to hoist over guns and ammunition. When the fog shifted, the pursuing English war-brig that had riddled the pirate saw nothing but the peaceful old tub ahead, and went on into the fog, looking for the other.

"Any port in a storm, Angel," remarked Captain Swarth, as he flashed his keen eyes over the rickety fabric aloft; "but we'll find a better one soon. How do the boys stand the pumping?"

Mr. Angel Todd, first mate and quartermaster, filled a black pipe before answering. Then, between the first and second deep puffs, he said: "Growlin' —dammum."

"At the work?"

"Yep, and the grub. And they say the 'tween-deck and forecastle smells o' bedbugs and bilge-water, and they want their grog. 'An ungodly witness scorneth judgment: and the mouth of the wicked devoureth iniquity.'" Mr. Todd had been educated for the pulpit; but, going out as a missionary, he had fallen into ungodly ways and taken to the sea, where he was more successful. Many of his old phrasings clung to him.

"Well," drawled the captain, "men get fastidious and high-toned in this business,—can't blame them, —but we've got to make the coast, and if we don't pick up something on the way, we must careen and stop the leak. Then they'll have something to growl about."

" S'pose the brig follows us in? "

" Hope she will," said Captain Swarth, with a pleasant smile and a lightening of his eyes—" hope she will, and give me a chance. Her majestic widow-ship owes me a brig, and that's a fine one."

Mr. Todd had never been known to smile, but at this speech he lifted one eyebrow and turned his saturnine face full at his superior, inquiry written upon every line of it. Captain Swarth was musing, however, and said no more; so the mate, knowing better than to attempt probing his mind, swung his long figure down the poop-ladder, and went forward to harass the men—which, in their opinion, was all he was good for.

According to his mood, Mr. Todd's speech was choicest English or the cosmopolitan, technical slang of the sea, mingled with wonderful profanity. But one habit of his early days he never dropped: he wore, in the hottest weather, and in storm and battle, the black frock and choker of the clerical profession. Standing now with one foot on the fore-hatch, waving his long arms and objurgating the scowling men at the pumps, he might easily have seemed, to any one beyond the reach of his language, to be a clergy-man exhorting them. Captain Swarth watched him with an amused look on his sunburnt face, and muttered: " Good man, every inch of him, but he can't handle men." Then he called him aft.

" Angel," he said, " we made a mistake in cutting the ports; we can't catch anything afloat that sees them, so we'll have to pass for a peaceable craft until we can drift close enough to board something. I think the brig'll be back this way, too. Get out some old tarpaulins and cover up the ports. Paint them, if you can, the color of the sides, and you might coil some lines over the rail, as though to dry. Then you can break out cargo and strike the guns down the main-hatch."

Three days later, with Cape St. Roque a black line to the westward, a round shot across her bows brought the old vessel—minus the black emblem now, and outwardly respectable—up to the wind, with maintopsail aback, while Captain Swarth and a dozen of his men—equally respectable in the nondescript rig of the merchant sailor—watched the approach of an English brig of war. Mr. Todd and the rest of the crew were below hatches with the guns.

The brig came down the wind like a graceful bird —a splendid craft, black, shiny, and shipshape, five guns to a side, brass-bound officers on her quarter-deck, blue-jackets darting about her white deck and up aloft, a homeward-bound pennant trailing from her main-truck, and at her gaff-end a British ensign as large as her mainroyal. Captain Swarth lazily hoisted the English flag to the bark's gaff, and, as the brig rounded to on his weather beam, he pointed to it; but his dark eyes sparkled enviously as he viewed the craft whose government's protection he appealed to.

"Bark ahoy!" came a voice through a trumpet. "What bark is that?"

Captain Swarth swung himself into the mizzen-rigging and answered through his hands with an excellent cockney accent: "*Tryde Wind* o' Lunnon, Cappen Quirk, fifty-one dyes out fro' Liverpool, bound to Callao, gen'ral cargo."

"You were not heading for the Horn."

" Hi'm a-leakin' badly. Hi'm a-goin' to myke the coast to careen. D'ye happen to know a good place? "

An officer left the group and returned with what Captain Swarth knew was a chart, which a few of them studied, while their captain hailed again:

" See anything more of that pirate brig the other day? "

" What! a pirate? Be 'e a pirate? " answered Captain Swarth, in agitated tones. " Be that you a-chasin' of 'im? Nao, hi seed nothink of 'im arter the fog shut 'im out."

The captain conferred with his officers a moment, then called:

" We are going in to careen ourselves. That fellow struck us on the water-line. We are homeward bound, and Rio's too far to run back. Follow us in; but if you lose sight of us, it's a small bay, latitude nine fifty-one forty south, rocks to the north, lowland to the south, good water at the entrance, and a fine beach. Look out for the brig. It's Swarth and his gang. Good morning."

" Aye, that hi will. Thank ye. Good marnin'."

In three hours the brig was a speck under the rising land ahead; in another, she was out of sight; but before this Captain Swarth and his crew had held a long conference, which resulted in sail being shortened, though the man at the wheel was given a straight course to the bay described by the English captain.

Late on the following afternoon the old bark blundered into this bay—a rippling sheet of water, bag-shaped, and bordered on all sides by a sandy beach. Stretching up to the mountainous country was a luxurious forest of palm, laurel, and cactus, bound and intertwined by almost impassable undergrowth, and about half-way from the entrance to the end of the bay was the English brig, moored and slightly careened on the inshore beach. Captain Swarth's seamanly eye noted certain appearances of the tackles that held her down, which told him that the work was done and she was being slacked upright. "Just in time," he muttered.

They brought the bark to anchor near the beach, about a half-mile from the brig, furled the canvas, and ran out an anchor astern, with the cable over the taffrail. Heaving on this, they brought the vessel parallel with the shore. So far, good. Guns and cargo lightered ashore, more anchors seaward to keep her off the beach, masthead tackles to the, trees to heave her down, and preventer rigging and braces to assist the masts, would have been next in order, but they proceeded no further toward careening. Instead, they lowered the two crazy boats, provisioned and armed them on the inshore side of the bark, made certain other preparations—and waited.

On the deck of the English brig things were moving. A gang of blue-jackets, under the first lieutenant, were heaving in the cable; another gang, under the boatswain, were sending down and stowing away the heavy tackles and careening-gear, tailing out halyards and sheets and coiling down the light-running rigging, while topmen aloft loosed the canvas to bunt-gaskets, ready to drop it at the call from the deck.

The second lieutenant, overseeing this latter, paced the port quarter-deck and answered remarks from Captain Bunce, who paced the sacred starboard side (the brig being at anchor) and occasionally turned his glass on the dilapidated craft down the beach.

" Seems to me, Mr. Shack," he said across the deck, "that an owner who would send that bark around the Horn, and the master who would take her, ought to be sequestered and cared for, either in an asylum or in jail."

" Yes, sir, I think so too," answered the second lieutenant, looking aft. " Might be an insurance job. Clear away that bunt-gasket on the royal-yard," he added in a roar.

Captain Bunce—round, rosy, with brilliant mutton-chop whiskers—muttered: " Insurance—wrecked intentionally—no, not here where we are; wouldn't court investigation by her Majesty's officers." He rolled forward, then aft, and looked again through the glass.

" Very large crew—very large," he said; " very curious, Mr. Shack."

A hail from the forecastle, announcing that the anchor was short, prevented Mr. Shack's answering. Captain Bunce waved a deprecatory hand to the first lieutenant, who came aft at once, while Mr. Shack descended to the waist, and the boatswain ascended to the forecastle steps to attend to the anchor. The first lieutenant now had charge, and from the quarter-deck gave his orders to the crew, while Captain Bunce busied himself with his glass and his thoughts.

Fore-and-aft sail was set and head-sheets trimmed down to port, square sails were dropped, sheeted home, and hoisted, foreyards braced to port, the anchor tripped and fished, and the brig paid off from the land-breeze, and, with foreyards swung, steadied down to a course for the entrance.

"Mr. Duncan," said the captain, "there are fully forty men on that bark's deck, all dressed alike—all in red shirts and knitted caps—and all dancing around like madmen. Look!" He handed the glass to the first lieutenant, who brought it to bear.

"Strange," said the officer, after a short scrutiny; "there were only a few showing when we spoke her outside. It looks as though they were all drunk."

As they drew near, sounds of singing—uproarious discord—reached them, and soon they could see with the naked eye that the men on the bark were wrestling, dancing, and running about.

"Quarters, sir?" inquired Mr. Duncan. "Shall we bring to alongside?"

"Well—no—not yet," said the captain, hesitatingly; "it's all right—possibly; yet it is strange. Wait a little."

They waited, and had sailed down almost abreast of the gray old craft, noticing, as they drew near, an appreciable diminution of the uproar, when a flag arose from the stern of the bark, a dusky flag that straightened out directly tward them, so that it was difficult to make out.

But they soon understood. As they reached a point squarely abreast of the bark, five points of flame burst from her innocent gray sides, five clouds of smoke ascended, and five round shot, coming with the thunder of the guns, hurtled through their rigging. Then they saw the design of the flag, a white skull and cross-bones, and noted another, a black flag too, but pennant-shaped, and showing in rudely painted letters the single word "Swarth," sailing up to the forepeak.

"Thunder and lightning!" roared Captain Bunce.

" Quarters, Mr. Duncan, quarters, and in with the kites. Give it to them. Put about first."

A youngster of the crew had sprung below and immediately emerged with a drum which, without definite instruction, he hammered vigorously; but before he had begun, men were clearing away guns and manning flying-jib downhaul and royal clue-lines. Others sprang to stations, anticipating all that the sharp voice of the first lieutenant could order. Around came the brig on the other tack and sailed back, receiving another broadside through her rigging and answering with her starboard guns. Then for a time the din was deafening. The brig backed her main-yards and sent broadside after broadside into the hull of the old craft. But it was not until the eighth had gone that Captain Bunce noticed through the smoke that the pirates were not firing. The smoke from the burning canvas port-coverings had deluded him. He ordered a cessation. Fully forty solid shot had torn through that old hull near the water-line, and not a man could now be seen on her deck.

" Out with the boats, Mr. Duncan," he said; " they're drunk or crazy, but they're the men we want. Capture them."

" Suppose they run, sir—suppose they take to their boats and get into the woods—shall we follow? "

" No, not past the beach—not into an ambush."

The four boat-loads of men which put off from the brig found nothing but a deserted deck on the sinking bark and two empty boats hauled up on the beach. The pirates were in the woods, undoubtedly, having kept the bark between themselves and the brig as they pulled ashore. While the blue-jackets clustered around the bows of their boats and watched nervously the line of forest up the beach, from which bullets might come at any time, the two lieutenants conferred for a few moments, and had decided to put back, when a rattling chorus of pistol reports sounded from the depths of the woods. It died away; then was heard a crashing of bush and branch, and out upon the sands sprang a figure—a long, weird figure in black frock of clerical cut. Into their midst it sped with mighty bounds, and sinking down, lifted a glad face to the heavens with the groaning utterance: "O God, I thank thee. Protect me, gentlemen—protect me from those wicked men."

"What is it? Who are you?" asked Mr. Duncan. "Were they shooting at you?"

"Yes, at me, who never harmed a fly. They would have killed me. My name is Todd. Oh, such suffering! But you will protect me? You are English officers. You are not pirates and murderers."

"But what has happened? Do you live around here?"

It took some time for Mr. Todd to quiet down sufficiently to tell his story coherently. He was an humble laborer in the vineyard of the Lord. He had gleaned among the poorest of the native population in the outskirts of Rio de Janeiro until his health suffered, and had taken passage home in a passenger-ship, which, ten days out, was captured by a pirate brig. And the pirate crew had murdered every soul on board but himself, and only spared his life, as he thought, for the purpose of amusement; for they had compelled him to dance—he, a minister of the gospel—and had made him drink under torture, and recite ribald poetry, and swear, and wash their clothes. All sorts of indignities had been heaped upon him, but he had remembered the injunction of the Master; he had invariably turned the other cheek when smitten, and had prayed for their souls. He told of the flight from the English war-brig, of the taking of the old bark in the fog and the sinking of the pirate craft, of the transfer of guns and treasure to the bark, and the interview at sea with the English brig, in which Captain Swarth had deceived the other, and of Captain Swarth's reckless confidence in himself, which had induced him to follow the brig in and careen in the same bay. He wound up his tale with a lurid description of the drunken debauch following the anchoring of the bark,—during which he had trembled for his life,—of the insane firing on the brig as she passed, and the tumbling into the boats when the brig returned the fire, of the flight into the woods, the fighting among themselves, and his escape under fire.

As he finished he offered an incoherent prayer of thankfulness, and the sympathetic Mr. Shack drew forth his pocket-flask and offered it to the agitated sufferer; but Mr. Todd, who could probably drink more whisky and feel it less than any other man in the pirate crew, declined the poison with a shiver of abhorrence. Then Mr. Duncan, who had listened thoughtfully, said: "You speak of treasure; did they take it with them?"

Mr. Todd opened wide his eyes, looked toward the dark shades of the forest, then at the three masts of the bark rising out of the water, and answered impressively:

"Gentlemen, they did not. They were intoxicated

—mad with liquor. They took arms and a knapsack of food to each man,—they spoke of an inland retreat to which they were going,—but the treasure from the passenger-hip—the bars of gold and the bags of diamonds—they forgot. They transferred it from their sinking vessel when sober, but when intoxicated they remembered food and left it behind. Gentlemen, there is untold wealth in the hull out there which your fire has sunk. It is, verily, the root of all evil; let us hope that it remains at the bottom of the sea."

"Bars of gold—bags of diamonds!" said Mr. Duncan. "Come on board, Mr. Todd; we'll see what the captain thinks."

At dinner in the brig's cabin that evening—as a prelude to which Mr. Todd said grace—his account of the wealth spread out on Captain Swarth's cabin table after the taking of the passenger-ship was something to arouse interest in a less worldly man than Captain Bunce. Virgin gold—in bars, ingots, bricks, and dust—from the Morro Velho mines of Brazil was there, piled up on the table until the legs had given way and launched the glittering mass to the floor. Diamonds uncut, uncounted, of untold value,—a three years' product of the whole Chapada district,—some as large as walnuts, had been spread out and tossed about like marbles by those lawless men, then boxed up with the gold and stowed among the cargo under the main-hatch. Again Mr. Todd expressed the hope that Providence would see fit to let this treasure remain where the pirates had left it, no longer to tempt man to kill and steal. But Captain Bunce and his officers thought differently. Glances, then tentative comments, were exchanged, and in five minutes they were of one mind, even including Mr. Todd; for it may not be needless to state that the treasure and the passenger-ship existed only in his imagination.

Pending the return of the boats the brig's anchor had been dropped about two hundred yards from the bark; now canvas was furled, and at eight bells all hands were mustered aft to hear what was in store. Captain Bunce stated the case succinctly; they were homeward bound and under general orders until they reported to the admiral at Plymouth. Treasure was within their reach, apportionable, when obtained, as prize-money. It was useless to pursue the pirates into the Brazilian jungle; but they would need to be watchful and ready for surprise at any moment, either while at work raising the bark or at night; for though they had brought out the two boats in which the pirates had escaped, they could find other means of attack, should they dare or care to make it. The English sailors cheered. Mr. Todd begged to say a few words, and enjoined them not to allow the love of lucre to tempt their minds from the duty they owed to their God, their country, and their captain, which was also applauded and forgotten in a moment. Then, leaving a double-anchor watch, provided with blue fire and strict instructions, on deck, the crew turned in to dream of an affluent future, and Mr. Todd was shown to a comfortable stateroom. He removed his coat and vest, closed the door and dead-light, filled and lighted his black pipe, and rolled into the berth with a seaman's sigh of contentment.

"That was a good dinner," he murmured, after he had filled the room with smoke—" a good dinner. Nothing on earth is too good for a sky-pilot. I'd go back to the business when I've made my pile, if it wasn't so all-fired hard on the throat; and then the trustees, with their eternal kicking on economy, and the sisters, and the donation-parties—yah, to h—l with 'em! Wonder if this brig ever carried a chaplain? Wonder how Bill and the boys are making out? Fine brig, this,—'leven knots on a bow-line, I'll bet,—fine state-room, good grub, nothin' to do but save souls and preach the Word on Sunday. Guess I'll strike the fat—duffer—for the—job—in —the—morn—" The rest of the sentence merged into a snore, and Mr. Todd slept through the night in the fumes of tobacco, which so permeated his very being that Captain Bunce remarked it at breakfast. "Smoke, Captain Bunce? I smoke? Not I," he answered warmly; "but, you see, those ungodly men compelled me to clean all their pipes,—forty foul pipes,—and I do not doubt that some nicotine has lodged on my clothing." Whereupon Captain Bunce told of a chaplain he had once sailed with whose clothing smelled so vilely that he himself had framed a petition to the admiral for his transfer to another ship and station. And the little story had the effect on Mr. Todd of causing him mentally to vow that he'd " ship with no man who didn't allow smoking," and openly aver that no sincere, consistent Christian clergyman would be satisfied to stultify himself and waste his energies in the comfort and ease of a naval chaplaincy, and that a chaplain who would smoke should be discredited and forced out of the profession. But later, when Captain Bunce and his officers lighted fat cigars, and he learned that the aforesaid chaplain had merely been a careless devotee of pipe and pigtail twist, Mr. Todd's feelings may be imagined (by a smoker); but he had committed himself against tobacco and must suffer.

During the breakfast the two lieutenants reported the results of a survey which they had taken of the wreck at daylight.

"We find," said Mr. Duncan, "about nine feet of water over the deck at the stern, and about three feet over the fore-hatch at low tide. The topgallant-forecastle is awash and the end of the bowsprit out of water, so that we can easily reach the upper ends of the bob-stays. There is about five feet rise and fall of tide. Now, we have no pontoons nor casks. Our only plan, captain, is to lift her bodily."

"But we have a diving-suit and air-pump," said Mr. Shack, enthusiastically, "and fifty men ready to dive without suits. We can raise her, captain, in two weeks."

"Gentlemen," said Captain Bunce, grandly, "I have full faith in your seamanship and skill. I leave the work in your hands." Which was equivalent to an admission that he was fat and lazy, and did not care to take an active part.

"Thank you, sir," said Mr. Duncan, and "Thank you, sir," said Mr. Shack; then the captain said other pleasant things, which brought other pleasant responses, and the breakfast passed off so agreeably that Mr. Todd, in spite of the soul-felt yearning for a smoke inspired by the cigars in the mouths of the others, felt the influence of the enthusiasm and bestowed his blessing—qualifiedly—on the enterprise.

Every man of the brig's crew was eager for the work, but few could engage at first; for there was nothing but the forecastle-deck and the bark's rigging to stand upon. Down came the disgraceful black flags the first thing, and up to the gaff went the ensign of Britain. Then they sent down the fore and main lower and topsail yards, and erected them as sheers over the bow and stern, lower ends well socketed in spare anchor-stocks to prevent their sinking in the sand, upper ends lashed together and stayed to each other and to the two anchors ahead and astern. To the sheer-heads they rigged heavy threefold tackles, and to the disconnected bobstays (chains leading from the bowsprit end to the stem at the water-line) they hooked the forward tackle, and heaving on the submerged windlass, lifted the bow off the bottom—high enough to enable them to slip two shots of anchor-chain under the keel, one to take the weight at the stern, the other at the bow, for the bobstays would pull out of the stem under the increased strain as the bark arose.

Most of this work was done under water; but a wetting is nothing to men looking for gold, and nobody cared. Yet, as a result of ruined uniforms, the order came from Captain Bunce to wear underclothing only or go naked, which latter the men preferred, though the officers clung to decency and tarry duck trousers. Every morning the day began with the washing of the brig's deck and scouring of brasswork—which must be done at sea though the heavens fall; then followed breakfast, the arming of the boats ready for an attack from the shore, and the descent upon the bark of as many men as could work.

Occasionally Captain Bunce would order the dinghy, and, accompanied by Mr. Todd, would visit the bark and offer interfering suggestions, after the manner of captains, which only embarrassed the officers; and Mr. Todd would take advantage of these occasions to make landlubberly comments and show a sad ignorance of things nautical. But often he would decline the invitation, and when the captain was gone would descend to his room, and, shutting the door, grip his beloved—though empty—black pipe between his teeth and breathe through it, while his eyes shone fiercely with unsatisfied desire, and his mind framed silent malediction on Bill Swarth for condemning him to this smokeless sojourn. For he dared not smoke; stewards, cooks, and sailors were all about him.

In three days the bark's nose was as high as the seven-part tackle would bring it, with all men heaving who could find room at the windlass-brakes. Then they clapped a luff-tackle on the fall, and by heaving on this, nippering and fleeting up, they lifted the fore-hatch and forecastle scuttle out of water—which was enough. Before this another gang had been able to slip the other chain to position abaft the mizzenmast, hook on the tackle, and lead the fall through a snatch-block at the quarter-bitts forward to the midship capstan. Disdaining the diving-suit, they swam down nine feet to do these things, and when they had towed the rope forward they descended seven feet to wind it around the capstan and ship the bars, which they found in a rack at the mainmast.

A man in the water weighs practically nothing, and to heave around a capstan under water requires lateral resistance. To secure this they dived with hammers and nails, and fastened a circle of cleats to catch their feet. Then with a boy on the main fiferail (his head out) holding slack, eighteen men— three to a bar—would inhale all the air their lungs could hold, and, with a "One, two, three," would flounder down, push the capstan around a few pawls, and come up gasping, and blue in the face to perch on their bars and recover. It went slowly, this end, but in three days more they could walk around with their heads above water.

The next day was Sunday, and they were entitled to rest; but the flavor of wealth had entered their souls, and they petitioned the captain for privilege to work, which was granted, to the satisfaction of the officers, and against the vigorous protest of Mr. Todd, who had prepared a sermon and borrowed clean linen from Mr. Shack in which to deliver it.

With luff-tackles on the fall they hove the stern up until the cabin doors and all deck-openings but the main-hatch were out of water, and then, with the bark hanging to the sheers as a swinging-cradle hangs from its supports, some assisted the carpenter and his mates in building up and calking an upward extension of the main-hatch coaming that reached above water at high tide, while others went over the side looking for the shot-holes of eight broadsides. These, when found, were covered with planking, followed by canvas, nails being driven with shackles, sounding-leads, and stones from the bottom in the hands of naked men clinging to weighted stagings— men whose eyes protruded, whose lungs ached, whose brains were turning.

Then, and before a final inspection by the boatswain in the diving-suit assured them that the last shot-hole was covered, they began bailing from the main-hatch, and when the water perceptibly lowered —the first index of success—a feverish yell arose and continued, while nude lunatics wrestled and floundered waist-deep on the flooded deck. The bark's pumps were manned and worked under water, bailing-pumps—square tubes with one valve—were made and plunged up and down in each hatch, whips were rigged, and buckets rose and fell until the obstructing cargo confined the work to the bark's pumps. Can-hooks replaced the buckets on the whips, then boxes and barrels were hoisted, broken into, and thrown overboard, until the surface of the bay was dotted with them. They drifted back and forth with the tide, some stranding on the beach, others floating seaward through the inlet. And all the time that they worked, sharp eyes had watched through the bushes, and a few miles inland, in a glade surrounded by the giant trees of the Brazilian forest, red-shirted men lolled and smoked and grew fat, while they discussed around the central fire the qualities of barbecued wild oxen, roast opossum and venison, and criticised the seamanship of the Englishmen.

With a clear deck to work on, every man and boy of the brig's crew, except the idlers (stewards, cooks, and servants), was requisitioned, and boxes flew merrily; but night closed down on the tenth day of their labor without sign of the treasure, and now Mr. Todd, who had noticed a shade of testiness in the queries of the officers as to the exact location of the gold and diamonds, expressed a desire to climb the rigging next afternoon, a feat he had often wished to perform, which he did clumsily, going through the lubber's hole, and seated in the maintop with Mr. Duncan's Bible, he remained in quiet meditation and apparent reading and prayer until the tropic day changed to sudden twilight and darkness, and the hysterical crew returned. Then he came down to dinner.

In the morning the work was resumed, and more boxes sprinkled the bay. They drifted up with the flood, and came back with the ebb-tide; but among them now were about forty others, unobserved by Captain Bunce, pacing his quarter-deck, but noted keenly by Mr. Todd. These forty drifted slowly to the offshore side of the brig and stopped, bobbing up and down on the crisp waves, even though the wind blew briskly with the tide, and they should have gone on with the others. It was then that Captain Bunce stepped below for a cigar, and it was then that Mr. Todd became strangely excited, hopping along the port-rail and throwing overboard every rope's end within reach, to the wonder and scandal of an open-eyed steward in the cabin door, who immediately apprised the captain.

Captain Bunce, smoking a freshly lit cigar, emerged to witness a shocking sight—the good and godly Mr. Todd, with an intense expression on his somber countenance, holding a match to a black pipe and puffing vigorously, while through the ports and over the rail red-shirted men, dripping wet and scowling, were boarding his brig. Each man carried a cutlass and twelve-inch knife, and Captain Bunce needed no special intelligence to know that he was tricked.

One hail only he gave, and Mr. Todd, his pipe glowing like a hot coal, was upon him. The captain endeavored to draw his sword, but sinewy arms encircled him; his cigar was removed from his lips and inserted in the mouth of Mr. Todd alongside the pipe; then he was lifted, spluttering with astonishment and rage, borne to the rail and dropped overboard, his sword clanking against the side as he descended. When he came to the surface and looked up, he saw through a cloud of smoke on the rail the lantern-jaws of Mr. Todd working convulsively on pipe and cigar, and heard the angry utterance: "Yes, d—n ye, I smoke." Then a vibrant voice behind Mr. Todd roared out: "Kill nobody—toss 'em overboard," and the captain saw his servants, cooks, and stewards tumbling over to join him.

Captain Bunce turned and swam—there was nothing else to do. Soon he could see a black-eyed, black-mustached man on his quarter-deck delivering orders, and he recognized the thundering voice, but none of the cockney accent of Captain Quirk. Men were already on the yards loosing canvas; and as he turned on his back to rest—for, though fleshy and buoyant, swimming in full uniform fatigued him—he saw his anchor-chains whizzing out the hawse-pipes.

He was picked up by the first boat to put off from the bark, and ordered pursuit; but this was soon seen to be useless. The clean-lined brig had sternway equal to the best speed of the boats, and now head-sails were run up, and she paid off from the shore. Topsails were sheeted home and hoisted, she gathered way, and with topgallantsails and royals, spanker and staysails, following in quick succession, the beautiful craft hummed down to the inlet and put to sea, while yells of derision occasionally came back to the white-faced men in the boats.

A month later the rehabilitated old bark also staggered out the entrance, and, with a naked, half-starved crew and sad-eyed, dilapidated officers, headed southward for Rio de Janeiro.

WHEN GREEK MEETS GREEK

"Thrice is he armed that hath his quarrel just."

BARD OF AVON.

"But 4 times he who gits hiz blo' in fust."

JOSH BILLINGS.

CAPTAIN WILLIAM BELCHIOR was more than a martinet. He was known as "Bucko" Belchior in every port where the English language is spoken, having earned this prefix by the earnest readiness with which, in his days as second and chief mate, he would whirl belaying-pins, heavers, and handspikes about the decks, and by his success in knocking down, tricing up, and working up sailors who displeased him. With a blow of his fist he had broken the jaw of a man helplessly ironed in the 'tween-deck, and on the same voyage, armed with a simple belaying-pin, had sprung alone into a circle of brandishing sheath-knives and quelled a mutiny. He was short, broad, beetle-browed, and gray-eyed, of undoubted courage, but with the quality of sympathy left out of his nature.

During the ten years in which he had been in command, he was relieved of much of the executive work that had made him famous.when he stood watch, but was always ready to justify his reputation as a "bucko" should friction with the crew occur past the power of his officers to cope with. His ship, the *Wilmington*, a skysail-yard clipper, was rated by sailormen as the "hottest" craft under the American flag, and Captain Belchior himself was spoken of by

213

consuls and commissioners, far and near, as a man peculiarly unfortunate in his selection of men; for never a passage ended but he was complainant against one or more heavily ironed and badly used-up members of his crew.

His officers were, in the language of one of these defendants, " o' the same breed o' dorg." No others could or would sign with him. His crews were invariably put on board in the stream or at anchorage —never at the dock. Drunk when coerced by the boarding-masters into signing the ship's articles, kept drunk until delivery, they were driven or hoisted up the side like animals—some in a stupor from drink or drugs, some tied hand and foot, struggling and cursing with returning reason.

Equipped thus, the *Wilmington*, bound for Melbourne, discharged her tug and pilot off Sandy Hook one summer morning, and, with a fresh quartering wind and raising sea, headed for the southeast. The day was spent in getting her sail on, and in the " licking into shape " of the men as fast as they recovered their senses. Oaths and missiles flew about the deck, knock-downs were frequent, and by eight bells in the evening, when the two mates chose the watches,—much as boys choose sides in a ball game, —the sailors were well convinced that their masters lived aft.

Three men, long-haired fellows, sprawling on the main-hatch, helpless from seasickness, were left to the last in the choosing and then hustled into the light from the near-by galley door to be examined. They had been dragged from the forecastle at the mate's call for " all hands."

" Call yourselves able seamen, I suppose," he said

with an oath, as he glared into their woebe-
gone faces.

"No, pard," said the tallest and oldest of the
three, in a weak voice. "We're not seamen; we
don't know how we got here, neither."

The mate's answer was a fist-blow under the ear
that sent the man headlong into the scuppers, where
he lay quiet.

"Say 'sir' when you speak to me, you bandy-
legged farmers," he snarled, glowering hard at the
other two, as they leaned against the water-tank.
"I'm pard to none of ye."

They made him no answer, and he turned away
in contempt. "Mr. Tomm," he called, "want these
Ethiopians in your watch?"

"No, sir," said the second mate; "I don't want
'em. They're no more use 'an a spare pump."

"I'll make 'em useful 'fore I'm done with 'em.
Go forrard, you three. Get the bile out o' yer giz-
zards 'fore mornin', 'f ye value yer good looks."
He delivered a vicious kick at each of the two standing men, bawled out, "Relieve the wheel an' lookout
—that'll do the watch," and went aft, while the crew
assisted the seasick men to the forecastle and into
three bedless bunks—bedless, because sailors must
furnish their own, and these men had been
shanghaied.

The wind died away during the night, and they
awoke in the morning with their seasickness gone and
appetites ravenous. Somber and ominous was their
bearing as they silently ate of the breakfast in the
forecastle and stepped out on deck with the rest in
answer to the mate's roar: "All hands spread dunnage." Having no dunnage but what they wore, they

drew off toward the windlass and conferred together while chests and bags were dragged out on deck and overhauled by the officers for whisky and sheath-knives. What they found of the former they pocketed, and of the latter, tossed overboard.

"Where are the canal-drivers?" demanded the chief mate, as he raised his head from the last chest. "Where are our seasick gentlemen, who sleep all night—what—what—" he added in a stutter of surprise.

He was looking down three eight-inch barrels of three heavy Colt revolvers, cocked, and held by three scowling, sunburnt men, each of whom was tucking with disengaged left hand the corner of a shirt into a waistband, around which was strapped a belt full of cartridges.

"Hands up!" snapped the tall man; "hands up, every one of ye! Up with 'em—over yer heads. That's right!" The pistols wandered around the heads of the crowd, and every hand was elevated.

"What's this? What d'ye mean? Put them pistols down. Give 'em up. Lay aft, there, some o' ye, and call the captain," blustered the mate, with his hands held high.

Not a man stirred to obey. The scowling faces looked deadly in earnest.

"Right about, face!" commanded the tall man. "March, every man—back to the other end o' the boat. Laramie, take the other side and round up anybody ye see. Now, gentlemen, hurry."

Away went the protesting procession, and, joined by the carpenter, sail-maker, donkey-man, and cook, "rounded up" from their sanctums by the man called Laramie, it had reached the main-hatch before the captain, pacing the quarter-deck, was aware of the disturbance. With Captain Belchior to think was to act. Springing to the cabin skylight, he shouted: "Steward, bring up my pistols. Bear a hand. Lower your weapons, you scoundrels; this is rank mutiny."

A pistol spoke, and the captain's hat left his head. "There goes your hat," said a voice; "now, for a button." Another bullet sped, which cut from his coat the button nearest his heart. "Come down from there—come down," said the voice he had heard. "Next shot goes home. Start while I count three. One—two—" Captain Belchior descended the steps. "Hands up, same as the rest." Up went the captain's hands; such marksmanship was beyond his philosophy. "'Pache," went on the speaker, "go up there and get the guns he wanted." The steward, with two bright revolvers in his hands, was met at the companion-hatch by a man with but one; but that one was so big, and the hand which held it was so steady, that it was no matter of surprise that he obeyed the terse command, "Fork over, handles first." The captain's nickel-plated pistols went into the pockets of 'Pache's coat, and the white-faced steward, poked in the back by the muzzle of that' big firearm, marched to the main-deck and joined the others.

"Go down that place, 'Pache, and chase out any one else ye find," called the leader from behind the crowd. "Bring 'em all down here."

'Pache descended, and reappeared with a frightened cabin-boy, whom, with the man at the wheel, he drove before him to the steps. There was no wind, and the ship could spare the helmsman.

" Now, then, gentlemen," said the tall leader, " I
reckon we're all here. Keep yer hands up. We'll
have a powwow. 'Pache, stay up there, and you,
Laramie, cover 'em from behind. Plug the first man
that moves."

He mounted the steps to the quarter-deck, and,
as he replaced empty shells with cartridges, looked
down on them with a serene smile on his not ill-
looking face. His voice, except when raised in ac-
cents of command, had in it the musical, drawling,
plaintive tone so peculiar to the native Texan—and
so deceptive. The other two, younger and rougher
men, looked, as they glanced at their victims through
the sights of the pistols, as though they longed for
the word of permission to riddle the ship's company
with bullets.

" You'll pay for this, you infernal cutthroats,"
spluttered the captain. " This is piracy."

" Don't call any names now," said the tall man;
" 'tain't healthy. We don't want to hurt ye, but I
tell ye seriously, ye never were nearer death than
ye are now. It's a risky thing, and a foolish thing,
too, gentlemen, to steal three American citizens with
guns under their shirts, and take 'em so far from land
as this. Hangin' 's the fit and proper punishment
for hoss-stealin', but man-stealin's 's so great a crime
that I'm not right sure what the punishment is.
Now, we don't know much 'bout boats and ropes,—
though we can tie a hangman's knot when necessary,—but we do know somethin' 'bout guns and
human natur'—here, you, come 'way from that
fence."

The captain was edging toward a belaying-pin;
but he noticed that the speaker's voice had lost its

plaintiveness, and three tubes were looking at him.
He drew inboard, and the leader resumed:

"Now, fust thing, who's foreman o' this outfit?
Who's boss?"

"I'm captain here."

"You are? You are not. I'm captain. Get up
on that shanty." The small house over the mizzen-
hatch was indicated, and Captain Belchior climbed it.
The tubes were still looking at him.

"Now, you, there, you man who hit me last night
when I was sick, who are you, and what?"

"Mate, d—— you."

"Up with you, and don't cuss. You did a cowardly thing, pardner—an unmanly thing—low down
and or'nary. You don't deserve to live any longer;
but my darter, back East at school, thinks I've
killed enough men for one lifetime, and mebbe she's
right—mebbe she's right. Anyhow, she don't like it,
and that lets you out—though I won't answer for
'Pache and Laramie when my back's turned. You
kicked 'em both. But I'll just return the blow."
The mate had but straightened up on top of the
hatch-house when the terrible pistol spat out another
red tongue, and his yell followed the report, as he
clapped his hand to the ear through which the bullet
had torn.

"Hands up, there!" thundered the shooter, and
the mate obeyed, while a stream of blood ran down
inside his shirt-collar.

"Any more bosses here?"

The second mate did not respond; but 'Pache's
pistol sought him out, and under its influence, and
his guttural, "I know you; get up," he followed his
superiors.

" Any more? "

A manly-looking fellow stepped out of the group, and said: " You've got the captain and two mates. I'm bo's'n here, and yonder's my mate. We're next, but we're not bosses in the way o' bein' responsible for anything that has happened or might happen to you. We b'long forrard. There's no call to shoot at the crew, for there's not a man among 'em but what 'ud be glad to see you get ashore, and get there himself."

" Silence, bo's'n," bawled the captain. But the voice of authority seemed pitifully ludicrous and incongruous, coupled with the captain's position and attitude, and every face on the deck wore a grin. The leader noticed the silent merriment, and said:

" Laramie, I reckon these men'll stand. You can come up here. I'm gettin' 'long in years, and kind o' steadyin' down, but I s'pose you and 'Pache want some fun. Start yer whistle and turn loose."

Up the steps bounded Laramie, and, with a ringing whoop as a prelude, began whistling a clear, musical trill, while 'Pache, growling out, " Dance, dance, ye white-livered coyotes," sent a bullet through the outer edge of the chief mate's boot-heel.

" Dance," repeated Laramie between bars of the music. *Crack, crack*, went the pistols, while bullets rattled around the feet of the men on the hatch, and Laramie's whistle rose and fell on the soft morning air.

The sun, who has looked on many scandalous sights, looked on this, and hid his face under a cloud, refusing to witness. For never before had the ethics of shipboard life been so outrageously violated. A squat captain and two six-foot officers, nearly black in the face from rage and exertion, with hands clasped over their heads, hopped and skipped around a narrow stage to the accompaniment of pistol reports harmoniously disposed among the notes of a whistled tune, while bullets grazed their feet, and an unkempt, disfigured, and sore-headed crew looked on and chuckled.   When the mate, weak from loss of blood, fell and rolled to the deck, the leader stopped the entertainment.

"Now, gentlemen," he said in his serious voice, "I'm called Pecos Tom, and I've had considerable experience in my time, but this is my fust with human creatur's so weak and thoughtless that they'll drug and steal three men without takin' their guns away from them.   And so, on 'count o' this shiftless improvidence, I reckon this boat will have to turn round and go back."

They bound them, rolled and kicked the two mates to the rail, lifted the captain to his feet, and then the leader said significantly:

"Give the right and proper order to yer men to turn this boat round."

With his face working convulsively, Captain Belchior glanced at his captors, at his eager, waiting crew, at the wheel without a helmsman, at a darkening of the water on the starboard bow to the southward, up aloft and back again at the three frowning muzzles so close to his head.

"One hand to the wheel!   Square in main and cro'-jack yards!" he called.   He was conquered.

With a hurrah which indicated the sincerity of these orders, the crew sprang to obey them, and with foreyards braced to starboard and head-sheets flat, the ship *Wilmington* paid off, wore around, and bringing the young breeze on the port quarter, steadied down to a course for Sandy Hook, which the captain, with hands released, but still under the influence of those threatening pistols, worked out from the mate's dead-reckoning. Then he was pinioned again, but allowed to pace the deck and watch his ship, while the two officers were kept under the rail, sometimes stepped upon or kicked, and often admonished on the evil of their ways.

Early passengers on the East River ferry-boats were treated to a novel sight next morning, which they appreciated according to their nautical knowledge. A lofty ship, with skysails and royals hanging in the buntlines, and jibs tailing ahead like flags, was charging up the harbor before a humming southerly breeze, followed by an elbowing crowd of puffing, whistling, snub-nosed tugs. It was noticeable that whenever a fresh tug arrived alongside, little white clouds left her quarter-deck, and that tug suddenly sheered off to take a position in the parade astern. Abreast of Governor's Island, topgallant-halyards were let go, as were those of the jibs; but no cluing up or hauling down was done, nor were any men seen on her forecastle-deck getting ready lines or ground-tackle. She passed the Battery and up the East River, craft of all kinds getting out of her way,—for it was obvious that something was wrong with her,—until, rounding slowly to a starboard wheel, with canvas rattling and running-gear in bights, she headed straight for a slip partly filled with canal-boats. Now her topsail-halyards were let go, and three heavy yards came down by the run, breaking across the caps; and amid a grinding, creaking, and crashing of riven timbers, and a deafening din of applauding tug whistles, she plowed her way into the nest of canal-boats and came to a stop.

Then was a hejira. Down her black sides by ropes and chain-plates, to the wrecked and sinking canal-boats,—some with bags or chests, some without,—came eager men, who climbed to the dock, and answering no questions of the gathering crowd of dock-loungers, scattered into the side-streets. Then three other men appeared on the rail, who shook their fists, and swore, and shouted for the police, calling particularly for the apprehension of three dark-faced, long-haired fellows with big hats.

In the light of later developments it is known that the police responded, and with the assistance of boarding-house runners gathered in that day nearly all of this derelict crew,—even to the cautious boatswain,—who were promptly and severely punished for mutiny and desertion. But the later developments failed to show that the three dark-faced men were ever seen again.

PRIMORDIAL

GASPING, blue in the face, half drowned, the boy was flung spitefully—as though the sea scorned so poor a victory—high on the sandy beach, where succeeding shorter waves lapped at him and retired. The encircling life-buoy was large enough to permit his crouching within it. Pillowing his head on one side of the smooth ring, he wailed hoarsely for an interval, then slept—or swooned. The tide went down the beach, the typhoon whirled its raging center off to sea, and the tropic moon shone out, lighting up, between the beach and barrier reef, a heaving stretch of oily lagoon on which appeared and disappeared hundreds of shark-fins quickly darting, and, out on the barrier reef, perched high, yet still pounded by the ocean combers raised by the storm, a fragment of ship's stern with a stump of mizzen-mast. The elevated position of the fragment, the quickly darting dorsal fins, and the absence of company for the child on the beach spoke, too plainly, of shipwreck, useless boats, and horrible death.

Sharks must sleep like other creatures, and they nestle in hollows at the bottom and in coral caves, or under overhanging ledges of the reefs which attract them. The first swimmer may pass safely by night, seldom the second. Like she-wolves, fiendish cats, and vicious horses, they have been known to show mercy to children. For one or both reasons, this child had drifted to the beach unharmed.

Anywhere but on a bed of hot sand near the equator the sleep in wet clothing of a three-year-old boy might have been fatal; but salt water carries its own remedy for the evils of its moisture, and he wakened at daylight with strength to rise and cry out his protest of loneliness and misery. His childish mind could record facts, but not their reason or coherency. He was in a new, an unknown world. His mother had filled his old; where was she now? Why had she tied him into that thing and thrown him from her into the darkness and wet? Strange things had happened, which he dimly remembered. He had been roused from his sleep, dressed, and taken out of doors in the dark, where there were frightful crashing noises, shoutings of men, and crying of women and other children. He had cried himself, from sympathy and terror, until his mother had thrown him away. Had he been bad? Was she angry? And after that—what was the rest? He was hungry and thirsty now. Why did she not come? He would go and find her.

With the life-buoy hanging about his waist—though of cork, a heavy weight for him—he toddled along the beach to where it ended at a massive ridge of rock that came out of the wooded country inland and extended into the lagoon as an impassable point. He called the chief word in his vocabulary again and again, sobbing between calls. She was not there, or she would have come; so he went back, glancing fearfully at the dark woods of palm and undergrowth. She might be in there, but he was afraid to look. His little feet carried him a full half-mile in the other direction before the line of trees and bushes reached so close to the beach as to stop him. Here he sat down, screaming passionately and convulsively for his mother.

Crying is an expense of energy which must be replenished by food. When he could cry no longer he tugged at the straps and strings of the life-buoy. But they were wet and hard, his little fingers were weak, and he knew nothing of knots and their untying, so it was well on toward midday before he succeeded in scrambling out of the meshes, by which time he was famished, feverish with thirst, and all but sunstruck. He wandered unsteadily along the beach, falling occasionally, moaning piteously through his parched, open lips; and when he reached the obstructing ridge of rock, turned blindly into the bushes at its base, and followed it until he came to a pool of water formed by a descending spray from above. From this, on his hands and knees, he drank deeply, burying his lips as would an animal.

Instinct alone had guided him here, away from the salt pools on the beach, and impelled him to drink fearlessly. It was instinct—a familiar phase in a child—that induced him to put pebbles, twigs, and small articles in his mouth until he found what was pleasant to his taste and eatable—nuts and berries; and it was instinct, the most ancient and deeply implanted,—the lingering index of an arboreal ancestry,—that now taught him the safety and comfort of these woody shades, and, as night came on, prompted him—as it prompts a drowning man to reach high, and leads a creeping babe to a chair—to attempt climbing a tree. Failing in this from lack of strength, he mounted the rocky wall a few feet, and here, on a narrow ledge, after indulging in a final fit of crying, he slept through the night, not comfortably on so hard a bed, but soundly.

During the day, while he had crawled about at the foot of the rocks, wild hogs, marsupial animals, and wood-rats had examined him suspiciously through the undergrowth and decamped. As he slept, howling night-dogs came up, sniffed at him from a safe distance, and scattered from his vicinity. He would have yielded in a battle with a pugnacious kitten, but these creatures recognized a prehistoric foe, and would not abide with him.

A week passed before he had ceased to cry and call for his mother; but from this on her image grew fainter, and in a month the infant intelligence had discarded it. He ate nuts and berries as he found them, drank from the pool, climbed the rocks and strolled in the wood, played on the beach with shells and fragments of splintered wreckage, wore out his clothes, and in another month was naked; for when buttons and vital parts gave way and a garment fell, he let it lie. But he needed no clothes, even at night; for it was southern summer, and the northeast monsoon, adding its humid warmth to the radiating heat from the sun-baked rocks, kept the temperature nearly constant.

He learned to avoid the sun at midday, and, free from contagion and motherly coddling, escaped many of the complaints which torture and kill children; yet he suffered frightfully from colic until his stomach was accustomed to the change of diet, by which time he was emaciated to skin and bone. Then a reaction set in, and as time passed he gained healthy flesh and muscle on the nitrogenous food.

Six months from the time of his arrival, another storm swept the beach. Pelted by the warm rain, terror-stricken, he cowered under the rocks through the night, and at daylight peered out on the surf-washed sands, heaving lagoon, and white line of breakers on the barrier reef. The short-lived typhoon had passed, but the wind still blew slantingly on the beach with force enough to raise a turmoil of crashing sea and undertow in the small bay formed by the extension of the wall. The fragment of ship's stern on the reef had disappeared; but a half-mile to the right—directly in the eye of the wind— was another wreck, and somewhat nearer, on the heaving swell of the lagoon, a black spot, which moved and approached. It came down before the wind and resolved into a closely packed group of human beings, some of whom tugged frantically at the oars of the water-logged boat which held them, others of whom as frantically bailed with caps and hands. Escorting the boat was a fleet of dorsal fins, and erect in the stern-sheets was a white-faced woman, holding a child in one arm while she endeavored to remove a circular life-buoy from around her waist. At first heading straight for the part of the beach where the open-eyed boy was watching, the boat now changed its course and by desperate exertion of the rowers reached a position from which it could drift to leeward of the point and its deadly maelstrom. With rowers bailing and the white-faced woman seated, fastening the child in the life-buoy, the boat, gunwale-deep, and the gruesome guard of sharks drifted out of sight behind the point. The boy had not understood; but he had seen his kind, and from association of ideas appreciated again his loneliness—crying and wailing for a week; but not for his mother: he had forgotten her.

With the change of the monsoon came a lowering of the temperature. Naked and shelterless, he barely survived the first winter, tropical though it was. But the second found him inured to the surroundings—hardy and strong. When able to, he climbed trees and found birds' eggs, which he accidentally broke and naturally ate. It was a pleasant relief from a purely vegetable diet, and he became a proficient egg-thief; then the birds built their nests beyond his reach. Once he was savagely pecked by an angry brush-turkey and forced to defend himself. It aroused a combativeness and destructiveness that had lain dormant in his nature.

Children the world over epitomize in their habits and thoughts the infancy of the human race. Their morals and modesty, as well as their games, are those of paleolithic man, and they are as remorsely cruel. From the day of his fracas with the turkey he was a hunter—of grubs, insects, and young birds; but only to kill, maim, or torture; he did not eat them, because hunger was satisfied, and he possessed a child's dislike of radical change.

Deprived of friction with other minds, he was slower than his social prototype in the reproduction of the epochs. At a stage when most boys are passing through the age of stone, with its marbles, caves, and slings, he was yet in the earlier arboreal period —a climber—and would swing from branch to branch with almost the agility of an ape.

On fine, sunny days, influenced by the weather, he would laugh and shout hilariously; a gloomy sky made him morose. When hurt, or angered by disappointment in the hunt, he would cry out inarticulately; but having no use for language, did not talk, hence did not think, as the term is understood. His mind received the impressions of his senses, and could fear, hate, and remember, but knew nothing of love, for nothing lovable appealed to it. He could hardly reason, as yet; his shadow puzzled, angered, and annoyed him until he noticed its concomitance with the sun, when he reversed cause and effect, considered it a beneficent, mysterious Something that had life, and endeavored by gesture and grimace to placate and please it. It was his beginning of religion.

His dreams were often horrible. Strange shapes, immense snakes and reptiles, and nondescript monsters made up of prehistoric legs, teeth, and heads, afflicted his sleep. He had never seen them; they were an inheritance, but as real to him as the sea and sky, the wind and rain.

Every six months, at the breaking up of the monsoon, would come squalls and typhoons—full of menace, for his kindly, protecting shadow then deserted him. One day, when about ten years old, during a wild burst of storm, he fled down the beach in an agony of terror; for, considering all that moved as alive, he thought that the crashing sea and swaying, falling trees were attacking him, and, half buried in the sand near the bushes, found the forgotten life-buoy, stained and weather-worn. It was quiescent, and new to him,—like nothing he had seen,—and he clung to it. At that moment the sun appeared, and in a short time the storm had passed. He carried the life-buoy back with him—spurning and threatening his delinquent shadow—and looked for a place to put it, deciding at last on a small cave in the rocky wall near to the pool. In a corner of this he installed the ring of cork and canvas, and remained by it, patting and caressing it. When it rained again, he appreciated, for the first time, the comfort of shelter, and became a cave-dweller, with a new god—a fetish, to which he transferred his allegiance and obeisance because more powerful than his shadow.

From correlation of instincts, he now entered the age of stone. He no longer played with shells and sticks, but with pebbles, which he gathered, hoarded in piles, and threw at marks,—to be gathered again, —seldom entering the woods but for food and the relaxation of the hunt. But with his change of habits came a lessening of his cruelty to defenseless creatures,—not that he felt pity: he merely found no more amusement in killing and tormenting,—and in time he transferred his antagonism to the sharks in the lagoon, their dorsal fins making famous targets for his pebbles. He needed no experience with these pirates to teach him to fear and hate them, and when he bathed—which habit he acquired as a relief from the heat, and indulged daily—he chose a pool near the rocks that filled at high tide, and in it learned to swim, paddling like a dog.

And so the boy, blue-eyed and fair at the beginning, grew to early manhood, as handsome an animal as the world contains, tall, straight, and clean-featured with steady eyes wide apart and skin—the color of old copper from sun and wind—covered with a fine, soft down, which at the age of sixteen had not yet thickened on his face to beard and mustache, though his wavy brown hair reached to his shoulders.

At this period a turning-point appeared in his life

which gave an impetus to his almost stagnant mental development—his food-supply diminished and his pebble-supply gave out completely, forcing him to wander. Pebble-throwing was his only amusement; pebble-gathering his only labor; eating was neither. He browsed and nibbled at all hours of the day, never knowing the sensation of a full stomach, and, until lately, of an empty one. To this, perhaps, may be ascribed his wonderful immunity from sickness. In collecting pebbles his method was to carry as many as his hands would hold to a pile on the beach and go back for more; and in the six years of his stone-throwing he had found and thrown at the sharks every stone as small as his fist, within a sector formed by the beach and the rocky wall to an equal distance inland. The fruits, nuts, edible roots, and grasses growing in this area had hitherto supported him, but would no longer, owing to a drought of the previous year, which, luckily, had not affected his water-supply.

One morning, trembling with excitement, eye and ear on the alert,—as a high-spirited horse enters a strange pasture,—he ventured past the junction of bush and tide-mark, and down the unknown beach beyond. He filled his hands with the first pebbles he found, but noticing the plentiful supply on the ground ahead of him, dropped them and went on; there were other things to interest him. A broad stretch of undulating, scantily wooded country reached inland from the convex beach of sand and shells to where it met the receding line of forest and bush behind him; and far away to his right, darting back and forth among stray bushes and sand-hummocks, were small creatures—strange, unlike those he knew, but in regard to which he felt curiosity rather than fear.

He traveled around the circle of beach, and noticed that the moving creatures fled at his approach. They were wild hogs, hunted of men since hunting began. He entered the forest about midday, and emerging, found himself on a pebbly beach similar to his own, and facing a continuation of the rocky wall, which, like the other end, dipped into the lagoon and prevented further progress. He was thirsty, and found a pool near the rocks; hungry, and he ate of nuts and berries which he recognized. Puzzled by the reversal of perspective and the similarity of conditions, he proceeded along the wall, dimly expecting to find his cave. But none appeared, and, mystified, —somewhat frightened,—he plunged into the wood, keeping close to the wall and looking sharply about him. Like an exiled cat or a carrier-pigeon, he was making a straight line for home, but did not know it.

His progress was slow, for boulders, stumps, and rising ground impeded him. Darkness descended when he was but half-way home and nearly on a level with the top of the wall. Forced to stop, he threw himself down, exhausted, yet nervous and wakeful, as any other animal in a strange place. But the familiar moon came out, shining through the foliage, and this soothed him into a light slumber.

He was wakened by a sound near by that he had heard all his life at a distance—a wild chorus of barking. It was coming his way, and he crouched and waited, grasping a stone in each hand. The barking, interspersed soon with wheezing squeals, grew painfully loud, and culminated in vengeful growls, as a young pig sprang into a patch of moonlight, with a dozen dingoes—night-dogs—at its heels. In the excitement of pursuit they did not notice the crouching boy, but pounced on the pig, tore at it, snapping and snarling at one another, and in a few minutes the meal was over.

Frozen with terror at this strange sight, the boy remained quiet until the brutes began sniffing and turning in his direction; then he stood erect, and giving vent to a scream which rang through the forest, hurled the two stones with all his strength straight at the nearest. He was a good marksman. Agonized yelps followed the impact of stone and hide; two dogs rolled over and over, then, gaining their feet, sped after their fleeing companions, while the boy sat down, trembling in every limb—completely unnerved. Yet he knew that he was the cause of their flight. With a stone in each hand, he watched and waited until daylight, then arose and went on homeward, with a new and intense emotion— not fear of the dingoes: he was the superior animal, and knew it—not pity for the pig: he had not developed to the pitying stage. He was possessed by a strong, instinctive desire to emulate the dogs and eat of animal food. It did not come of his empty stomach; he felt it after he had satisfied his hunger on the way; and as he plodded down the slope toward his cave, gripped his missiles fiercely and watched sharply for small animals—preferably pigs.

But no pigs appeared. He reached his cave, and slept all day and the following night, waking in the morning hungry, and with the memory of his late adventure strong in his mind. He picked up the two stones he had brought home, and started down the beach, but stopped, came back, and turned inland by

the wall; then he halted again and retraced his steps
—puzzled. He pondered awhile,—if his mental proc-
esses may be so termed,—then walked slowly down
the beach, entered the bush a short distance, turned
again to the wall, and gained his starting-point.
Then he reversed the trip, and coming back by way
of the beach, struck inland with a clear and satisfied
face. He had solved the problem—a new and hard
one for him—that of two roads to a distant place;
and he had chosen the shortest.

In a few hours he reached his late camping-spot,
and crouched to the earth, listening for barking and
squealing—for a pig to be chased his way. But
dingoes hunt only by night, and unmolested pigs do
not squeal. Impatient at last, he went on through
the forest in the direction from which they had come,
until he reached the open country where he had first
seen them; and here, rooting under the bushes at the
margin of the wood, he discovered a family—a mother
and four young ones—which had possibly contained
the victim of the dogs. He stalked them slowly and
cautiously, keeping bushes between himself and them,
but was seen by the mother when about twenty yards
away. She sniffed suspiciously, then, with a warning
grunt and a scattering of dust and twigs, scurried
into the woods, with her brood—all but one—in her
wake.

A frightened pig is as easy a target as a darting
dorsal fin, and a fat suckling lay kicking convulsively
on the ground. He hurried up, the hunting gleam
bright in his eyes, and hurled the second stone at the
little animal. It still kicked, and he picked up the
first stone, thinking it might be more potent to kill,
and crashed it down on the unfortunate pig's head.

It glanced from the head to the other stone and struck a spark—which he noticed.

The pig now lay still, and satisfied that he had killed it, he tried to repeat the carom, but failed. Yet the spark had interested him,—he wanted to see it again,—and it was only after he had reduced the pig's head to a pulp that he became disgusted and angrily threw the stone in his hand at the one on the ground. The resulting spark delighted him. He repeated the experiment again and again, each concussion drawing a spark, and finally used one stone as a hammer on the other, with the same result—to him, a bright and pretty thing, very small, but alive, which came from either of the dead stones. Tired of the play at last, he turned to the pig—the food that he had yearned for.

It was well for him, perhaps, that the initial taste of bristle and fat prevented his taking the second mouthful. Slightly nauseated, he dropped the carcass and turned to go, but immediately bounded in the air with a howl of pain. His left foot was red and smarting. Once he had cut it on a sharp shell, and now searched for a wound, but found none. Rubbing increased the pain. Looking on the ground for the cause, he discovered a wavering, widening ring of strange appearance, and within it a blackened surface on which rested the two stones. They were dry flint nodules, and he had set fire to the grass with the sparks.

Considering this to be a new animal that had attacked him, he pelted it with stones, dancing around it in a rage and shouting hoarsely. He might have conquered the fire and never invoked it again, had not the supply of stones in the vicinity given out, or those he had used grown too hot to handle; for he stayed the advancing flame at one side. But the other side was creeping on, and he used dry branches, dropping to his hands and knees to pound the fire, fighting bravely, crying out with pain as he burned himself, and forced to drop stick after stick which caught fire. Soon it grew too hot to remain near, and he stood off and launched fuel at it, which resulted in a fair-sized bonfire; then, in desperation and fear, he hurled the dead pig—the cause of the trouble—at the terrible monster, and fled.

Looking back through the trees to see if he was pursued, he noticed that the strange enemy had taken new shape and color; it was reaching up into the air, black and cloud-like. Frightened, tired mentally and physically, and suffering keenly from his burns, he turned his back on the half-solved problem and endeavored to satisfy his hunger. But he was on strange territory and found little of his accustomed food; the chafing and abrading contact of bushes and twigs irritated his sore spots, preventing investigation and rapid progress, and at the end of three hours, still hungry, and exasperated by his torment into a reckless, fighting mood, he picked up stones and returned savagely to battle again with the enemy. But the enemy was dead. The grass had burned to where it met dry earth, and the central fire was now a black-and-white pile of still warm ashes, on which lay the charred and denuded pig, giving forth a savory odor. Cautiously approaching, he studied the situation, then, yielding to an irresistible impulse, seized the pig and ran through the woods to the wall and down to his cave.

Two hours later he was writhing on the ground

with a violent stomach-ache. It was forty-eight hours after when he ate again, and then of his old food—nuts and berries. But the craving returned in a week, and he again killed a pig, but was compelled to forego eating it for lack of fire.

Though he had discovered fire and cooked food, his only conception of the process, so far, was that the mysterious enemy was too powerful for him to kill, that it would eat sticks and grass but did not like stones, and that a dead pig could kill it, and in the conflict be made eatable. It was only after months of playing with flints and sparks that he recognized the part borne by dry grass or moss, and that with these he could create it at will; that a dead pig, though always improved by the effort, could not be depended upon to kill it unless the enemy was young and small,—when stones would answer as well, —and that he could always kill it himself by depriving it of food.

It is hardly possible that animal food produced a direct effect on his mind; but the effort to obtain it certainly did, arousing his torpid faculties to a keener activity. He grasped the relation of cause to effect—seeing one, he looked for the other. He noticed resemblances and soon realized the common attributes of fire and the sun; and, as his fetish was not always good to him,—the sun and storm seeming to follow their own sweet will in spite of his unspoken faith in the life-buoy,—he again became an apostate, transferring his allegiance to the sun, of which the friendly fire was evidently a part or symbol. He did not discard his dethroned fetish completely; he still kept it in his cave to punch, kick, and revile by gestures and growls at times when the sun was hidden, retaining this habit from his former faith. The life-buoy was now his devil—a symbol of evil, or what was the same to him—discomfort; for he had advanced in religious thought to a point where he needed one. Every morning when the sun shone, and at its reappearance after the rain, he prostrated himself in a patch of sunlight —this and the abuse of the life-buoy becoming ceremonies in his fire-worship.

In time he became such a menace to the hogs that they climbed the wall at the high ground and disappeared in the country beyond. And after them went the cowardly dingoes that preyed on their young. Rodent animals, more difficult to hunt, and a species of small kangaroo furnished him occupation and food until they, too, emigrated, when he was forced to follow; he was now a carnivorous animal, no longer satisfied with vegetable food.

The longer hunts brought with them a difficulty which spurred him to further invention. He could carry only as many stones as his hands would hold, and often found himself far from his base of supply, with game in sight, and without means to kill it. The pouch in which the mother kangaroo carried her young suggested to his mind a like contrivance for carrying stones. Since he had cut his foot on the shell, he had known the potency of a sharp edge, but not until he needed to remove charred and useless flesh from his food did he appreciate the utility. It was an easy advance for him roughly to skin a female kangaroo and wear the garment for the pocket's sake. But it chafed and irritated him; so, cutting off the troublesome parts little by little, he finally reduced it to a girdle which held only the pouch.

And in this receptacle he carried stones for throwing and shells for cutting, his expeditions now extending for miles beyond the wall, and only limited by the necessity of returning for water, of which, in the limestone rock, there were plenty of pools and trickling springs.

He learned that no stones but the dry flints he found close to the wall would strike sparks; but, careless, improvident, petulant child of nature that he was, he exhausted the supply, and one day, too indolent to search his hunting-tracts to regain the necessary two, he endeavored to draw fire from a pair that he dug from the moist earth, and failing, threw them with all his strength at the rocky wall. One of them shivered to irregular pieces, the other parted with a flake—a six-inch dagger-like fragment, flat on one side, convex on the other, with sharp edges that met in a point at one end, and at the other, where lay the cone of percussion, rounded into a roughly cylindrical shape, convenient for handling. Though small, no flint-chipping savage of the stone age ever made a better knife, and he was quick to appreciate its superiority to a shell.

Like most discoveries and inventions that have advanced the human race, his were, in the main, accidental; yet he could now reason from the accidental to the analogous. Idly swinging his girdle around his head, one day, and letting go, he was surprised at the distance to which, with little effort, he could send the stone-laden pouch. Months of puzzled experimenting produced a sling—at first with a thong of hide fast to each stone, later with the double thong and pouch that small boys and savages have not yet improved upon.

To this centrifugal force, which he could use without wholly understanding, he added the factor of a rigid radius—a handle to a heavy stone; for only with this contrivance could he break large flints and open cocoanuts—an article of good food that he had passed by all his life and wondered at until his knife had divided a green one. His experiments in this line resulted in a heavy, sharp-edged, solid-backed flint, firmly bound with thongs to the end of a stick,—a rude tomahawk,—convenient for the *coup de grâce*.

The ease with which he could send a heavy stone out of sight, or bury a smaller one in the side of a hog at short range, was wonderful to him; but he was twenty years old before, by daily practice with his sling, he brought his marksmanship up to that of his unaided hand, equal to which, at an earlier date, was his skill at hatchet-throwing. He could outrun and tomahawk the fastest hog, could bring down with his sling a kangaroo on the jump or a pigeon on the wing, could smell and distinguish game to windward with the keen scent of a hound, and became so formidable an enemy of his troublesome rivals, the dingoes, —whose flesh he disapproved of,—and the sharks in the lagoon, that the one deserted his hunting-ground and the other seldom left the reef.

He broke or lost one knife and hatchet after another, and learned, in making new ones, that he could chip them into improved shape when freshly dug, and that he must allow them to dry before using— when they were also available for striking fire. He had enlarged his pocket, making a better one of a whole skin by roughly sewing the edges together with thongs, first curing the hide by soaking in salt water and scraping with his knife. His food-list now embraced shellfish and birds, wild yams, breadfruit, and cocoanuts, which, even the latter, he cooked before eating and prepared before cooking. Pushed by an ever-present healthy appetite, and helped by inherited instincts based on the habits and knowledge of a long line of civilized ancestry, he had advanced in four years from an indolent, mindless existence to a plane of fearless, reasoning activity. He was a hunter of prowess, master of his surroundings, lord over all creatures he had seen, and, though still a cave-dweller when at home, in a fair way to become a hut-builder, herdsman, and agriculturist; for he had arranged boughs to shelter him from the rain when hunting, had attempted to block up the pass over the wall to prevent the further wanderings of a herd of hogs that he had pursued, and had lately become interested in the sprouting of nuts and seeds and the encroachments and changes of the vegetation.

Yet he lacked speech, and did his thinking without words. The deficiency was not accompanied by the unpleasant twisted features and grimacing of mutes, which comes of conscious effort to communicate. His features were smooth and regular, his mouth symmetrical and firm, and his clear blue eye thoughtful and intent as that of a student; for he had studied and thought. He would smile and frown, laugh and shout, growl and whine, the pitch and timbre of his inarticulate utterance indicating the emotion which prompted it to about the same degree as does an intelligent dog's language to his master. But dogs and other social animals converse in a speech beyond human ken; and in this respect he was their inferior, for he had not yet known the need of language, and did not, until, one day, in a section of his domain that he had never visited before,—because game avoided it,—down by the sea on the side of the wall opposite to his cave, he met a creature like himself.

He had come down the wooded slope on the steady jog-trot he assumed when traveling, tomahawk in hand, careless, confident, and happy because of the bright sunshine and his lately appeased hunger, and, as he bounded on to the beach with a joyous whoop, was startled by an answering scream.

Mingled with the frightful monsters in the dreams of his childhood had been transient glimpses of a kind, placid face that he seemed to know—a face that bent over him lovingly and kissed him. These were sub-conscious memories of his mother, which lasted long after he had forgotten her. As he neared manhood, strange yearnings had come to him—a dreary loneliness and craving for company. In his sleep he had seen fleeting visions of forms and faces like his reflection in a pool—like, yet unlike; soft, curving outlines, tinted cheeks, eyes that beamed, and white, caressing hands appeared and disappeared—fragmentary and illusive. He could not distinctly remember them when he wakened, but their influence made him strangely happy, strangely miserable; and while the mood lasted he could not hunt and kill.

Standing knee-deep in a shallow pool on the beach, staring at him with wide-open dark eyes, was the creature that had screamed—a living, breathing em-bodiment of the curves and color, the softness, bright-ness, and gentle sweetness that his subconsciousness knew. There were the familiar eyes, dark and lim-pid, wondering but not frightened; two white little teeth showing between parted lips; a wealth of long brown hair held back from the forehead by a small hand; and a rounded, dimpled cheek, the damask shading of which merged delicately into the olive tint that extended to the feet. No Venus ever arose from the sea with rarer lines of beauty than were combined in the picture of loveliness which, backed by the blue of the lagoon, appeared to the astonished eyes of this wild boy. It was a girl—naked as Mother Eve, and as innocently shameless.

In the first confusion of his faculties, when habit and inherent propensity conflicted, habit dominated his mind. He was a huntsman—feared and avoided: here was an intruder. He raised his hatchet to throw, but a second impulse brought it slowly down; she had shown no fear—no appreciation of what the gesture threatened. Dropping the weapon to the ground, he advanced slowly, the wonder in his face giving way to a delighted smile, and she came out of the pool to meet him.

Face to face they looked into each other's eyes— long and earnestly; then, as though the scrutiny brought approval, the pretty features of the girl sweetened to a smile, but she did not speak nor attempt to. Stepping past him, she looked back, still smiling, halted until he followed, and then led him up to the wall, where, on a level with the ground, was a hollow in the formation, somewhat similar to his cave, but larger. Flowering vines grew at the entrance, which had prevented his seeing it before. She entered, and emerged immediately with a life-buoy, which she held before him, the action and smiling face indicating her desire that he admire it.

The boy thought that he saw his property in the

possession of another creature and resented the spoliation. With an angry snarl he snatched the life-buoy and backed away, while the girl, surprised and a little indignant, followed with extended hands. He raised it threateningly, and though she did not cower, she knew intuitively that he was angry, and feeling the injustice, burst into tears; then, turning from him, she covered her eyes with her hands and crouched to the ground, sobbing piteously.

The face of the boy softened. He looked from the weeping girl to the life-buoy and back again; then, puzzled,—still believing it to be his own,—he obeyed a generous impulse. Advancing, he laid the treasure at her feet; but she turned away. Sober-faced and irresolute, not knowing what to do, he looked around and above. A pigeon fluttered on a branch at the edge of the wood. He whipped out his sling, loaded it, and sent a stone whizzing upward. The pigeon fell, and he was beneath it before it reached the ground. Hurrying back with the dead bird, he placed it before her; but she shuddered in disgust and would not touch it. Off in the lagoon a mis-guided shark was swimming slowly along,—its dorsal fin cutting the surface,—a full two hundred yards from the beach. He ran to the water's edge, looked back once, flourished his sling, and two seconds later the shark was scudding for the reef. If she had seen, she evidently was not impressed. He returned, picked up his tomahawk on the way, idly and nerv-ously fingered the pebbles in his pocket, stood a moment over the sulky girl, and then studied the life-buoy on the ground. A light came to his eyes; with a final glance at the girl he bounded up the slope and disappeared in the woods.

Three hours later he returned with his discarded fetish, and found her sitting upright, with her life-buoy on her knees. She smiled gladly as he approached, then pouted, as though remembering. Panting from his exertion, he humbly placed the faded, scarred, and misshapen ring on top of the brighter, better-cared-for possession of the girl, and stood, mutely pleading for pardon. It was granted. Smiling radiantly,—a little roguishly,—she arose and led him again to the cave, from which she brought forth another treasure. It was a billet of wood,—a dead branch, worn smooth at the ends,—around which were wrapped faded, half-rotten rags of calico. Hugging it for a moment, she handed it to him. He looked at it wonderingly and let it drop, turning his eyes upon her; then, with impatience in her face, she reclaimed it, entered the cave,—the boy following, —and tenderly placed it in a corner.

It was her doll. Up to the borders of womanhood —untutored, unloved waif of the woods—living through the years of her simple existence alone—she had lavished the instinctive mother-love of her heart on a stick, and had clothed it, though not herself.

With a thoughtful little wrinkle in her brow, she studied the face of this new companion who acted so strangely, and he, equally mystified, looked around the cave. A pile of nuts in a corner indicated her housewifely thrift and forethought. A bed of dry moss with an evenly packed elevation at the end— which could be nothing but a pillow—showed plainly the manner in which she had preserved the velvety softness of her skin. Tinted shells and strips of faded calico, arranged with some approach to harmony of color around the sides and the border of the floor, gave evidence of the tutelage of the bower-birds, of which there were many in the vicinity. And the vines at the entrance had surely been planted—they were far from others of the kind. In her own way she had developed as fully as he. As he stood there, wondering at what he saw, the girl approached, slowly and irresolutely; then, raising her hand, she softly pressed the tip of her finger into his shoulder.

In the dim and misty ages of the past, when wandering bands of ape-like human beings had not developed their tribal customs to the level of priestly ceremonies,—when the medicine-man had not arisen, —a marriage between a man and young woman was generally consummated by the man beating the girl into insensibility, and dragging her by the hair to his cave. Added to its simplicity, the custom had the merit of improving the race, as unhealthy and ill-favored girls were not pursued, and similar men were clubbed out of the pursuit by stronger. But the process was necessarily painful to the loved one, and her female children very naturally inherited a repugnance to being wooed.

When a civilized young lady, clothed and well conducted, anticipates being kissed or embraced by her lover, she places in the way such difficulties as are in her power; she gets behind tables and chairs, runs from him, compels him to pursue, and expects him to. In her maidenly heart she may want to be kissed, but she cannot help resisting. She obeys the same instinct that impelled this wild girl to spring from the outstretched arms of the boy and go screaming out of the cave and down the beach in simulated terror—an instinct inherited from the prehistoric mother, who fled for dear life and a whole skin from a man behind armed with a club and bent upon marriage.

Shouting hoarsely, the boy followed, in what, if he had been called upon to classify it, might have seemed to him a fury of rage, but it was not. He would not have harmed the girl, for he lacked the tribal education that induces cruelty to the weaker sex. But he did not catch her; he stubbed his toe and fell, arising with a bruised kneecap which prevented further pursuit. Slowly, painfully, he limped back, tears welling in his eyes and increasing to a copious flood as he sat down with his back to the girl and nursed his aching knee. It was not the pain that brought the tears; he was hardened to physical suffering. But his feelings had been hurt beyond any disappointment of the hunt or terror of the storm, and for the first time in his life since his babyhood he wept—like the intellectual child that he was.

A soft, caressing touch on his head aroused him and brought him to his feet. She stood beside him, tears in her own eyes, and sympathy overflowing in every feature of the sweet face. From her lips came little cooing, gurgling sounds which he endeavored to repeat. It was their first attempt at communication, and the sounds that they used—understood by mothers and infants of all races—were the first root-words of a new language. He extended his arms, and though she held back slightly, while a faint smile responded to his own, she did not resist, and he drew her close—forgetting his pain as he pressed his lips to hers.

www.ingramcontent.com/pod-product-compliance
Lightning Source LLC
Chambersburg PA
CBHW020556030726
47497CB00007B/1967